JONATHAN'S SHIELD

CHANNING TURNER

Jonathan's Shield
A Red Adept Publishing Book

Red Adept Publishing, LLC
104 Bugenfield Court
Garner, NC 27529
http://RedAdeptPublishing.com/

ISBN-13: 978-1-940215-65-5
ISBN-10: 194021565X

First Print Edition: March 2016

Cover and Formatting: Streetlight Graphics

For Lucille McDowell, the first person who encouraged me to put stuff down on paper

CHAPTER ONE

Saul and his son Jonathan and the men with them were staying in Gibeah in Benjamin, while the Philistines camped at Micmash.

1 Samuel 13:16 NIV

"**B**ERAL, WAKE UP! WHAT DO you make of this?"

I opened my eyes and quickly rolled to one knee, reaching for the pointed staff stuck upright in the gritty dirt next to my sleeping mat. Darkness still covered our sleeping army's camp, although outlines of surrounding hilltops had begun to emerge in the rose-colored predawn. Prince Jonathan stood nearby, hands on hips with his back toward me, staring off toward the Micmash pass. I got to my feet. "My lord?" I asked.

Jonathan kept his gaze fixed away. "Look there—at the top of the hill, Seneh. Do you see them?" He pointed at the crest of a hill next to the pass. I came alongside him, running my fingers through my tangled hair to push it away from my eyes. He clapped me on the shoulder. "Good morning, Beral." He smiled.

I sniffed. "Good morning, my lord."

He pointed again. "Use your sharper eyes, Beral. Look at the very top."

I opened my eyes wider then squinted at the distant hill. Tiny figures, backlit by the growing dawn, moved about on its flattened top. I saw the glint of polished metal and turned to Jonathan in shock.

"Are those Philistines?" I asked.

He nodded grimly. "I fear that they are."

The Philistines must have climbed Seneh during the night, probably using a goat path on the other side to scramble up by moonlight, carelessly kicking down loose rocks and shale, knowing none of our sentries waited nearby to hear them. Now visible at first light, two dozen of them stood on the rocks overlooking the pass to Micmash, hooting like monkeys and slapping their backsides at us.

Unlike most of the sea people, their leader, who looked to be a big man, sported a beard, its reddish color contrasting with the black hair of his followers. He preened too far away to be seen clearly, but he likely smiled at us as he raised his battle kilt and started to urinate down the steep slope in our direction. The whole band joined him and accompanied the act with exaggerated obscene gestures for our benefit.

After a few days, we grew accustomed to their outpost watching our camp. They, in turn, wearied of jeering at us, so we simply looked at each other. Behind them crouched an army that spies said numbered nearly one hundred thousand. The combined smoke of their dung cooking fires spread across half of the northern sky. Facing them, our Israelite army had six hundred men, mostly Benjamite kinsmen of King Saul. Soldiers from the other tribes, once so enthusiastic after Saul's early victories at Jabesh-Gilead and Geba, now melted away like an early snowfall at the sight of the invaders. We who stayed and waited for the Philistines to attack saw to our weapons and prayed. I'd never observed so many hardened men at prayer as in that camp in those days. A sense of foreboding settled throughout the encampment.

Truthfully, I could hardly blame the deserters. None of us had ever faced chariots before, and these heathens brought more than three thousand of their war wagons and teams. No soldier in Saul's army even carried a decent weapon. The Philistines had long ago banned ironworkers in Israel so that after years of subjugation, our war implements were simply sharpened farm tools.

I, Beral, am also of the tribe of Benjamin. In those days, I followed my lord Jonathan, Saul's eldest son, into battle carrying only a stout oak stave tipped with a bronze point. I did this willingly, for I was his armor bearer, and I was responsible for him.

I remember clearly our first battle together. Jonathan led fighters against the Geba Philistines. My limbs shook when we waded into their dusty ranks, but then the bloodlust took me as I clubbed them away from his back. That was a glorious day for both of us.

My father, Ammiel, was a friend of Saul's, if it can be said that a king truly has any friends. He sent me to serve in the king's household as a youth. General Abner, the king's cousin, then selected me to attend the eldest prince, only a few years older than me. Jonathan and I became as brothers. We sported together and roamed the surrounding Judean hills for game. We talked often when alone. Although he appeared tall and dark like his father, I still marveled that Jonathan could be of Saul's mercurial blood.

One morning, a week after the Philistines occupied Seneh, Prince Jonathan came whistling to my thatched shelter, showing the hint of a smile as he sat down in its shade. In our youth, that same little grin would take us out into the fields to hunt—or somewhere else to mischief. Not so many seasons before, I sometimes received beatings from our elderly tutors for those pranks we did together. Jonathan, of course, was only struck by his father the king, and rarely at that.

He settled back on one elbow. "Beral, are you rested for a walk?"

Although pleased by his presence, I felt wary, having learned long before that the prince's idle questions were the ones with purpose. "Of course, my lord, but where?"

He made a vague gesture with his free hand, indicating everywhere and nowhere at the same time. "Out. Beyond the camp. I need to stretch my legs." He kept grinning at me, and I knew not to ask what amused him so. Jonathan would tell me in his own manner and time.

I rose and rummaged in my gear. "Are we going to hunt?" I picked up my bow and quiver, noticing as I did so that he carried none of his own hunting gear. His smile became tight-lipped.

"No, Beral. Leave your little coney shooter here. Bring your staff and my shield. There are Philistines about. We will likely see some."

I dutifully hefted his wood-and-bronze buckler over my back, where it rode clean and unscratched in a cloth sack. My fighting staff lay in the crook of my arm as I stood before him, my face quizzical.

He looked me up and down. "Tighten your sandals," he said. I bent and retied my footwear, kept loosely fastened in camp. He nodded and turned to lead the way.

Fighting men sitting at their fires raised hands in greeting, and Jonathan returned the waves informally as we passed. He knew every soldier in his brigade and each man's father as well. Should I ever fall, a dozen of those men would be standing before his tent that same day, asking to take my place and walk a step behind him as I did.

That day, he made a casual inspection of our encampment. We walked the perimeter then out into the small herd of horses and camels, where he suddenly stopped. He craned over the neck of a riding mare to look back at our tents and brush shelters.

"What do you think, Beral? Are we seen from here?"

I shaded my eyes to study the camp. By then I understood that he meant to leave without being observed. My stomach churned with the lightness that always came with his ideas of adventure. "No, my lord. No one looks in this direction."

"Good. Duck down and follow where I go."

Together, we bent and eased our way from among the animals and down into a dry, barren wadi that no water had coursed through in years. It led away from our army. I still had no idea what he intended.

At first, we traveled eastward then left the wadi to circle in a wide arc to the north and back through large scattered boulders toward the pass at Micmash. Within an hour, we were closer to the Philistine positions than our own, but I wasn't alarmed. If they tried to run us down out there with chariots, their teams of small horses would beat the carts to pieces on the rocks while we slipped easily away. Even mounted scouts would have difficulty intercepting us on that broken ground. Sometimes it was a begrudging compliment when other peoples called us goats.

But then, as we approached Seneh, I sucked in my breath. Jonathan headed directly toward its base. "My lord?" I questioned softly.

"There's no need to speak quietly, Beral," he replied. "They already know we're here."

Certainly enough, at the top of that steep knoll, the Philistine detachment lined up like a row of curious birds, peering over the rocks at us. Their reddish captain stood high on a boulder with hands on his hips. We must have looked odd, wandering about aimlessly in that dangerous ground between opposing armies. No doubt they took us for more deserters from King Saul.

8

Jonathan turned to me. "Come now, Beral. Let's go closer and see these uncircumcised fellows. Maybe Yahweh will favor us today. Nothing will stop Him if He chooses to act on our behalf."

I couldn't spit. My grip tightened on my staff while I tried not to let my knees tremble. To approach those Philistines seemed like madness. Certainly Yahweh would take us into His protection under ordinary circumstances, but to tempt His disapproval by deliberately walking toward death did not sound proper to me.

But that didn't matter. Jonathan was my prince, friend, and brother. We shared water and rations. I had attended him at his wedding to the princess Reina. I'd held his infant children. And long before that, as younger men, we had teased each other about the maidens we fancied, and I knew when and to whom he lost his virginity. Braver than any of his soldiers, he still honored the old veterans. Yahweh spoke to Jonathan more than to me, and I knew my prince listened. Maybe Yahweh would protect us today, maybe not. However, even if mad, Jonathan belonged to me, and I would go with him, one step behind.

"Do all you intend, Prince Jonathan." I spoke formally, as if we were at the royal court. "Lead me. I am with you, heart and soul." He smiled broadly and clapped me on the shoulder.

"Come then. Let's go closer and let them get a better look at us." He paused with a finger to the side of his nose, the gesture he used when thinking. "They will keep yelling at us. If they say, 'Wait there, and we will come to kill you,' why then, we will wait. But..." and here he paused again. "If they say, 'Why don't you come up to us?' then that will be our sign that the Lord has given them into our hands." He spoke with such confidence that I could not doubt him. Surely, he listened to Yahweh.

As we came nearer, the Philistines did shout to us. Jonathan and I understood enough of their language to make out the gist of their taunts. With great crude humor, they described our bestial ancestry and what they would do with a pair of Hebrew sheep like us.

The taunting paused for a long moment when we reached the bottom of the hill. I heard the muted surprise in their voices when Jonathan stopped and reached back for his shield, which I uncovered and placed on his arm. The little buckler offered more mobility than protection.

A true warrior of the line would never carry one like it, but its royal emblem identified my prince to the watching Philistines as surely as if he had shouted out his name to them. The tone of their insults changed.

"So… it is the *prince* himself who comes to visit us! We are honored. Such a handsome prince—King Saul's eldest." Then came the words I dreaded to hear: "Why don't you come up to us? We would entertain you, noble prince. Perhaps you will learn something." They laughed uproariously. The men fell against each other and rubbed away tears from their eyes.

Jonathan craned his head back to see them clearly. The words he said were soft and to me alone. "There is our calling, Beral. Come." He started the long climb upward, and I followed.

CHAPTER TWO

Jonathan climbed up, using his hands and feet,
with his armor-bearer right behind him…

1 Samuel 14:13a NIV

SUN-BAKED ROCKS LAY TUMBLED TOGETHER like giant loaves of bread spilled from a tray. We scrabbled over and around them to climb the steep face of the hill toward the Philistines. The pagans yipped and hurled insults as we labored upward, searching out hand-and footholds. Any one of them could have heaved a boulder on us, but they only watched expectantly. I knew they weren't being noble. They simply anticipated an easy killing. Their captain waited, giant hands on hips, eyeing Jonathan grimly. The only Philistine not laughing, he was a grizzled fighter with gray flecks in his rust-colored beard.

The chatter died when we stopped just beneath the crest, the only sounds our breathing and the breeze, playing over us. My nose wrinkled at the strong scents of their unwashed armpits and crotches. The captain hopped down from his rock and stepped back as a sign that we could come up the rest of the way unimpeded. When we reached their level, he extended an arm while he inclined his head in a mock bow.

"Welcome, young prince, most royal Prince Jonathan. I believe I shall entertain you myself." He turned his head to address his men, arranged in a loose arc behind him. "And *only* myself." His detachment laughed with the throaty rumble of an animal pack.

Jonathan stood and waited until the noise died away before he nodded in return. "You may surrender," he said quietly in their language. "It is not yet too late to save yourselves."

The large captain blinked in confusion, probably unable to believe what my prince had just said. I confess I shared his disbelief.

Jonathan faced an opponent easily half again his weight and probably his strength as well, but my prince could move like a desert cat. Whenever he and I sparred with padded weapons, I always finished with bruised arms and body. But even knowing this, I feared for him, for I was no Philistine captain.

The Philistine's face turned crimson. "Piglet boy!" he shouted. He lunged like an enraged beast.

Jonathan slipped to his left, and the captain's overhead swing only hissed through the air. Before he could recover, Jonathan stepped up and swung backhanded into the back of the larger man's neck, slicing through the leather guard. The Philistine crashed to the ground with a clattering of shield and sword while Jonathan yanked his own blade out of the dead man's severed spine. It ended that quickly.

I positioned myself behind my prince to protect his back. Too many Philistines stood there for me to watch well, but the pagans stayed motionless, shocked at their leader's sudden defeat. Jonathan jumped at the center of their line while the captain's body still twitched. In all our battles together, I had never seen him like that before. That day, he became a madman, fighting his way forward in a frenzy.

He killed the next one with a quick sideways jab to the armpit before that fighter could raise his shield. Jonathan wheeled and crashed into the soldier on his left. The man toppled backward, going down in a tangle of limbs along with the fellow next to him. Jonathan put deep slashes in both their necks. Shaken out of their stupor, the remaining Philistines swarmed furiously, trying to attack him from all sides.

I stayed close at his back. Yahweh was with us that day, for in their fervor to slay King Saul's son, they dismissed me completely even as I swatted them from his back like flies.

Jonathan lunged forward, swinging his sword and buckler side to side, growling like a cornered animal. The Philistines stayed back on their heels except for those who tried to circle him. And there they circled into me. He was the maddened bull—I was the scorpion's sting. He stabbed, feinted, and slashed. I cracked their skulls. In the mad, dusty violence on that half acre of hilltop, the clang of one sword against another and the thump of sword on shield covered the sharp rap of my wooden staff. The thick oak bashed heads, and the bronze point punched into throats and eyes while the heathens lay stunned on the ground.

The Philistines' grab for an easy victim turned instead into a fight for their own lives. We downed most of them. Only four remained to break and run when they finally teetered at the back slope. Jonathan and I stood panting side by side as we watched them tumbling down the hill, heedless of the rocks and gravel spilling down with them. They slid to tethered mules at the bottom and jumped onto their bare backs, wrapping their arms around the mules' necks. Frantic heels drummed into the animals' sides. We chuckled at their clumsy riding. When the terrified riders galloped into their distant camp and scattered sentries to each side, we turned back around to our hilltop.

Twenty Philistine bodies lay scattered in a loose line laid out from the dead captain's corpse to where we stood. Not all of them were dead. Mortally wounded ones groaned and tried to rise in the dirt.

Jonathan walked to the nearest living one. "Come, Beral, we should end their suffering." He knelt down and grabbed the man by his black hair. Blood still dripped from his sword's blade as he raised it for the death stroke.

"No!" I cried. I moved next to him and pushed his arm down.

Jonathan's mouth went slack as if he did not recognize me.

"This is not a task for you, my prince," I said. "You should not have to kill those who are already dying. I will do this."

He nodded slowly and stood up. "Perhaps you are right, Beral." He gazed around at those he and I had slain and wounded. "I will wait there." He indicated the back slope, overlooking the Philistine camp.

I took his place at the dying man's side. The Philistine gurgled from a thrust into his neck, one of Jonathan's downed victims. I finished his throat with my dagger. I moved swiftly from one groaning body to the next to dispatch them. Too many still breathed. Some looked younger than me, one barely a man, with a beard like black goose down. A few were conscious of me and knew what I did. Feeble voices begged me. Those were my worst memories of that fight, but I had been right. A prince should not do this.

13

I didn't loot the dead but took only the captain's sword and shield when I finished. The sword's handle had been fashioned as a pair of intertwined bronze serpents whose heads met at the hilt. It was a fine, distinctive weapon.

I rose up and looked about at the scene again. It brought back to mind a day long before.

When I had been a young boy, my father once took me on a trading journey. After some days' travel, we came across a death struggle in the wilderness. We watched from atop a rock outcropping as a wild ox tried to fight off a pack of jackals. I could tell the ox was old. A few seasons earlier, the little dogs would never have tried to bring him down as they did then. Even so, his massive horns still made them pay a terrible price for their attack. One after another, he pitched many of them yelping against the rocks.

But he could not turn fast enough to protect his flanks. The jackals swarmed up and over his haunches while he wheeled about, futilely trying to catch them. Blood began to flow from rips on his sides. The old bull's bravery moved me, and I wanted to come to his assistance. I loaded my sling, but my father placed his arm across my chest.

"No," he said. "It is better that the old warrior die fighting here than to limp away and bleed out his life alone."

So in the end, the pack of snarling jackals brought the weakened ox down, his horns swinging until he was pinned to the ground. They began to eat while he still moved feebly.

Seeing how it troubled me, my father laid his hand on my shoulder. "The bull ox died at the hands of creatures that could only face him boldly in numbers. But he did not die alone, Beral, because we watched him make this stand. We will honor him whenever we tell the tale of what we saw here."

He pointed to a rising patch of dust moving down a wadi in the distance. "See, he did not die in vain, either. There goes his herd, the cows and young ones he protected with his own life. The calves will live today because of him. We should not feel much sadness that he died like this. We should only hope that, when we die, we die for a cause like his." He looked back down at the feeding jackals with a wry expression. "I suppose it would be vanity to perhaps hope that someone would witness our bravery too as we witnessed his." I can't remember anymore what my father's business was on that trip, but I never forgot that wild ox's solitary fight or his death.

That day at the top of Seneh, Jonathan had just faced his own pack of grimacing, scrambling jackals. But there I stood behind him, and his flanks were guarded. That gave me some comfort since my mood had fallen away from the immediate flush of victory. Killing the wounded had soiled my spirit, and I wanted only to wipe the blood off my hands.

Jonathan stood at the edge of the hilltop with his back to me, watching the Philistine encampment. "Beral, come here. Look at this!"

As I came and stood beside him, my eyes widened, and I caught my breath.

Below us in the distance, the Philistine camp boiled in uproar. The men fleeing our hilltop had apparently kicked up a maelstrom of dust and shouting. The heathens ran everywhere in confusion. We could even hear the distant clanking of sword on sword. Horses milled about while unmanned chariots circled at a gallop, running down hapless dozens in their way. Smoke rose from burning tents. A wild panic overwhelmed their army.

I looked at Jonathan. "What's happening? What caused this?"

His laugh sounded like a bark, and he gripped my shoulder. "I think we did."

Jonathan saw the advantage before I did. "Beral," he exclaimed, "now is the time to attack the Philistines!" He started running toward the front slope facing our forces. "We have to tell my father," he shouted over his shoulder.

He reached the edge and raised his sword and buckler to signal but then lowered both arms in disbelief. When I reached him, I saw why. Our army, in ranks and moving briskly, was already marching forward toward the pass below us.

CHAPTER THREE

Then Saul and all his men assembled and went to the battle.

1 Samuel 14:20a NIV

I LEARNED FROM KING SAUL'S GUARDS what happened in the Israelite camp after Jonathan and I slipped away. They told me what they saw then, but not until we were breakfasting on meat and bread together the next morning. I only wish my prince and I had heard it much sooner.

King Saul sat in the morning shade of a fruit tree, grimly pondering his army's prospects. Two men had been seen climbing Seneh, but no one could identify them at that distance. Soon after that, a fight on the hilltop kicked up dust and noise, and men paused to watch. Saul heard the excited mutterings of the sentries and got up for a better look. In those days, he had the sharp eyes of a coasting vulture.

"What's happening up there?" he demanded. "Are they brawling amongst themselves?"

"I don't know, my lord," answered Ben-Ami, the captain of his bodyguards. "There *is* fighting at the top of the pass."

"I can see that, fool, but what does it mean? *Who* is fighting?" He turned to Abner, standing next to him. "Did you send men up there to capture Seneh against my orders?"

"No, my lord. I did not." He shaded his eyes and squinted. "But the scuffle appears to be done."

The dust settled on the Philistines' hill position, and the sounds of fighting died away. Suddenly smoke and dust appeared in the enemy's distant main camp. Disjointed noises sounded there, horses running, swords clashing.

"This makes me uneasy," said the king. "Something is wrong. If this is some trick, I won't be caught here sucking on a pomegranate."

Ahijah waited nearby, wearing a linen ephod and looking as bewildered as everyone else.

"Come here, Priest," said Saul quietly. He spoke to the man of God in hushed tones. "Bring up the ark. Have the Kohathites ready to carry it."

"Yes, sire." The young priest clapped his hands and sent an assistant running to gather up the Levite clan from the hill country of Ephraim, designated since Moses's time to carry Israel's Ark of the Covenant on their shoulders.

Saul stilled as Ahijah placed a hand on his shoulder to bless him. Sounds of the tumult in the enemy camp increased to a roar easily heard.

"Sire, they're scattering! The Philistines run in all directions!" Ben-Ami practically hopped with excitement.

Saul shook off the priest's touch. "Not now, Ahijah. Remove your hand. I must be about this business." He shouted to his commanders, "Muster the ranks and hurry with your formations! And someone is up on Seneh. Find out who."

Captains bustled throughout the encampment, kicking men out of midmorning naps to strap on crudely made shields. Fathers, sons, and cousins ran to stand beside each other as the army responded. At the order from Abner, brigade commanders stood at the head of their men and gave strength counts—all the commanders except one.

Jeronn was Prince Jonathan's second-in-command, and he trotted forward to take the vacant commander's post in front of the first rank. "Sire, Prince Jonathan is not here," he called.

"'Not here'? What do you mean, 'Not here'?" Saul paced while Nathon, his armor bearer, struggled to fasten the king's breastplate. "Go and find him. Send Beral to bring him from the latrine."

"Sire, Beral is not here either. He and the prince are both gone."

"Both of them? Gone?" Saul stopped to stare at Jeronn in disbelief then spun around to face the pass at Micmash. He shaded his eyes and studied the top of Seneh. None of the Philistine lookouts could be seen anymore. "Could it be?" he muttered.

"My king," said Abner quietly, "I believe your son is on that hilltop. Alive or dead, I do not know, but he has opened up the Philistine camp for us. We should enter before the pagans recover from their confusion and close it again."

Saul answered in a detached voice as he continued to watch Seneh. "Yes, you're right, Abner. We must not let this chance leave us." He lowered his hand and turned to his general. "Order the men forward. Bring the ark with us. I will lead." He stood still and let Nathon finish the bindings while Abner bellowed orders. He looked back again at the deserted Philistine outpost before he went to take his place in the already moving army. He swung his sword back and forth. As it swished, he shouted, "I curse any man who eats before sunset today, before we finish, before I have avenged myself on my enemies, these accursed Philistines!" The men roared in reply. They loved him in that moment.

No man ever called King Saul a coward. A conspicuous head taller than any other soldier of Israel, he strode at the center of the first rank, just ahead of the hoisted Ark of the Covenant. The mostly untrained army moved forward in loose ranks, parting around large boulders and stumbling past smaller ones. They could see burning tents and complete panic in the Philistine camp. Closing on the Micmash pass, the ranks saw a man standing at the top of Seneh. The figure raised his sword and shield then lowered them abruptly. Another man joined him.

"It's Prince Jonathan!" The cries rose as men recognized him.

King Saul's face brightened like a silver spoon when he saw his eldest, the apparent victor of a fight, standing unhurt high above him. He beckoned the prince down.

———— ◦◦◦◦ ————

"Come, Beral, it's time to rejoin our brethren," Jonathan said. We slid down on our backsides, only slightly less comically than the Philistine survivors who'd fled from us earlier. My prince ran to his father, who embraced him for an instant before sending him to his men. I followed a step behind. Jeronn looked relieved at the appearance of his commander.

None of the Philistines noticed our army until we burst into their camp. Jonathan strode at the head of lions downing sheep when we fell upon that roiling mass of panicked men. Our commanders tried to keep order, but soldiers broke away in packs after fleeing enemy groups. The Philistines deserted the battle. They dropped their weapons and ran from the slaughter. Hebrew farmers and tradesmen gleefully picked up swords and spears to continue the pursuit. Jonathan paused in the midst of the choking smoke to put his hands down and watch as fighting men boiled out of the encampment to disappear down wadis and over hills. Standing beside him, I could hear Philistines screaming far away.

Suddenly, a flicker of movement behind us caught the corner of my eye. A nearby collapsed tent heaved up on one side, and a burly Philistine struggled out from underneath it. Apparently caught inside when the tent fell, he looked about, wild-eyed and bewildered, until he saw Prince Jonathan. He yanked a spear out of the tangled wreckage and started forward. I moved to intercept him as he rushed my prince's back. The soldier swerved, moving the spear tip around toward me. I knocked it aside with my staff and stepped inside the point. While he tried to draw his sword, I clubbed him on the side of the head. He staggered back, and I finished him with a thrust under the shield into his groin.

Jonathan had turned around at the sound of the clash, sweat streaking his dusty face. He grunted as the Philistine slammed into the dirt in a death spasm. Then he smiled broadly at me. "What do you think, Beral? Yahweh has taken our cause today, has He not?"

"Yes, my lord. I see that He has." I was still breathing hard from the brief fight.

"He does even more. Look at that." He gestured to a group near the center of the destroyed camp.

Saul stood surrounded by Ben-Ami and his guards while a gray-headed man knelt before him. A large number of men gathered behind the old man, all fallen to their knees. The old man jabbered and shook his head as he held out his hands. He looked familiar.

"Sire, isn't that Mihovil?" I asked.

Mihovil, one of the Hebrew clan leaders who had left Saul and allied with the Philistine army, was pleading for his life. The king smiled at the traitor and motioned him to his feet. The old scoundrel leapt up and kissed Saul on both cheeks. His clansmen cheered and waved their spears. The king spoke again, pointing toward the few scattered enemy still in sight. Mihovil and his men turned as one and ran to give chase, baying as if they pursued a chicken-stealing fox. The scene disgusted me. I would have beheaded him and every tenth one of his men. Yet they received the king's pardon and rejoined us.

I looked at Jonathan in dismay.

He raised his eyebrows and shrugged, palms up. "Beral, a king must have soldiers if he is to carry the day. Mihovil is a leader with many soldiers. He will be loyal to us from this day on. Yahweh gave him back to us."

I remained unconvinced. Rats that run once from a burning barn will leave the next time even faster.

Jonathan tapped me with his sword. "Come on. There are more sea people about." With but a handful of our brigade still intact, he led us from the encampment to find and kill more Philistines.

Just outside the burning camp, we came across more repentant traitors, men skulking about, searching for Saul to declare that they had always, in fact, been loyal to him. Seeing Jonathan, they tried offering their services, but he shook his head, saying it was a matter to take up with his father. We continued after the fleeing enemy. Still more Israelites knelt as we trotted past, ones who had simply deserted to hide in caves and cisterns. With their bravery restored at sighting the invaders' backs, they cheered my prince and joined us. I resigned myself to it. At least those men hadn't actually joined themselves with the heathens as Mihovil had. I smiled to myself. I was starting to reason like a king.

The Philistines ran like Samson's foxes. Many lost their weapons, but they received no mercy, for they were heathens, enemies of Yahweh. By late afternoon, our army, exhausted and famished, paused at the edge of a cedar thicket. Some of the men staggered in the heat. I wanted to rest before we entered the woods to flush out the remnants of the sea people. However, Abner gave the command to advance.

Men banged their newfound swords or spear butts against shields as we stepped into the shade of the trees. We slowed, eyes searching the shadows for any cowering foe. Bees buzzed listlessly ahead of us.

Someone shouted, "Honey!" and I saw the amber fluid oozing from splits and holes in the hollow wood of a downed log.

"Look here, Beral," Jonathan said excitedly. "Lend me your staff." I handed my fighting oak to him, having already cached the unfamiliar weaponry from the dead Philistine captain. Jonathan stood back from the swarming bees and dipped the butt into a pocket of honeycombs. He shucked half the honey onto his hand and let me take the rest. Nothing had ever tasted better to me than that first scoop of honey. Jonathan's eyes lit up, and we grinned at each other as we took turns dipping out of the log. Neither of us noticed that no other soldier joined in.

One of the spearmen, Zamir, finally spoke. "Sire, this morning your father bound the army under a strict oath, saying, 'Cursed be any man who eats food today!' That is why the men are faint. No one has eaten since morning."

"Zamir, I fear my father has made trouble for us," Jonathan replied. "See how much better I feel now? Beral too. I will not tell you to break the oath, but it would have been much better if the men could eat some of the plunder they have already taken from our enemies. Wouldn't we kill so many more if we had full bellies?"

The men shifted their feet and looked down at the ground, but still no one else ate any honey.

CHAPTER FOUR

Saul said, "May God deal with me, be it ever so
severely, if you do not die, Jonathan."

1 Samuel 14:44 NIV

ABNER CALLED THE CHASE OFF at sundown. He had to, for our army was staggering, hollow-eyed, and spent. We had run the Philistines more than ten miles that day. Along the way, we'd rounded up and brought with us several head of the enemy's cattle and sheep. Philistines scrabbled away in the twilight even as our men stopped near the village of Aijalon to build fires. They butchered the livestock and immediately hoisted quarters on makeshift spits over the roaring flames.

I ate as ravenously as the others, my honey meal long since gone. Blood and juice dripped from every face, the barely singed meat delicious to famished soldiers.

Jonathan would not eat any of it, although I carried a chunk of shoulder to him. "Take it to the sentries, Beral," he said. He sounded distracted in the encroaching darkness. I delivered the meal to our perimeter posts and returned to the feast fires.

The perimeter guards shouted challenges, and I knew King Saul had arrived. He appeared at the largest fire atop his riding mule. General Abner and Ahijah the priest rode with him while Ben-Ami and his bodyguards paced alongside on foot, more fatigued than any one of us.

Abner looked pleased as he dismounted. He walked over to Jonathan and the other commanders. "Well done, Prince Jonathan. Well done, each of you." He placed a hand on Jonathan's shoulder, a gesture one fighting man gave to another.

All seemed well at first. The new arrivals gathered around the fires to slice off strips of the sizzling meat for themselves. Suddenly, a horrified shout stopped everyone.

Ahijah, with rounded eyes and a hand to his mouth, still sat on his mule, surveying the sight of blood-splattered armed men. He must have finally realized all that blood hadn't come from fighting. "Look!" he cried. "The men are sinning against the Lord by eating meat that has blood in it."

The priest spoke the truth. The Law did forbid us from eating meat until the blood had been properly drained, but I thought surely the Law would flex in times of need. The army had fought all day for Yahweh, and that evening our stomachs rumbled. The king, however, agreed with Ahijah. He spoke to the leaders around him. "You have broken faith," he said.

Looking around in the firelight, he pointed to a large boulder with a flattened top. Half a dozen men sat on the rock, wiping grease from their hands onto their tunics.

"Roll that stone here," Saul ordered. He towered over us in his anger. "Now!"

They hopped up and heaved at it, using spear shafts for leverage. While they manhandled it toward the fire, Saul turned back to his commanders. "Go out among the men and tell them to bring the captured cattle and sheep to this rock. Slaughter them here and eat them instead. Drain the blood and do not sin against the Lord further by eating any more meat with blood still in it."

I went with Jonathan as the leaders scattered to pass on the king's instructions. Not many complained. We had broken the Law and been caught at it. I felt Saul's quick response to our trespass should dispel Yahweh's wrath. When we returned to the firelight with men and oxen, we found others stacking stones to build an altar under Ahijah's watchful eye, the first altar Saul ever built to Yahweh.

We slaughtered more animals and then consumed purified meat with clean consciences. Our compliance didn't calm Saul, however. While he and Jonathan ate together near the dying fire, he kept casting an eye about, taking in his warriors as they started to lean back with sated appetites. Finally standing, he hitched his tunic closer against the night chill and climbed onto another large boulder. He stood there, backlit by glowing embers, until every eye turned toward him.

He raised a fist. "Men of Israel, you have won a great victory here today. Our Lord's enemies still run from us as sheep scatter before hyenas."

Soft chuckles sounded from the reclining soldiers, and some of them thudded sword and spear hafts on the ground.

But the king hadn't finished. "Let us go down after the Philistines again tonight and plunder them till dawn, and let us not leave one of them alive," he said.

No one moved in the silence that followed. I watched men, weary to the bone, roll their heads to look at each other. Next to me, Jonathan stared down at his lap for a moment before he noisily got to his feet. I rose to lean on my staff beside him.

My prince met the eye of every captain and commander in the firelight. "Come, men. We have more to do," he said. He spoke softly, yet every warrior heard him. Jeronn and other captains stood up wearily. Other soldiers also got up.

"Do whatever seems best to you," one commander said. Farther away in the darkness, some muttered other things.

"Wait." Ahijah, still wearing the ephod, had watched everything in silence until then. He stepped forward and addressed the king. "Sire, I believe we should know Yahweh's will first. Let us inquire of God here."

Saul looked exasperated, but he shrugged. "Very well," he said. He looked up at the night sky and spread his arms, palms up. In that posture, standing atop the rock, he at least looked like a prophet speaking to God. "Lord, shall I go down after the Philistines? Will you give them into Israel's hand?" His voice rose to heaven alongside sparks from the fire dying behind him. We barely breathed, waiting for Yahweh's answer. Ahijah raised his face to the starlight and closed his eyes. Crackling fires and the remaining bawling oxen were the only sounds. The moment dragged on for a long minute until Saul lowered his head. He exchanged a look with the priest.

Ahijah shook his head. "There is no answer, sire," he said sadly, his head bowed. "Shall I consult the Urim and Thummim?"

King Saul's face flushed. "Someone has sinned, Ahijah. Yahweh turns his face from us because of someone's guilt. Yes, cast the lots. But

24

do not ask Yahweh whether we fight on. Ask instead who has done this. Ask who has sinned against Israel." He stepped down from the boulder. "Come here, you leaders of the army. We will find out what sin has been committed today." He drew his sword. "As surely as the Lord who rescues Israel lives, even if it was my son, Jonathan"—he pointed the sword tip at his eldest son—"he must die."

Not one of the assembled men said a word. Ahijah stared at Jonathan and me with horrified eyes. He knew. Almost every man knew that their prince, not having heard of Saul's reckless vow, had been cursed by that vow. The king himself seemed unaware of the mute tension in his army. He addressed the heads of each family and clan. "You stand over there with your ranks. I and Jonathan my son will stand here."

"Do what seems best to you," came a reply from the darkness. Men shuffled, their faces sullen. The king raised his face to heaven once again. "O Lord God of Israel, give me the right answer that I may act to purge this sin from us." He stepped down from the rock and turned to the priest. "Cast the lots."

Ahijah performed the ritual with shaking hands. One at a time, he approached the tribal leaders. Facing that man, he withdrew one sacred gem from the pouch on the ephod and threw it down while heads craned forward to see. Every throw turned up a Thummim, exonerating whoever stood before him and the soldiers he led. I waited behind my prince. Nathon cast a pitying look at me from the front rank. Finally, the priest finished. Every man in the army had passed the trial by lot except Saul and Jonathan. And me.

The priest approached us. His whole being trembled. "Sire?" he asked.

"Cast the lot between me and Jonathan my son." Saul glowered at the ground, his anger building.

Ahijah stood before Jonathan and drew a stone. The Urim. And Jonathan proved guilty. Saul's eyes flashed as he twirled to face his son. I stayed behind my prince even as I gripped my fighting staff.

"Tell me what you have done," said the king, his rage threatening to boil over, knuckles white on his sword hilt.

"I merely tasted a little honey with the end of a staff. And now must I die for that?" It was the first time I'd ever heard Jonathan's voice

25

tremble. Yet, even then, he protected me by leaving out my name. Saul wasn't fooled, though. His eyes pierced me, and he looked pointedly at my staff.

"May God deal with me, be it ever so severely, if you do not die, Jonathan. I have already sworn this to God," the king said.

Jonathan only bowed his head, his silence speaking more than words. I stepped up to stand at his shoulder, still holding the staff.

"Sire," said the priest. He drooped with apology. "Your son, the prince, did not know of the vow. In this case, I feel forgiveness would be justified. Perhaps a rite of purification—"

"Silence! You already *knew* of this, Ahijah?" Saul said. Incredulous, eyes bulging, he turned to the army, still waiting in ranks. "Am I the only one who stands here ignorant of what sins my own son has committed today?" His address went out to a restless, moving mass of armed men, anonymous in the darkness beyond the firelight, their murmuring rising with no individual voice. Finally, one man spoke clearly: Jeronn.

"My king, should Jonathan die now after he has brought about this great deliverance in Israel? I think it should not be so. Never! Not by our hand. As surely as the Lord lives, not a hair of his head will fall to the ground. He killed the first Philistines today with God's help, and he should now have God's protection." His voice grew as he spoke. Men roared their agreement, and swords battered shields. The cacophony rose as men of war threatened to become a mob. They shouted Jonathan's name. Even Mihovil the traitor raised a spear and called for my prince's pardon as he himself had been spared.

Saul was shaken. No one was supporting him, and even I knew that when a king loses the precious loyalty of his army, he loses everything. Looking like a beaten pugilist, he held his arms out in a gesture of surrender. The clamoring subsided.

"Very well," Saul said. "I will release my son Jonathan from a vow I made in haste." He turned and embraced my prince to the cheers of the army. Jonathan returned the grip.

Soon, peace settled upon our camp. Men finished eating. Guards were changed. We sought out sleeping spots, and everything became quiet.

But I saw two things that night. I saw the dark look on Saul's face as he sat alone by the dying fire. He brooded to himself for a long time, looking first at the men sleeping around him, then toward Jonathan and me. I think he feared his son then and hated me. While my name had never been mentioned, my fate always intertwined with Jonathan's. Had he died that night, I would have as well, only not with my head bowed in submission as an Isaac. And my prince would not have died until Saul's guards killed me at my place defending his back.

And earlier, the other sight was Jonathan's face. I saw the sad eyes when he embraced his father. He kept his thoughts to himself, but I think I knew them. Saul would have killed him that night, but not to honor an oath to Yahweh. The volatile king wore the mantle of obedience to a sacred oath only in order to cover his own pride. No, Jonathan wouldn't have died because of Yahweh. He would have been executed because his father was too prideful to admit an error.

CHAPTER FIVE

...whenever Saul saw a mighty or brave man, he took him into his service.

1 Samuel 14:52b NIV

THE PHILISTINES WITHDREW TO THEIR lands, and we returned to Saul's home in Gibeah. My prince never mentioned the incident of the honey after that night, at least not to me. He and his father avoided each other for weeks. I only observed them speak sparingly to each other in the evenings when they sat to eat at the king's table while I stood against the wall behind them. We all felt the unease in the banquet hall, but no one spoke of it. Even the cooking-area gossips were muted.

After Micmash, Saul decided to push back against the enemies surrounding Israel. First, he turned to the Moabites, making the announcement at one of those stony evening meals.

"I have decided to turn eastward and press an attack against the Moabites. They will be the first to feel Yahweh's wrath and mine as well," he said. He took a long draw from his wine cup and continued without looking up. "You, Jonathan, will command the three brigades of the army's right wing."

I couldn't see Jonathan's expression, but his head jerked at the news of his promotion. He inclined it slightly. "As you wish, my king."

I struck my staff against the stone floor in approval.

Saul slammed his empty cup down. "It is time for Abinadab and Malki-Shua to finally campaign as well. I am placing them with you. Make them your aides, and see that no harm comes to either of them."

I smiled inwardly. Prince Jonathan's arrogant younger brothers would surely chafe at being under his command. Neither would ever be his equal, in my opinion.

———— ✦✧✦ ————

On the day our army left Gibeah, Prince Jonathan walked at its head beside his father's mule. He could have had a squad of bodyguards, but he declared he needed only me. I walked proudly behind him.

We charged the Moabites whenever we encountered them. They never fought as well as the Philistines. None of the other peoples did— not the Ammorites, the Edomites, the Amalekites, nor the kings of Zobah. King Saul, as always, walked in the front rank. Everyone fought harder when he led. Only his eldest son, my prince, could inspire and lead like him. And we were skillfully led, for General Abner played the fox, usually finding a way to surprise an enemy's flank. With Yahweh, we seemed invincible.

Sometimes, Jonathan stepped out beyond our first rank, and I stepped out with him. As always, I scrambled behind him whenever he went into the fight. When he ran ahead of our lines, his commanders, worried for his safety, hurried their companies forward. At other times, he advanced leisurely with ranks of men abreast on either side of him. The Moabites never knew which Prince Jonathan they faced, but either way I stayed at his back. No one ever struck him from behind. I killed several who tried.

That day when the last Moabite battle ended, our men busied themselves rooting out and killing their stragglers. I stood beside my prince in the narrow valley where the fighting had taken place, surrounded by dead and dying men still clutching broken weapons. All around and above us, the heathens screamed as they were being dragged from their hiding places in caves and rock clefts. Their cries were pitiful.

Jonathan stared up at the hillsides and listened for a few moments before he sheathed his sword and turned to me. "There's nothing more here that needs us, Beral," he said. "You and I are going back to Gibeah. Jeronn can finish this slaughter."

"Home, my lord?"

That morning, word had reached the army that Reina had given birth to a boy. I knew Jonathan was anxious to see his son, whom he had declared he would name Mephibosheth.

"Yes," he said. "I will go and take leave from my father. Go and gather up my things and yours."

"Yes, my lord." I hurriedly packed provisions and our sleeping mats. In a matter of minutes, we were moving briskly toward home, carrying sacks and leaving the final acts of carnage behind us. Abner sent along a squad of ten as an escort for us through the Judean hill country, still infested with bandits even in the midst of warring armies. We jogged most of the way, stopping to rest every few miles. It was during one of those rest halts that Prince Jonathan changed my life.

He and I sat on rocks, apart from the others, alongside the dirt track we were following home. I gnawed on a lump of cheese as hard as my fist while he sucked on the remains of a grilled goat's leg.

He leaned back and threw the thighbone away. "Beral, where is that sword and shield you took at Micmash?" The question surprised me. I had almost forgotten those weapons.

"They are stored at Gibeah, my lord. This bashes heads much better." I grinned as I twirled my oak staff with one hand before burying its bronze point in the dirt. He licked his fingers. That damned little smile that always preceded trouble crept over his face while he watched me from the corner of his eye.

"I think when we get back, you should have the shield oiled." He nodded to himself. "Get the sword sharpened too."

I was startled. "Why, my lord? This oak serves both of us much better. It's what I can best use at your back."

Jonathan reached down to pick up some pebbles and roll them between his palms as he answered. "I know that, Beral. Your bronze-tipped staff has saved me many times already. It suits an armor bearer well… but you're not going to be my armor bearer after today."

"What?" My face sagged. "My lord, have I done wrong to you?"

"Be at ease, Beral." He smiled and pulled my staff out of the ground. "This is a good, stout staff, certainly, but it isn't suitable gear for a commander of a hundred fighting men."

"My lord?"

He clapped me on the back. "Beral, you're going to be one of my commanders. You're going to have a hundred new soldiers under you. And I want you to start training them as soon as we get back." His smile broadened. "You may find there's more to do there than step with them in the line."

"But, my lord," I sputtered, "I've never commanded anyone before. And who'll carry your shield? Who will guard your back?"

Jonathan held me by both shoulders and looked me directly in the eyes. "Beral, every man in Israel knows of your bravery and the deeds you have done. Haven't you seen how they part for you now when you walk by? You'll have no problem leading any of them. And as for my back…" He turned and whistled at the lounging soldiers waiting behind us. They stiffened and sat up. "Zelig, send Herzi to me," he called.

The squad leader nodded before he turned to tap the shield of one of his men. That one stood quickly and trotted over to where we sat. He looked as jittery as a colt being led to his castration, yet he managed to stand still in front of Jonathan. I studied him closely. He was young— very young. I doubted his balls sported anything hairier than silk. He had a stout build, though, with shoulders as strong looking as any man's.

"My lord?" His voice cracked as he spoke.

Jonathan looked sideways at me. "What do you think, Beral? Will he do?"

I didn't like what was happening. "My prince, he looks to be only a boy," I said.

But Jonathan only smiled. "Herzi is two years older than you were when you first carried your staff at my back. A head taller too." He turned to the youth. "You are Herzi, son of Lavan?"

"Yes, my lord."

"You fought at Micmash? You killed a Philistine captain there?"

"Yes, my lord." The boy squared and raised his chin a little. I had to admit I did like him.

"Good. You will be my shield bearer. Do you know of Beral here?"

Herzi's eyes flicked to me then back to my prince. "Yes, my lord. Everyone knows of Beral, son of Ammiel."

"Good. Walk beside him the rest of the way. Beral will tell you what your duties are." He looked at me while he spoke to his new armor bearer. "In Gibeah, Beral will train you to use the staff and what to do in battle at my back. He will also tell you about the ways of the palace—which royals to avoid. Listen to him and learn quickly. He will have other things to do when we return. Do you understand all this?"

"Yes, my lord." Herzi's eyes opened wide, whether in eagerness or dread I did not know.

"Good," Jonathan said. "Now go and gather your gear. Return here quickly. You and Beral can talk from here on. Go."

The youth hurried away, probably as dazed by the sudden change to his life as I was.

Jonathan spoke quietly to me. "Abner checked him and his family before recommending him to me. He's fought bravely in the front rank already. Herzi will be a good man." He paused for a long time before he went on. "He'll be a good man, but he won't be you, Beral. I doubt I'll have another friend like you." He looked off at the low hills ahead of us.

"Then why, my lord? Why are you sending me away?" My eyes watered.

"I'm not sending you *away*, Beral. I'm letting you rise to be the leader you should be. It's part of what being a future king means. I need a good armor bearer behind me... and good commanders beside me." He grasped me at the elbow. "Now go and start training this boy. You won't have much time for him at Gibeah."

We walked the remaining miles while I told Herzi the things he would need to know. I hesitated to confide all the habits and preferences of my prince, feeling as though I would be betraying him. Jonathan, however, knew me.

He came forward to where we walked ahead of him. "Tell him everything, Beral, including how I pout if the wine is spoiled. Tell him of Reina's moods too." He slapped both of us on the back before he slowed to rejoin the rest.

I knew what he meant. The princess Reina suffered from harsh dreams during the night and developed headaches. The palace servants knew to stay away from her at those times. I think she resented me because of the friendship her husband had with me, never understanding the bond between men who walk into combat together. She often ordered me to do household tasks when Jonathan was absent. I hoped she would not be such a disdainful mistress to this young boy. He seemed anxious and eager to learn.

When we arrived at Gibeah, Jonathan took Herzi into the royal household, and for the first time, I didn't follow. I watched them walking away, feeling strange at seeing Herzi with my prince's shield slung over his back. After that moment, changes came too quickly for me to ponder on them any further. Katriel, one of Abner's aides, awaited me at the barracks.

"Welcome and congratulations, Commander Beral," he gushed. "Prince Jonathan has arranged everything for you. Come this way, please."

I dropped my gear and followed him to the training ground, wondering how many others already knew of this promotion before I did. We came to the open sand-covered yard where fighting drills were conducted. A loose crowd of men and youths waited there, shuffling from foot to foot and looking off in every direction like sheep without a shepherd. They straightened a bit when Katriel and I arrived. Armed guards stood watch around the perimeter of the area.

Katriel turned to me with a half bow. "These are your men, Commander Beral. A fine-looking group of fighting men for Israel. I wish you success in training them as you see fit." A mealy smile covered his oiled face, and I knew he hadn't meant a single word. He was mocking me.

I felt sure Katriel had wanted the company himself. He indicated a mounting block I should stand on to address my new command. Then, no doubt anticipating my failure and hardly able to control his giggles at that prospect, he faced about and left.

When King Saul had decided earlier that he needed to establish a trained army, he toured Israel on his mule, looking for young men over twenty with promise, whether tending fields or flocks. Any strong lad he saw soon ended up taken by the king's entourage for service in the ranks. Families grumbled that this was what the prophet Samuel had predicted a king would do, but the army needed their sons, so we took them. Most of them would strike out for their homes if given a chance.

As I stood before nearly a hundred of these reluctant boys, I was rooted to the spot, with no idea of what I should do. On the road home from battle, I had told Herzi of his duties while giving no thought to my own. My new company, the guards, and even some idlers who dropped by—they all watched me. I walked to the block with legs like wood, my mind roiling. What would I say to these men? What did I know about training any of them? I climbed up to stand there, dry mouthed and speechless. I cleared my throat.

"My name is Beral. You and I have one thing in common, men of Israel," I began. "You are untested as fighting men. I am untested as a commander." I stopped and swept my gaze left and right.

Some of them watched me. Others stared at the ground.

"But I have been the shield bearer for Prince Jonathan, King Saul's eldest and our future king. I know how to fight, and I have kept him from harm. I will see that you learn how to fight as well." Most of the group looked at me now, but every fifth man or so still kicked at the earth as if refusing to acknowledge my presence.

A voice rumbled behind me like a grindstone, causing the whole company to stiffen. "Stand straight before your commander! Look like men! You are soldiers now, not manure haulers!"

I turned to see who had spoken. Zelig and his squad of ten stood just to my right side. Barrel-chested and squat, as solid as a cedar stump, he planted himself with a characteristic wide stance. Scars lined his face and laced his arms. Two left fingers had been lost long before to a hacking Moabite sword.

He touched a palm to his chest in salute. "May I assist you, Commander Beral?" he asked.

Zelig was one of Jonathan's favorites. A grizzled old veteran and leader, he should have been one of the king's generals by this time, but he refused any advancement beyond squad leader. "You don't kill as many Philistines when you have to tell others to do it," he'd always growled. He had led that same squad that escorted us back that day, and he had tapped Herzi to report to Prince Jonathan. Did *everyone* know about my promotion to commander of a company except Herzi and me?

"Yes, Zelig. I am grateful for your help," I replied. A wave of relief washed through my insides.

He touched his chest again before he addressed the men. "All right, listen to me, all of you. Step up closer. The commander and I don't want to be screaming at you. You're not goats we call home to their pen. Here. You... and you"—Zelig pointed at two of his men—"line them up in two ranks. Swat them on the butt if they don't move." In the confusion of men jostling each other, he turned around to face me.

He spoke quietly so no one else could hear his words. "Remember this, Beral. A line soldier needs his legs more than his arms. Always his legs. When you run out of anything else to do, run them a mile. You should run with them too, but not today."

Zelig wheeled about to face the ragged lines. "This is an abomination! Can you goatherds even *pretend* to stand in a straight line?" He pointed at a distant tree. "Do all of you see that dung heap next to the tree?" Men craned to look where he pointed. "You do? Good! Now run to it and run back. The last two of you will catch the flat of my sword on your backsides. Now run, damn you!"

The confused and scared men ran, accompanied by the guards and Zelig's veterans. Headscarves and robes flapped, and the slap of sandals went with them.

Zelig watched for a moment, hands on his hips. His eyes twinkled when he looked back at me. "Running also gives us time to talk," he said.

Jonathan had planned that, knowing the battle-scarred old warrior would become my strong right hand.

CHAPTER SIX

They were brave warriors, ready for battle and able to handle
the shield and spear. Their faces were the faces of lions,
and they were as swift as gazelles in the mountains.

1 Chronicles 12:8b NIV

ISRAEL HAD HAD FIGHTING MEN since the time of Joshua—men from the twelve tribes who came together to stand against our enemies when needed. Herdsmen and farm youths, sturdy from hard labor and able to hunt with slings and bows, always formed our front wall in battle before, but King Saul intended that the young men he conscripted would become the mainstay of a true standing army. The hundred assigned to me were some of the first. I had no idea what to do with them.

I ran with the recruits for two days in the surrounding hills before I decided to have the men spar as Jonathan and I used to do. I walked among the dueling pairs, giving them instructions and encouragement. I expected Zelig to do the same, but he only stood to the side, watching with folded arms as our fighters clanged their captured swords on opponents' shields. The clatter sounded like a sackful of metalware tumbling down a stairway.

"This is a desert donkey trying to hump a camel! Men will be slaughtered dancing around this way," Zelig growled when I stopped beside him. "Proper blade work takes months for goatherds to learn. If we have to lead these boys against the Philistines before then, most of them will die, and you'll be listening to the wailing of their mothers and sweethearts for days. Are you ready to hear all of that, Commander? They will want your head as well."

Zelig spoke to me without deference, and I accepted it. The old veteran knew sword and shield and the techniques of fighting. Every soldier respected him. Still, I was startled by his words even though, as his commander, I tried to act confident.

"Wh-What are you saying?" I stammered. "Fighting men *have* to know how to fight."

"Of *course* they need to know how to fight! That's not what I mean." His voice came from deep in his chest. "Truly, they already know just enough to kill, but not this way, circling each other like bristling cats, too cautious to attack and too afraid to run." He made a slicing motion at the group. "Give me the ones on this side for an hour. You take the rest. Then we'll mock battle—your sixty men against my forty, including my ten veterans. Just give me this time, and you'll see what I mean."

I pretended to mull it over, having no idea what he intended. After a suitable moment, I nodded. "Very well, Zelig. Take them."

He grinned at me, a disconcerting act since Zelig never smiled. He turned to gather his forty men, calling back over his shoulder as he trotted away. "When we return here in an hour, you can either attack or defend—it doesn't matter."

"Certainly," I replied, a plan forming in my head. If Zelig wanted to use fewer men, I would make him see the mistake in that.

Zelig took his group out of sight around a storage building while I gathered the remaining sixty. I divided them so that twenty practiced against forty—one man sparring against two. I showed them how simple it would be for a pair to separate so that one of them could circle behind a single fighter. "It's an easy kill when he doesn't have an armor bearer," I said. They laughed, knowing of my history with Prince Jonathan in battle. "Then, when you have dispatched that opponent, you join a comrade who's fighting alone and do it again. That way, we cut them all down," I continued.

Everyone smiled.

Zelig's forty returned in rough order, trying to march in a single file. Zelig walked alongside, snarling at the ones who lagged. He halted them in front of me then turned and swept his arm over the ragged file in a grand gesture. "Commander Beral, here are your opponents, men of the line. Do you wish to attack or defend?"

I hesitated for an instant. "We will attack."

He saluted with a fist to his chest. "Very well, Commander. We will ready ourselves." He spun around and bellowed. "Form the line. Move!"

His recruits shuffled into a line facing me, the ten seasoned men scattered among them. The new ones moved awkwardly but with a purpose, each one looking to his left and right.

Zelig paced back and forth behind them, lashing their bare calves with a switch to position them. "Form a *rank*, damn you, not a snake's belly! Your fathers' donkeys line up better than this." I have heard overloaded camels that did not criticize as loudly as Zelig. Finally, he conceded that was as good as they would get. He stepped through the line and faced me. "We are ready, Commander," he said.

My sixty waited forty paces away from that uneven line that did not look at all formidable. I directed my men to form pairs. "Use the flat of your blade or the butt end of your spear," I said. "If you are struck on the head or trunk, yield and sit down with your shield over your head. If I see one of you who does not, I will thump you with this." I held up a spear shaft as the men laughed again. It would do no good to have men kill each other in practice.

At my command, we spread out and started a brisk walk toward our outnumbered foes. Zelig went back behind his line, a poor place for a leader, I thought.

Suddenly his voice boomed. "Close!" His group of fighters shuffled again, this time moving sideways, left and right, until every man's shield touched the ones on either side. His ill-formed gaggle transformed into a wall of shields with legs beneath them and eyes above.

Uh oh.

The shields were mismatched articles, mostly of wood and leather, crude and sometimes flimsy, but when we struck against them, our attack looked like pebbles being pitched against a house. My tactic of circling pairs proved useless against their solid front. We hammered and poked at them while they flailed back over the tops of their wall. In the excitement, many of them forgot about using the flats of their blades, yet the ineptness on both sides caused little injury.

I stepped back to watch while the pounding continued. We would not break through, but I saw a way to beat them. Taking four men who hung back from the melee, I tried to lead them around our right side. "This way! Follow me!" I yelled.

Zelig was watching us from behind his wall. When we came around the flank, he had moved a reserve of four experienced men to that side. They formed another solid front as he angled his left side back, moving men with his switch and his bellowed orders.

"Back, you fool! Back one step. Just one step." He scampered behind the line, sometimes moving men by grabbing their shoulders from the rear and shouting, always shouting. "Hold! Keep your shields together. Now back another step. Shields together, you dung eaters!"

My flank attack foiled, I stopped to think. Both sides paused, and the sounds fell away except for labored breathing and moaning. Two of my attacking force sat on the ground holding their heads. Zelig's side would win if I did not do something now.

"Shields together. One step forward. Move!" Zelig bawled. "Move, I said!" His switch hissed behind their wall. "Now two steps forward... Move!" Shields banged together as the entire line of fighters stepped forward and stopped. "Two more steps forward... Move!" Zelig was attacking. His outnumbered force lumbered ahead two steps at a time. Their line was clumsy. It lurched like a child learning to walk, but we fell back before it.

"Hold!'" I yelled. "Hold."

Perhaps ten stood to hack at the moving wall. The rest were cowed and continued to back away. Their fight was over.

I looked across the line at Zelig. "Cease fighting," I said.

He nodded back. "That's enough," he bellowed. "Stop where you stand. Shields down."

Both sides stopped, sides heaving, to set their shields on the ground and lean on spears plundered from the Philistines. Zelig stepped through his line of fighters. "Well done, you goatherds," he told them. He turned to address all of the hundred. "Form up. Four ranks. Hurry now. Sit down where you form up. You can rest for a few minutes. You five, go and fetch water jugs. Move. Move!"

I had said nothing since stopping our skirmish. Zelig's forty men had clearly bested my sixty. Zelig looked over the seated men for a moment before he spoke to me. "Come, Commander Beral. Let's take a moment to talk while they rest." We walked away.

"You did well just then, Commander," he said.

I watched the ground in front of me. "Zelig, don't be polishing a broken sword. I know we were beaten, and I couldn't find a way to change that. I am afraid Prince Jonathan made a mistake in picking me for this."

Zelig stopped short, seizing my arm at the elbow. "What nonsense is this? Beral, if I want to hear crying and whining, I go sit at home with my wife and daughters. Do you know what you just did back there?"

I nodded. "Yes. I lost a scrimmage that I should have won."

"I agree. You certainly did that," he replied. "But do you know all the things you did right?"

"Nothing."

"By the beard of Pharaoh!" he exclaimed in disgust. He raised a hand, and for a second I thought he would strike me, but instead he counted on his fingers.

"You did several things. You organized those sixty raw, untrained boys into an attack. You gave them instructions on tactics—bad instructions, of course, yet still you taught them something. You led them in that attack—not always a good thing, but then you corrected that by stepping back to observe. Then you changed your tactics when you saw your frontal assault wasn't working. I wondered if you would try our flank, and you did. Finally, you realized you couldn't win and you halted the exercise. Of course, in battle you can't just cry, 'Stop!' You retreat and maintain order as you do."

I lifted my eyes from the sand. "You make it sound as though we actually won," I said.

"No, of course not," he scoffed. "Don't talk foolishness. And don't go back there to your men and tell them that you won. They'll know you're lying." He looked back at our recruits still sitting in ranks, already starting to jest with each other. "They would have all died today, you know, had we been fighting Philistines or the damned Amalekites." He turned around to me. "Even the ones I led. That slipshod line they formed would never stand against a real army."

40

I didn't know what to say. He laid his hand on my shoulder. "So, Commander, I've told you some things you did right. Now tell me... what else did you *learn*?"

"I don't know that I learned anything. Perhaps that I shouldn't command soldiers?"

He laughed. "No, Beral. You should be a commander. Only Prince Jonathan himself would do better than this in his first exercise." He began to count with his fingers again. "You learned that a wall of shields will defeat a loose rabble. The youths on my side are no better warriors than yours. I simply made them lock together so that you couldn't pass through. Remember this. You never want your enemy to get in amongst you as if they were wolves raiding your sheep pens."

"I never thought of that," I replied.

"I know you didn't. Now, the second thing you learned is to have reserves. I thought you might try to flank us, and so there stood my reserve when you did."

Zelig paused before he went on. "And that uncovers the most important thing you need to know. Always, *always* have a second plan, a second route or another position to fall back to. You actually did that. You changed your method of attack when you tried to go around us. That was a good change of plan." He paused to grin. "It wasn't as good as mine, but it showed you have a commander's eye. You will learn more each day. You will be a fine commander, Beral."

I took a deep breath, dejected. I didn't feel like a fine commander. Zelig had anticipated my every action, making me look quite the fool. I had lost respect from the very men I should lead.

"Zelig, I may have learned something, but how can I expect them to follow me after this? Even these raw recruits could see how badly we fared against you. They will never listen to me again."

The old warrior lowered his voice. "Here's the thing, Commander. *They* don't know you piddled in your own bed. Go back and praise them for their effort and act as though the outcome was what you planned all along to show them why we lock shields. Tell them we will drill them on that for weeks. Trust me, Beral. They will think you are brilliant."

His eyes bored into mine. "I will be loyal to you even as you are to our prince and king. You can listen to my counsel or not, but you will be the one to decide and lead. This is my role, and that will be yours."

I looked over his shoulder. Men were finishing the water jugs and stretching. Some watched us curiously. Zelig had just told me that I was capable of walking this road. My stumble today didn't end the journey. I locked eyes with him again. "Yes, Zelig, I believe you are right." We walked back, Zelig at my side and one step behind. I went to the mounting block and stepped up to address my command.

"Stand up!" Zelig yelled. Men pushed themselves to their feet, eyeing him cautiously.

I let my eyes roam over them before I spoke. "Today you learned something. Today you saw that a hasty and untrained shield wall can beat back a loose mob." I paused. "But this is the last day you can say you are untrained. From this time forward, we run, we drill, and we lock shields until we are the best soldiers in Israel. I can do this. *You* can do this. Now take hold of your shields. We run to the dung heap and back. You remember where it is."

The company turned in their files as I climbed down from the block. Zelig met my eye and nodded once, quietly.

CHAPTER SEVEN

The name of [Saul's] older daughter was Merab,
and that of the younger was Michal.

1 Samuel 14:49 NIV

As one of the king's military commanders, I could sometimes attend royal banquets where I reclined at Jonathan's table with his other officers. The hall was familiar to me, for I had already spent years there, standing against the wall behind my prince. But when I twisted about to see, it was Herzi who guarded Jonathan's back. I heard he had been doing an adequate job in defending and serving my prince—*his* prince. I wondered if Jonathan talked to him as openly as he had to me. I hoped not.

I looked forward to King Saul's feasts even though he did not have the luxuries I heard Philistine rulers enjoyed. Truthfully, his house seemed more a small fortress than a palace. However, he did bring in musicians to play for us, and the meat and wine were better than barracks food. Yet that had nothing to do with my reasons for enjoying the time there.

King Saul had two daughters who attended those elaborate meals. The older one, Merab, reminded me of a hen caught out in the rain, peevish and easily irritated. That manner of hers marred the beauty in her face and carriage. She could be hard, and I knew the servants feared her. Her father hadn't yet found anyone who wanted to try her. But then there was Jonathan's younger sister, Michal.

I had taken the favors of a few maidens and women. Jonathan and I both did so when the occasion arose. He preferred the ones from prominent families, although I found that a cook's helper offered the same delights without the entanglements. While every wealthy father urged his daughters upon Jonathan, no one cared who his armor bearer lay with. Once, back in those times, my prince ruefully admitted that I had the better lot.

He acknowledged that on a day years before as we were leaving Bezer. We had spent a week in that village while patrolling eastward for Ammonite raiders and chasing them from our lands. A daughter of the village headman wailed from her rooftop when we marched out.

I had barely made that march on time because of a final quick dalliance with a serving woman in an alcove behind her cooking area.

"Hurry and finish this, Beral. I have more to do here than service young soldiers," she murmured.

Afterward, I pulled away to adjust my tunic while the woman let her robe drop. She brushed her hair back with her fingers.

"We'll be coming back soon, Tamara," I said.

She smiled knowingly. "You all say that. I'm sure you will too." She looked toward the doorway. "Now go. They're calling for you."

A chorus of voices outside shouted for stragglers. She slapped my backside as I hurried out to join them on the road.

As we marched away, the cries from the headman's daughter faded behind us, although I felt certain she and her father still watched, forlornly hoping Jonathan would turn around for her. Jonathan's face turned red, and I could hear soft chuckles from the men walking close behind us.

"Beral, you are fortunate," he said. "The kitchen girl you're leaving behind doesn't follow us, clutching at your tunic and pleading for marriage."

I looked at him, startled. How did he know about that servant?

"Sire, it's only because of your great handsomeness," I said. "All the maidens in Israel want to marry you and bed you, perhaps not even in that order." I glanced back to see spearmen in the column smiling.

Our prince attracted young women without effort, and the men took great pride in that.

However, Jonathan only wagged his head side to side. "No, Beral. If only that were all of it. You see, one day you will find a maiden you burn for. You will marry her, and all Judea will say, 'Ah, isn't that a good thing? Jonathan's man has married and settled down. How wonderful.'" He threw his arms up as if shouting for joy. "But for me, every girl I tumble goes to sleep that night, dreaming of being the next queen of Israel. In the morning, her father starts looking for a new robe he can wear to the wedding feast. And so you see, when the day comes that I actually do betroth someone, all those women and their families will shout, 'That scoundrel, Prince Jonathan, betrayed us! He is a thieving stallion, only adding to his harem of mares. Oh, my poor, innocent daughter.'" He pressed his lips together and shook a mock fist in the air.

"Sire," I replied. "Perhaps then you should stop sampling the flavors of so many sweets."

He threw back his head and laughed. "Ah, Beral. You know *that* is something I cannot do." He laughed again, and the soldiers behind us did too, a hearty, boisterous sound that bounced off the rocks around us as we tramped back to Gibeah.

In those times, before my beard had sprouted, I never thought about any woman of high social rank. The servant and field girls I approached were all I needed, and I always expected to take one of them to wife someday when the time seemed right. But then, Prince Jonathan promoted me and changed everything.

There I sat in the same room as the king, at the same table with Jonathan, my beard thick as wild spring grass. I combed it each morning while I finally dared to think of her, the king's daughter.

Michal, several years younger than myself, was like a songbird. Her laughter trilled through her father's household, and she moved with the gazelle's grace. Strings of small polished stones graced a forehead framed by tumbling black hair. Her teeth were perfect pearls. Every young officer wanted to catch her eye. Every wealthy family dragged out at least one promising son to court her long before she was old enough to wed. Those breasts were only rosebuds when the young men began to appear at Saul's gate, hoping to impress both him and his daughter. I had watched it for years from behind Jonathan's seat at the banquets, never bold enough myself to dream of her.

Yet I had some reason to hope since I no longer stood as a fixture along the wall. She and I played eye games at the banquet tables, catching each other's glances across opposite ends of the hall. Her eyes were polished onyx, and she giggled when I quickly looked away, feeling the heat rising in my face. I began to sense that she looked forward to my presence there. Jonathan noticed all of it.

He came out to the training site one day to see the progress of my recruits. Standing together, we watched them drill as a shield wall, locking together with a solid thump. They were improving, and Zelig barely cursed at them anymore.

The old veteran walked behind them, watching and calling cadence. "Left foot. Step. Step."

The line advanced slowly, stomping in unison with shields forward. I had four men heaving a heavy post like a battering ram against individual shields at random. If it collapsed a man, the line closed the gap until he got up. They did it all well. I felt pleased, but then Jonathan's words struck me unexpectedly in a flank I didn't know was exposed.

"Ho, Beral, I see you would like to be my brother-in-law," he said, his posture casual as a town idler.

"My lord?" I replied. Did he always know my thoughts?

Jonathan laughed at my discomfort. "You know that the kitchen pot cleaners are whispering behind their hands about Beral and the honey-eyed looks he gives my little sister. Soon someone at my father's court will be asking me what I'm going to do about it and shouldn't I tell the king?"

"My lord, I meant no harm. I only... I only meant—"

"Relax." He slapped me on the back and shook me playfully. "I know *exactly* what you meant." A grin split his beard. "And I have no objection. Michal could certainly fare worse than to marry my Beral. I sometimes feared she would throw her catch net toward one of those crowing cocks that lounge in the banquet hall, one of those young men who boast of deeds they have not yet done." He looked directly into my face. "I have seen your deeds, Beral, and I know what you do still. You are a worthy man."

My heart hammered in my chest. Following my prince into a spear fight had never made me as nervous as speaking aloud to him about Michal. "Th-Thank you, my lord. I only hope... I mean, I don't know... I haven't done anything. Not yet. I mean that I *wouldn't* do anything unless—"

Another slap on the back. "Beral, stop talking. It's not something you do well. I understand what you're trying to say." He narrowed his eyes. "Beral, have you even spoken to my sister? A single word?"

I shook my head and looked to the side. "No, my lord."

"Ah, I see. I had thought as much." His thinking finger tapped his nose. "That may be a good thing for you now. Michal is still like a child in some ways. Our father will not be ready to betroth her for a while yet, and Merab will have to marry first, of course. That gives you time, but Beral... you should be a little bolder in your actions. Make your intent plain. Michal's more accustomed to her suitors having drooling tongues in their mouths and stiffened organs under their tunics. You'd fit in well among them if you behaved more like a rutting goat." He laughed. "Beware, though. My sister will tease a man. That beauty of hers can cast a spell."

He turned away from me and watched my recruits. The drill had changed. Half of them backed slowly, shields kept locked, while the other half beat at them with spear butts. At the end of the practice field, they reversed roles. It was a practice they enjoyed, and Zelig didn't switch their legs anymore.

"Your men are looking very good, Beral," Jonathan said. "They are beginning to look like line infantry soldiers. I think they will be ready when we campaign again. You and Zelig should be pleased with them and yourselves."

"Thank you, my prince. I will tell Zelig. He will be pleased." I hesitated and then decided to say nothing more.

An uncomfortable silence lay between us.

He stared at the men for a long time before he spoke again. "There is something you should realize." He still looked away, toward the training exercise. "While I myself have no objection, that might not be so with my father. A daughter is a valuable commodity to a king—someone he can use to seal an alliance or perhaps a loyalty. I believe my father loves Michal—he dotes on her actually—but he may feel compelled to barter her if he has the need. Only a proven and great warrior sitting at his table could hope to overcome that reality. Do you understand what I say?"

"I understand." And I did. For me, even as a commander in Saul's army, to gain the hand of his daughter, I would have to prove myself very worthy of that prize. I would have to cover myself in glory. I was anxious to have that chance.

In the spring, with our other enemies pushed back, I knew the king was considering a move against the Amalekites. Like their Edomite cousins, the Amalekites counted Esau as their ancestor, making them kinsmen of Israel in a distant way. However, they reserved a special animosity for us, going back to the time of Moses and Joshua. Samuel, the prophet, wanted Saul to war against them so as to blot out even their memory. Such was the will of Yahweh.

"Now go and attack the Amalekites," thundered the elderly man of God. "Punish them for what they did to Israel as Israel came up from Egypt." He referred to an old, bitter hatred, still alive because neither God nor the prophet nor the Amalekites ever forgot.

I stood mute at the rear of that war council as Samuel urged the king to take action.

"Do not spare them; put to death men and women, children and infants, cattle and sheep, camels and donkeys," the prophet railed.

Saul listened and agreed.

CHAPTER EIGHT

So Saul summoned the men and mustered them at Telaim...

1 Samuel 15:4a NIV

OUR HISTORY WITH THE AMALEKITES didn't concern me, but my stomach jumped at the prospect of battle. Zelig and I had drilled the recruits hard for months at Gibeah while experienced units fought Saul's foes without our help. Abner's judgment held that we weren't ready and weren't needed... until that campaign, a war that would be more than a series of skirmishes. Israel would need all of its standing army, including my hundred.

The morning after the king's decision, all the recruit companies, soon to be thrown into a battle for the first time, crowded into the training area while General Abner and Jonathan came to look at us. Jonathan nodded silently to me and the other commanders, one of them Katriel, the same aide who had scornfully greeted me not so long before. Katriel had received his own company shortly after mine. I noted Herzi standing proudly behind Jonathan.

"Good morning, Commanders. Are your men ready?" Abner never wasted words.

"Yes, sir!" we chorused.

"We'll see."

Each unit hurled javelins at a line of targets. We did not distinguish ourselves from the others since nearly every Israelite boy could spear a rabbit. We marched no worse than any except for Katriel's company. He beamed as his men paraded by in step, beating a marching cadence on their shields. They looked impressive.

"Nice," commented Abner.

But then we began simulated battles, company against company. It amazed me to see that no one else had drilled on the shield wall. Zelig called out our march while I directed us into ranks and double ranks, always with shields tight together and spears bristling out. By comparison, the others were a loose collection of fighters throwing themselves at us, usually to fall back as a spent wave. We stayed on the field longer than any other company. Abner sent two, then three companies against us in the choking dust. I formed the company into a defensive square. Finally, they overran us. Our square fell back on itself in fatigue, and we were defeated. Katriel's band had been among those who eventually beat us down.

I seethed at Katriel's smugness as we waited for Abner and Jonathan. They conferred at the far edge of the field while we stood panting in a casual formation. Other units finished up their own exercises, and gradually the area quieted.

Katriel strolled over to where I stood. "Don't feel too bad, Commander Beral. I'm sure your recruits fought their best for you." Even his voice sounded like oil.

"They did," I answered. "I could not have asked for more from them."

"Ah no, I'm sure you couldn't have," he purred, "but you lost anyway, didn't you?"

"We held our ground." I spoke through clenched teeth. My men stirred behind me.

"Yes, for a while at least," he said. "But no matter now. Here come General Abner and your prince." *Your prince?* I sensed disdain in Katriel's words.

Abner and Jonathan walked up to us. Both of them smiled at our tired men.

"A well-done stand, men of Beral," Jonathan shouted to them. "Beral, I think I shall call your company crocodiles. They stand and hold like their hides are armored, and they leap forward with their teeth snapping."

"Very well done, Commander Beral," Abner said.

I was pleased and embarrassed, catching Zelig's eye as he stood unobtrusively in the ranks. He nodded at me, a gesture that made me flush with pleasure even more than the praise of my superiors. I also saw Katriel's face fall, which might have been the greatest pleasure of all.

He stepped forward. "Sires," he said, "you saw my troops overrun his? They cracked that hide, did they not?"

Jonathan and the general exchanged a glance.

Abner turned aside to Katriel. "Yes, we did see that. Your company beat down these crocodiles… with the help of two others… after this wall stood off previous attacks and then counterattacked. Yes, Commander Katriel, we saw that." He gestured to the assembled units. "I also see your company is sitting with their weapons lying across their knees like all the rest—except one."

I looked left and right. Every other company sat resting. Only mine stood, still gripping spears. Sweat still ran down every face. They had heard General Abner's comments, and they waited for mine.

I stepped toward them and pointed away from the training area. "Men, we have more to do. Do you see that dung heap next to the tree?"

They answered with nods and shouted replies, standing taller with chests out. Some of them grinned, sensing what was coming.

"You do? Good. Now run to it and back here again. Zelig will run behind you. Anyone who finishes after him will get the flat of his sword. Now go!"

The men pivoted and ran, and no guards escorted them. Instead of the slap of sandals, the whole training ground heard the rhythm of swords rapping on shields as they ran in formation. Zelig trotted behind, but no one fell back to him. Abner and Jonathan stared after them before they turned to look at me.

"Would you excuse me, sires?" I said. "I should run with my company."

Abner jerked his head. "Go," he said.

I loped away, enjoying the disbelieving looks from other units. The general and my prince left before we returned from the mile run. I discovered then that I had made a mistake. Because I'd started so far behind the company, I had been content to follow it at a distance. My men waited for me at the finish. I didn't realize at first why so many of them were smiling.

"Commander Beral, you finished behind me, did you not?" Zelig asked, as grim as a Levite priest.

Afterward, we marched back to the barracks, my buttocks stinging from the flat of Zelig's blade. It had been a good morning.

The king declared war against the Amalekites two days later. The call went throughout Israel, and young men from every tribe gathered at Telaim, in the southernmost area of the tribe of Judah. Twenty thousand tribesmen camped there in high spirits even before Saul's army arrived. His earlier successes gave everyone confidence. These volunteer soldiers had already proven themselves against our enemies many times, but still I noticed the deference they paid the standing army when we marched into the encampment. We who had trained for warfare numbered only about six thousand, yet we would be the salt to season this throng.

We moved overnight to hide in ravines near the city of Amalek. When we arrived, the army and low-ranking commanders such as myself nestled down in the rocks to rest before sunrise. The king, General Abner, and the brigade commanders met in council while we slept.

"Beral, wake up. Time to relieve your bladder and strap on your sword. You can dream about your love later." My eyes flashed open. Jonathan was rapping the soles of my sandals with his sword. The walls of the gully brooded gray in the darkness. It looked to be yet another hour before the sun rose. I yawned and stood up. Herzi watched nearby.

"It's fortunate, sire, that I *wasn't* dreaming of my love, or I would have stayed there in her perfumed bed instead of standing here shivering with you."

"Perfumed bed? Beral, you *are* dreaming. Cattle don't have perfumed beds." He took my arm and pulled me along with him. "Come. There's something you should see."

He led me along the ravine until we came to a footpath snaking up its steep side. Removing our bronze headgear to avoid glinting in the moonlight, we climbed in the dimness until we could see over the edge toward Amalek.

"Look there," he said.

We faced the city's main gate, less than a mile away, where a heavily laden caravan of camels and mules streamed out in the moonlight.

Hundreds of robed figures trudged alongside, traveling the road that would bring them past the mouth of our ravine.

"Should we move before they see us?" I asked.

Jonathan shook his head. "No, look closer. Do you see the children with them? That's not a trade caravan. Those are Kenites, friends of Israel for generations. We slipped Judeans into the city during the night to warn them." He squinted at the travelers. "I see they took our advice to leave. But I didn't bring you here to stare at young mothers on donkeys. Do you see the highway they travel? See the little slope they climb now?"

I finger-combed my beard. A little beyond bowshot from the gate, the Kenite band had reached a point where the highway rose gently before it leveled again.

"I see it," I replied. "You woke me so I could look at a road bump under the moon?"

"Exactly. Look at that rise, Beral. Learn its position. That bump is where you and your crocodiles will begin to give us today's victory." Jonathan gripped my shoulder tightly as he talked. His words and intensity lit an eagerness in me.

"What are you telling me, sire?"

Jonathan slid down a few feet to rest against a rock outcropping. "Look here, Beral."

I joined him as he quickly sketched a crude map in the side of the ravine.

"Our army—but only our regulars—will march abreast to that rise in the road before daybreak. At sunrise, the Amalekites should be provoked to come out and fight us when they see how greatly we are outnumbered. We fight and then fall back until we pass the mouth of this ravine. At that time, the rest of our force—our volunteer army—falls upon the Amalekite flank and rear. I will be leading that attack." He looked up from his drawing. "It's Abner's plan, and I think it's a good one. What do you think?"

Under the bright moon, I stared at the crude map in the dirt, fingering my beard again. Jonathan expected me to be frank. It *was* a good plan but with a flaw.

Jonathan read my troubled posture. "What is it?"

"Sire, this could work, except that..."

"Except that what, Beral? What is it you distrust?" He looked at me anxiously.

"Only that this is the same ruse Israel used to defeat the king of Ai a generation ago. All the pagan tribes know that old story, when Joshua first fled before he turned and destroyed them. If we run today, I don't think these Amalekites would actually follow us very far from their walls." I looked down, embarrassed at having to contradict my prince.

Jonathan only smiled and gripped my shoulder again. "And *that*, dear Beral, is why you are a commander and not a shield bearer. You are right. Even the Amalekites wouldn't be fooled if we took to our heels when they sally out their gates. That is why you and your company will be at the center of our line. We do not intend to run from them like sheep. The heathens have to believe we retreat grudgingly and only because we are hard pressed by them. If we fight hard yet back away, the Amalekites will sense blood and then try to drive us even more. They would have no thought of looking about for an ambush."

He wiped out the drawings, and we stood up.

"Do you have doubts?" he asked.

I shook my head. "No, my lord. We can do this."

Jonathan looked intently at me, his serious expression wiping away goodwill and humor. "That's good, Commander Beral, because we need your company. You *must* hold the center in front of the city gate. Our army will align on you. We will back as you back. General Abner and I expect some of the troops to waver. They may even break and run. But, if this is to work, our center must hold. *You* must hold. Abner will send a courier to you when it's time to retreat. Keep your crocodiles together in good order, and with Yahweh's help, we will win this battle."

"I do have one question, sire," I said.

"Ask it."

"Why us?" I asked. "Why is my company chosen to hold the center?"

My prince actually chuckled. "Oh, to be sure, not everyone thought your scaled reptiles should be given that position. Veteran commanders wanted the honor. It took Abner and me together to convince my father that you could hold and maneuver."

"General Abner?"

"Of course. Why not? He saw your drills, Beral. Your men can back and still maintain a shield wall. You impressed him with your moving wall when you scrimmaged with the other companies." He crossed his arms and eyed me. "Your training was impressive enough, Beral, but that's not the only reason I wanted you where the fighting will be heaviest." He turned and started down toward the wadi's bottom, where Herzi waited.

I hurried after him. "Wait, my lord," I called. "What other reason is there?"

He stopped and faced me. "I heard about the thwacking Zelig gave your butt the other day. You should have run faster." He smiled broadly. "No other commander would have allowed that swat. Actually, very few commanders would have even run with their men after a day of training. You do what they do, Beral, and your men love you for it. They love you, and they will fight for you. As long as you stand firm, they will stand firm. *That* is why I want you at our center."

He wheeled, talking over his shoulder as he left. "See to your company, Commander. I must deal with other matters."

I watched him stride away, Herzi trotting close behind. When I started back to my company's area, I walked through thousands of waking men, sitting up, spitting and scratching. The army was stretching itself like a thousand cats.

I found Zelig's sleeping position by following the snores, sounds that could have come from a grumbling lion. I tapped his sandal. "Zelig, wake up. Time to relieve your bladder and strap on your sword."

CHAPTER NINE

Saul... set an ambush in the ravine.

1 Sam 15:5 NIV

ZELIG AND I ROUSED THE company in the darkness and hurried them toward the highway. I watched the last Kenites pass the ravine's mouth, where we stayed in shadows, hidden from the city. They walked by close enough for me to inhale the soft plops of dust they stirred up. The adults glanced furtively at us before turning to look straight ahead—not so with the children. Sleepy little ones stared openly at us with fingers in their mouths as nervous parents hustled them along the moonlit roadway.

"They don't want to get involved," said Zelig. "They're scared."

Out on the road, the last laden donkey went by, goaded by a young boy's stick.

Never taking my eyes from the pair, I replied, "So am I."

Zelig's head swung around to regard me.

"I have seen many battles, Zelig, as have you. This is only another for both of us. I don't fear dying in battle, for I have made my peace with Yahweh, but I am afraid for them." I nodded toward the company resting farther back in the ravine.

Zelig stood there in a long silence, and I feared I had said too much. Finally, he hawked up something in his throat and spat. "Commander, I've trembled for my squad before each fight, wondering which ones would die for some monkey-brained mistake of mine. Every squad leader feels that fear. Not enough commanders do." He smiled wryly.

"Now, the old soldiers I worried about are themselves squad leaders in Commander Beral's crocodile company. Serves them right."

"Commander!" The low call came from behind. A man pointed to a group coming up toward us in the dark ravine.

"There's our order to move out," said Zelig. He peered back in the shadows. "It appears we may have a guest. I guess we shouldn't be surprised."

I gasped when I saw one head looming over the rest. Saul, dressed in battle gear and wearing his customary crown and armband, walked with the entourage. Nathon followed with his shield.

Soldiers scrambled to their feet as he passed through their midst. He came directly to where Zelig and I stood.

"Good morning, Commander. Your men are ready for this?" He stared intently at me. Behind him, Abner watched, his expression hidden in the shadow of his helmet.

I placed a fist to my chest before I answered. "Yes, my king. We are ready." To my own surprise, my voice didn't quaver.

"Good. Then let's be about the task Yahweh has set before us. I will fight alongside your men."

"It is an honor, my king."

Zelig moved among the company, sending them out onto the road while I positioned each squad as it emerged into the moonlight. Saul and his staff watched without comment. At last, when we had two ranks stretched across the highway, Abner took me aside.

"Get your men up to the knoll before the sun is fully up while their last night watch is still dozing on the walls. The rest of the regulars will deploy to your left and right."

"I understand, General," I answered. Already, I could hear the scraping and clanking of thousands of armed men marching in the ravine behind us.

"Another thing, Beral. The Amalekites will recognize our king today. Don't lose him. Nothing should befall the king of Israel."

"I will be at his side as long as there is any danger."

He nodded. "I expect that, Beral, but don't let him know you take extra pains to protect him. Saul likes to fight as a soldier. He refuses even to put Ben-Ami and his guards around him. Let him believe Yahweh alone watches over him."

"And his shield bearer," I said.

"Yes, Nathon too. He does allow that." Abner grinned. He stepped away from me, looking back into the ravine, where the marching sounds grew louder. "Be on your way, Commander," he said. "May Yahweh be with your crocodiles. I will send someone to you when it's time to retreat." He turned and walked toward his approaching army. I went to my company.

King Saul waited there, shifting his weight and anxious to start. "It's time, Commander," he said.

"Yes, my king, if you would honor us by standing here in the front rank between Nissim and Yair, two of my best," I replied.

The two spearmen were indeed good men, but they both stood weak kneed at that moment. Months before, they had only been throwing rocks at dogs while guarding sheep. Now they found themselves about to protect the king in their first combat.

Saul regarded Nissim closely. "You are a Benjamite. I know your father, Hador," he said. When he turned to Yair, he asked, "What tribe is your father's?"

"We are of Ephraim, sire," the awed young man answered.

"Ephraim? Good. But remember—today we are all Israelites."

I thought both men would have gladly died for their king at that moment.

Saul looked at me. "And where will you be, Commander?"

"Sire, I will be right behind you."

"Behind me?" He sniffed.

I could sense what he felt, but I had protected his eldest son for years. Saul knew I was no coward.

"Yes, sire, it's where I can best direct our movements," I explained.

He dismissed me with a wave and positioned himself in our first line of foot soldiers. Nathon stood behind him.

I moved to the side. "March us forward, Zelig."

"All right, men. Forward!" he called. He didn't address them as *goatherds* anymore.

Our two ranks filled the roadway and spilled onto its shoulders on either side. Zelig used a slow cadence to keep the flanks from stumbling as the darkness gradually lifted. Sunrise had barely lipped over the eastern hills when I finally got a good look at the city of Amalek.

It was larger than any other town I had ever seen and looked prosperous. Stone and mud-brick structures towered in a display of wealth and power. Torches still blazed along sections of the stone wall even as the first rays of sunlight touched it. Pennants hung idly at the main gates. Heads dotted the top of the wall, no doubt trying to see who approached them so noisily out of the fading night. The gates began to open then abruptly stopped and swung shut again.

While we walked forward on the road, the rest of our regulars exited the mouth of the ravine. Companies trotted to catch up and align with us. I could hear the clattering and cursing as men tripped on the rough ground.

"Slow the pace, Zelig," I called.

Daylight increased as we drew closer. More heads peered over the city wall at us. A trumpet blared behind the wall, and drums pounded. The city awoke to our presence.

"Halt us here, Zelig," I said.

The ground gently sloped down from us toward the enormous main gate. Zelig busied himself straightening the ranks. I studied the gate and scanned the wall for archers. We were well beyond bowshot, but I was nervous having the king standing in the middle of the road, an obvious target. His polished gold crown gleamed now in the full light of morning. As if to make certain that no Amalekite failed to notice him, Saul stepped forward out of the front rank.

"Come with me, Nathon," he said without looking back, "and you also, Commander Beral."

"Yes, sire," I said.

Nathon and I slipped through the gap before Nissim and Yair closed it. We stood next to the king while he stared at the city before us. More drums thumped inside. Marching cadences.

"What do you see, Beral?" Saul asked.

I looked closely at the walls. Most of the helmeted men crowding the ramparts earlier had disappeared, probably climbing down to join others massing at the gate.

59

"It looks as if they may be preparing to sortie out, my king."

"Let's see if we can cause them to hurry." He took another step toward the city wall and stopped. Deliberate and measured, Saul planted his sandals wide in the dust on the road and folded his arms, his golden armband plainly visible. "This should draw some of them out." He raised his chin to regard the city once more.

Quickly, about a dozen new heads appeared on top of the wall. Archers. They drew back as one, and a brace of arrows took sudden flight at us. They reached their apex and fell to our front, thudding into the roadway twenty cubits away. Every arrow struck in a dense grouping directly in front of the king. I let my breath out. Even when out of range, no man is immune to that tightening in his gut when war arrows drop from the sky.

Saul seemed unperturbed, although his jaw clenched when the arrows reached out for him. "Nathon, fetch one of those arrows." He spoke casually, as if asking for a downed bird.

"Yes, sire." The armor bearer trotted forward on the road. He reached the closest arrow and yanked it out of the packed ground before the archers on the wall could chance another shot. Upon returning, he handed it to the king.

Saul accepted the trophy and held it up in a mock salute to the bowmen. Then he snapped it in two, much to the delight of my company, who erupted in a chorus of laughter.

I turned around. "Zelig, give the men 'rest'!" I shouted.

"'Rest,' Commander?"

"Yes, tell them to ground their shields since these pagans don't want to fight."

Soon every shield was down, leaning against the leg of its owner. The men looked puzzled. I walked back and forth in front, speaking softly to them. "Look like you haven't a care, but stay alert. The Amalekites won't be able to ignore our king taunting them while we stretch our limbs. Watch the gate. When it cracks open, I will give the command, and then we pick up shields as one man." I went back to stand beside Saul.

He looked sideways at me. "That's a good trick, Beral. They'll come now."

60

"I hope so, sire," I answered, looking at the gate. The drums inside the city stopped.

A trumpet blared, and the gate swung open quickly. A column eight men across began to double-time through to the outside. They split left and right to deploy against us in wide ranks.

I looked back and shouted over my shoulder. "Shields up!" Zelig and squad leaders echoed me as the company bent to fasten the round shields on their arms.

"Lock shields!" Zelig yelled.

Before my eyes, the men transformed into a leather-covered wall. Saul watched it too, nodding. I fretted at his nonchalance.

"My king, I think it is time to rejoin the ranks," I said.

Saul wheeled around to see the Amalekites completing their formation. They didn't move, but the drums started up again.

"Yes, you're probably right, Beral." He grinned. As we slipped back through the gap between the two spearmen, Saul smiled at them. "Ho, Nissim, I will tell your father how you fought today. Yair, I will send word to Ephraim and your father about you." He raised his voice so that the entire company heard him. "Come, Israelites! Now let us attend to Yahweh's wishes!"

They roared in reply, and at that moment, the Amalekites advanced. They came straight at us in a dense maelstrom of infantry, numbering probably three times our decoy force, but no chariots rolled with them, and the only archers I saw stayed on their city wall. This would be shield to shield. For a moment, I felt the anxious fear Zelig had told me about. My company faced its first test with the king of Israel in our ranks. I prayed silently to Yahweh for all of them. Then I forgot myself in the battle.

CHAPTER TEN

Then Saul attacked the Amalekites...

1 Sam 15:7a NIV

A HAILSTORM OF JAVELINS FLEW AT us just ahead of their infantry's advance. Our shields went up, and the little spears thunked into them. Eitan, a man in the front rank, fell with a wound in his thigh. We hardly had time to shake the javelins off our shields before the Amalekites banged into our line.

They struck as a loose collection of fighters, each one attacking the shield in front of him. We didn't thrust back directly but jabbed with short, heavy spears at openings to the right whenever a foe raised his sword arm. When Amalekites fell, they were pierced in their right armpits.

The loudest sounds were thumps of colliding shields joining the clack of Amalekite sickle swords on our shields. Everywhere, soldiers on both sides shouted gibberish. Men grunted when they lunged and growled at each other without knowing it. Sandaled feet scrabbled on the dry ground and churned up dust until we fought in a haze. We coughed as it caked our faces. A quick gasp and a shriek punctuated the din when a spear point stabbed deep. Somewhere to my right, a man farted in his effort, but no one laughed.

Saul fought with his heavy sword. Nathon and I stayed behind him in the second rank, stabbing around him when necessary. My eyes stung with sweat. I wiped it off with my forearm and stepped back to look up and down our line. Another man had fallen. Gidon, a Judean, crawled feebly back through the legs of his friends.

The Amalekites kept pressing, driven forward by the sheer mass of their rear troops, but my untested men held. The thin spot in our line was King Saul himself, although he fought mightily, swinging his big sword with great effectiveness. Many of the enemy fell before him, some simply overawed by his presence. But he had never practiced fighting as we did that day—within a bristling wall of shields held closely together. His weakness lay in that he stepped out from it repeatedly and opened up the line behind him. Nathon and I followed the king through the gap. We guarded his sides and tried to keep the Amalekites away from that opening. This day, I jabbed and struck with a spear instead of a bronze-pointed oak staff, but otherwise, it felt the same as those days when I watched Jonathan's back.

Saul had entered into the blood-rush of battle. No longer the king of Israel, he became a foot soldier, using his sword to kill any foe he could reach and enjoying the feel of his blade going deep. I knew that rush of killing the enemy who tried to kill you. It could overcome a fighting man until he forgot all else. However, I had to attend to my company.

"Sire," I cried. "Sire!"

I stepped up beside him and tapped my shield against his before he noticed me. "Stand away, Beral," he roared. "You hinder my stroke."

"Sire," I yelled back, desperate to be understood. "We must fall back into the line." Together, we skewered an Amalekite charging headlong at the king. "My king, remember what we are to do here."

He kept his shield up, swinging it side to side, looking for the next foe while I stabbed at another man being pushed up to us. "You're right, Commander. Killing these dogs made me forget," the king said.

We stepped backward toward our line. Amalekites followed, clawing at us right up to the shield wall, which widened enough to allow us passage along with a relieved Nathon.

"Well done, Nissim! Well done, Yair of Ephraim!" Saul boomed.

I moved farther back to stand free of the fight and see better. More of our men were down, yet the enemy had suffered far worse in front of our wall. Amalekite warriors crumpled in heaps before us or crawled away, moaning. We could have held that gentle knoll for hours. The companies beside us also sent Amalekites reeling back, but at a higher cost. They fought loosely, without the organization Zelig had brought to us. The heathens managed to force their way inside those lines to do their killing. Wounded and dead Israelites lay all about them.

Far behind us, I could see Abner on the highway near the ravine where we had waited the night. The general looked on with an assortment of aides and priests. As I watched, a courier detached himself from the group and ran forward toward our position. I turned about to check our lines when something whooshed past my ear and thudded behind me. A stone the size of a hen's egg skipped away in the roadway. I held my shield up. The Amalekites must have brought out their slingers, knowing a good one could outrange a bow. We had to begin our retreat soon. I prayed that would be the message coming from Abner.

"Commander Beral!" The youth came up, wheezing from his long sprint. Clearly excited to be so near the fighting, his eyes were rounded like little moons.

"Speak, boy. What does Abner say?" I never took my eyes from the struggling men in front of me.

Another stone struck near us. They were aiming at me behind the lines in order not to hit one of their own.

"General Abner says it is time. He said you would know what that means."

"Yes. Tell Abner we start now."

"Yes, Commander." The boy turned to go. No doubt the incoming stones unnerved him and made him anxious to leave.

"Wait," I said. "Tell him this too. Tell him to be wary of the companies on our flanks. They will need help soon." I looked more closely at him. "You're Shalev, son of Baruch, aren't you? It's important that you tell him this, Shalev."

"Yes, Commander. The companies on your flanks will need help. I'll report that."

"Good lad. Now go!" The boy started off, and I turned back to the fight. I never saw the stone that must have struck Shalev in the back of his head then. Hours later, his body still lay crumpled in the road behind us. Abner never received my warning.

We stood fast, but we were like a desert rock when wind starts to blow away the sand around it. Standing behind the fighting, I could see the companies on each side of us giving way slowly, weakened by the constant battering. I feared they would not hold much longer. In front of us, the enemy looked exhausted. They paused outside our spears' reach while they gathered their breath for another bout.

"Second rank forward!" I bellowed.

The rear line of spearmen stepped up and through the first rank as we had practiced. They clamped together. Before the dazed Amalekites realized what was happening, a new wall of locked Israelite shields faced them.

"Zelig, come to me!" I yelled.

The old warrior had used the shift as a chance to place himself in the front row. He slipped back a step and barked orders, making certain the gap closed before he made his way toward me in the roadway. He heaved like a spent bull while we shouted at each other an arm's length behind the fighting clamor, which had started again.

"Commander?"

"We start to withdraw now, Zelig. Start us back slowly."

He nodded before looking to each side. Pointing at our right flank, he said, "Perhaps I should call a fast cadence going back. Katriel's company is nearly behind us already."

I turned to follow his outstretched arm. I hadn't realized until that moment that Katriel led the company beside mine. He paced behind his men, shouting and waving a sword. I couldn't hear him, but he looked frantic. Their line bent back and, as I watched, began to give way again.

"Yes, you're right. Speed us a little," I agreed. "Call cadence. I'll go bend our flank." I hurried to the threatened right side of our shield line while gathering up my reserve, which was depleted to five men, the others having gone to plug positions of the fallen.

If Katriel's company next to us backed any farther, the enemy would swarm around through the gap. The five set themselves on the end at an angle, to hold back an Amalekite tide. I trotted back to the center. Zelig had the lines moving backward.

"Two steps back! Two steps! Move!" The men retreated two steps and stopped. The Amalekites also halted in surprise before they rushed us again. Our withdrawal emboldened them, and they fell on us with renewed enthusiasm, thinking we were at last breaking. Curved sickle blades tried to hook our weapons. Their hammering against our shields was worse than a hailstorm. "Two steps back! Move!" Zelig bawled. We backed again.

Once more, King Saul was almost our undoing. His instinct rebelled at stepping backward before a foe.

"Sire, you must come back with us!" I yelled at his back, but he didn't move. I reached out and seized his belted tunic. "Back! Get back!" I screamed.

He shook off my grip angrily before returning to the line, still thrashing at any foe who dared face him.

"Four steps back! Move!" Zelig's cadence calls came faster, and we moved farther each time.

I disengaged from the fighting and joined him behind our ranks.

"We're in trouble, Commander," he said grimly.

I looked where he pointed. Katriel's men were spilling back in confusion before the mass of warriors that threatened to overwhelm them. They were completely behind us now. Some started to turn away from the fight while squad leaders thumped them with spear butts. The Amalekites, sensing a blood rout, began howling like dogs. My flank guard was already engaged—soon, they would be turned.

"Hurry us back!" I yelled at Zelig. "Keep them moving. No stops!" I stepped up into the second rank beside Nathon, who stabbed valiantly at anyone near his king.

The melee centered around Saul as the heathens tried to catch him outside our wall.

I spoke loudly into Nathon's ear. "You must take the king back to Abner. We're about to be flanked." He looked at me blankly before he nodded. I backed up to get beside Zelig.

"Step back," he roared. "Steady step. No stopping!"

We started backing away once more. The Amalekites' clamor rose even more when we no longer paused in our withdrawal. I could sense the weight of their army as they pressed us. Saul finally appeared out of the ranks, followed closely by Nathon. The king was shaking his head in disapproval at me as they passed to the rear. I couldn't hear his words.

"Steady. Steady," Zelig yelled over the noise.

Our sandals crunched backward. More men fell. For the first time, I was afraid our dam wouldn't hold. I glanced back. Abner's group still waited on the road behind us. Saul and Nathon walked rapidly toward them, the king's posture indicating his displeasure at leaving the fight. I didn't have time to wonder why Abner hadn't sent reinforcements to our flanks because, at that moment, the company beside us broke and ran.

I saw Katriel running with the rest of his men. Javelins and sling stones struck some of them. Amalekites shouted in triumph as they pursued easy prey. Then the Israelite company on our left broke. We continued to retreat steadily as enemy soldiers poured past us on both sides. The pressure to our front faded away, but I knew they would soon turn back for us. We were still a very long way from the ravine and help.

"Form the square! Form the square!" I shouted.

Zelig and squad leaders took up the cry. Egyptian foot soldiers could possibly have done this maneuver better, but we were good too. In short order, we made a crude square—two ranks with wounded inside. I counted seventeen men down, and seven of those lay bleeding but alive inside our perimeter. To my shock, King Saul and Nathon stood there too. They had turned back to us when the other companies collapsed, seeing the battleground was too far overrun to chance going to Abner. I thought later that Saul simply did not want to be seen running in front of an enemy.

"It seems that Yahweh wills me to fight alongside you today after all, Commander," Saul said.

"My king, we are grateful for your presence," I said, mouthing words I did not mean.

The Amalekites left us alone while they pursued the rest of our broken army, but they pulled up well short of the ravine. Clearly, even in victory they weren't going to stray far from their city walls. They returned, waving spears with Israelite heads on them. I looked for Katriel's, but it wasn't displayed. Soon, a laughing mob surrounded our square, shaking those bloody trophies at us. We knew what they were screaming even though we couldn't speak their pagan tongue.

"They won't use the archers or slingers." I spoke loud enough for the compact formation to hear. "The king is with us. They want to capture him, but they won't. They won't because *we* are here. We are the ones who did not run." I turned to Saul. "We are here, my king, and you are safe."

He nodded. We all knew anyway that Saul would not be taken alive. If it became certain that the king would be captured, Nathon, his armor bearer, had orders to kill him.

CHAPTER ELEVEN

He fought valiantly and defeated the Amalekites, delivering
Israel from the hands of those who had plundered them.

1 Sam. 14:48 NIV

O
UR RETREAT TOWARD THE RAVINE was ended. Abner's help
would have to reach us instead. He and Jonathan would come,
but they might not come soon enough for us.

The Amalekite mob still circled, screaming just beyond our spear
tips. Hordes crowded against each other as they taunted us, making
grotesque faces and trilling like women. The shrill screeching pierced
my head until I could barely think. My shield-wall spearmen glanced
back at me, taking their cues from my face. They would stand and fight,
but they needed me to lead. I couldn't let them see me tremble.

"Grip your spears," I shouted over the noise. "Hold fast! We stand
here." In truth, we could do nothing else. I squeezed Zelig's upper arm
and leaned into hm. "The dung eaters are waiting for something. Let's
round the corners," I yelled in his ear. "We mustn't just stand and wait.
We'll start to think."

He nodded. A circle would be easier to defend than a misshapen
square with vulnerable corners. He and I walked along our second rank
to shift men forward or back. I touched each man as I positioned him
since speaking was almost impossible. The Amalekites kept up their
incessant noise but still made no new move against us.

I glanced toward Saul. I had forgotten about the king when I
repositioned the men. With his towering height, he was looking over the
heads of our wall, his eyes smoldering as he pivoted to see Amalekites

crowding us on every side. Next to him, Nathon looked as if he might vomit. I cupped my hands to speak into Zelig's ear. "The king wants to get in the front rank again. Best to keep him here in the center. We must give him something to do."

The old warrior shrugged and put his face against my ear. "Let him make a speech. He's a king. He can do it."

I snorted, but Saul was already edging his way into our second rank. If I didn't stop him, he would soon be up between Nissim and Yair again. The heathen mob saw him and began to mock him. Some soldiers fell to their knees. Others made exaggerated bows, laughing all the while. My jaw tightened. Even not knowing their tongue, I felt the insult. They jeered at the king of Israel, the king of Yahweh's people. Saul's face darkened as he glared back at them.

I moved to intercept him. "Sire, my company takes its courage from your presence here. Perhaps you could stay in the center and address them when it quiets."

He turned to stare through me. "I'll fight where I please."

"Yes, sire."

My head still throbbed from the incessant screaming. I rolled my shoulders and turned away to look back along the road toward the ravine. No Israelites spilled out of its mouth yet to come to our relief. At this point the entire Amalekite army encircled us. My company was a tortoise surrounded by a pack of slavering dogs. We pulled heads and arms in behind our shields and waited for them to try to open the shell.

Suddenly, within the space of two deep breaths, the shouting ceased. The howling mass quieted until the only sounds were crunching sandals and the clank of weapons. A murmuring started at the outer edge of the mass. Soldiers parted along the roadway leading to the city's main gate. A chariot drawn by two superb white horses appeared there and approached us. Ostrich plumes bounced on the horses' headstalls. A slave, chained to the vehicle via a neck collar, trotted alongside. One man stood in the chariot behind the driver.

He could only be Agag, the Amalekite king. He wore a white linen robe trimmed with purple embroidery, far finer than anything I had ever seen Saul wear. A golden circlet sat atop his black hair. His oiled and braided beard gleamed in the sun. He held his portly frame erect and haughty. In his right hand, he lightly held a spear shaft as polished and black as ebony with a tip that looked like silver. The driver reined in the chariot team at thirty paces from our shields. Saul moved to the front rank facing Agag.

The slave was an Israelite. He looked at us, his own race, with sad, frightened eyes. Agag yanked the chain, talking loudly and watching Saul. The slave glanced at his captor and cowered away. He stared at the ground in front of the chariot while he translated Agag's jabbering in a loud monotone. "The most high Lord and King Agag of the glorious Amalekite people greets his fellow king, Saul of the Hebrews. He wishes to spare you and the lives of your guards. He offers all of you the chance to lay down your weapons. He will take you into his service or allow you to be ransomed."

Saul replied almost before the shamed slave could finish. "No Israelite except you will ever surrender to your pig's butt of a king!" he thundered. "And you tell him I said that." He pointed at the translator. "I don't know you or how you came to be in this pagan's service, but you tell him exactly what I called him. Beware, you. I understand enough of his gibberish speech to know if you leave anything out."

The shocked slave shrank back, looking at Saul with his eyes pleading, his body shivering. He spoke to Agag in a quavering voice. The Amalekite king cuffed the captured translator to the ground with his spear shaft and hissed at the downed man before he cruelly jerked him back up by the iron collar. The Amalekite soldiers laughed at the wretch's misery. We shifted uneasily. Agag rattled the slave's chain while he ranted at him. Finally, the captive spoke to us again.

"Brave soldiers of Israel," the slave said, "you have fought hard for your king today. Now he would lead you all to your deaths for no reason except his own glory. So the noble King Agag makes his offer directly to you. He says, 'Give Saul over to me, and I will allow all of you to leave safely with your arms. Only turn over this fellow who would have you killed, and you can go free. Otherwise, you will all die here on this road, far away from your homes and your god.'"

King Saul's face went pale then reddened. Our ranks stirred. I had protected Prince Jonathan for years, and I would not desert his father, my king, to those heathen brutes. I felt confident my company would stand with him too.

"Bang your shields!" I roared. "Make them thunder." I began thumping my spear shaft against the flat of my shield, pounding rhythmically and slowly.

Zelig joined me, and then the men joined until the whole circle of warriors beat as one heart in a synchronized clashing of weapons. Agag tried to shout above our noise but could not. Suddenly, Saul snatched Nissim's spear. He hefted it once and then flung it overhanded. It struck the Israelite slave in the center of his chest, driving him backward to collapse in a shuddering spasm of blood when the chain jerked taut. Our clanging stopped.

"No Israelite should live as a slave under any uncircumcised Amalekite and surely not under this one," Saul cried. "Take care, Agag, you foul king. The Lord God of Israel will see your city destroyed this day."

Agag gripped the chariot with both hands as the reinsman wheeled it about in the road. Amalekite soldiers scattered before it, and the team trotted back to the city gate, dragging the bouncing, lifeless body of the translator behind.

Soldiers in both armies watched quietly, rooted where they stood. I bent to pick up another spear lying next to the wounded. Wordlessly, I stepped up and placed it in Nissim's hand.

"Tighten your wall," I said in that brief moment of calm.

Shields scraped closer together, and our circle compacted. Amalekite and Hebrew stared at each other in silence until one of their officers bellowed. Then they fell upon us like the walls of a collapsing well.

Never had I been so tightly packed in combat. We fought in two ranks, our circular position less than ten long strides across. Spears thrust out from the ring, and the pagans threw themselves upon our bristling tips. Men on both sides fell in that grunting mass to be trampled underfoot as our wall shrank ever smaller. Zelig and I became the only reserves. We plugged holes when a man went down until the gap closed again. At one point he and I exchanged a look and then a salute to the chest. I expected to die there.

The Amalekites howled as before. Gleeful shouts came from their rear while those being skewered by us in front only grunted. Saul fought

71

like a champion, using that heavy-bladed sword to clear out dozens of enemies who dared to face him.

Suddenly, a great shouting erupted behind me, and Hebrew voices sounded over the din. I knew without looking that Abner had come. The Amalekite soldiers stopped, their faces betraying confusion then shock and fear as they began to realize what was happening. Israelites surged around them on all sides. The enemy attacking us turned to face their new foe, leaving us forgotten. We could have struck at their backs then, but I held the company still. Even King Saul made no protest. We were exhausted. We stayed there in our tight circle, mutely watching the destruction of the Amalekite army.

Everything changed quickly. Throngs of Israelite militia chased the remaining pagans back through the gates into their city. My company stood silent in the middle of a churned landscape littered with bodies. Soon smoke arose behind the walls as our army carried out Yahweh's command to destroy the Amalekites totally. I could hear women screaming inside. Activity swirled around us as couriers hurried past in every direction, but the fighting had moved on. I made a hasty count. Fifty of us stood there with five wounded still alive inside our circle. Men looked at one another, forever changed by that day.

"Commander Beral."

I started. I hadn't seen General Abner come up. He and some of his staff stood nearby outside our shields. They were looking about at piles of dead and wounded on every side. Moans came from men struggling to get out from under corpses.

"Commander, you may stand down now. Relax your men. The danger is past."

"Yes, sir. Of course." I turned to Zelig and nodded.

"Unstrap your shields. Sit." Zelig spoke softly at last.

We moved like old men. Weariness soaked through everyone. The company slumped down in the same rough circle where we had stood fighting. Young boys with wineskins had come along with Abner. We guzzled, and wine dripped off our chins. While we drank, General Abner approached the king.

Saul looked wild-eyed, his hair matted with sweat when he removed his crown. He panted as he spoke excitedly. "That was a fight like no other! We held them back. Did you see us, Abner? We held them back!"

"Yes, my king. We all saw your stand. It was bravery such as I have never seen before." His voice shook with sincerity I didn't hear often from any man. "Sire, are you all right? Have you been wounded? We were concerned."

The king waved him off. He extended his arm and swept it around the circle of my soldiers. "With men like this at my side, do you think I could come to any harm?" He raised his voice to a shout. "The men of this company are indeed crocodiles!"

The effect was immediate. My men, sitting hollow-eyed an instant before, leaped to their feet and cheered. They cheered Saul, and I realized with a guilty start, they cheered me. The king beamed at them while I held my arms up for silence.

"My king, it was our honor to serve with you." I stumbled over the words. "You are welcome to join in our ranks anytime."

"And I shall do so!" He laughed.

The company whooped its approval as General Abner led the king away.

"Sire, there are still matters for your attention," the general said. "Agag has fled through another gate. Many of his forces are still with him. We can organize a pursuit—"

Saul stopped him abruptly. He turned around and looked at me. Our eyes met, and he nodded. "Beral," he said quietly, "I should have believed my son about you." He started to turn away but stopped again. "Thank you, Commander."

As I watched him walk away in triumph toward the captured city, my ears seemed to ring.

"Commander." Zelig gestured behind me.

Jonathan waited there, hands on his hips, face shining. "Well done, Beral," he said.

CHAPTER TWELVE

*He took Agag king of the Amalekites alive, and all his
people he totally destroyed with the sword.*

I Samuel 15:8 NIV

FOR TWO DAYS WE CLEARED the dead from the battlefield. We
wrapped fallen Israelites carefully and placed them aside as
brothers to be carried home in carts. The Amalekite corpses were
thrown onto huge piles to be set afire. The stench of burning human
flesh gagged us. Handling the dead made everyone unclean for seven
days, but it didn't matter much here. Ahijah and the other priests would
perform the purification rites on us before the men got back to wives
and families.

At night, we camped beside the desolation that had been the city
of Amalek. Nothing moved behind its scorched walls except wisps of
curling grey smoke, where building timbers still smoldered. Most of the
plunder went into the same flames that served as the pagans' funeral
pyre. Saul spared only the best cattle and sheep and a few horses. I
looked for the fine chariot team of white stallions, but Agag must have
taken them.

I saw those horses three days later, when King Saul and Abner
returned in Agag's chariot. The dejected Amalekite king walked behind,
chained to it with perhaps the same collar that had once held his Israelite
slave. He had been running to Egypt when elements of our army caught
up to him at Shur. None of his men survived the onslaught, but Saul
had let Agag live. I could not see why.

King Saul was in high spirits. "We have carried out Yahweh's command!" he shouted to our assembled ranks while he paraded his captive before us.

Dust kicked out from the chariot's wheels, and Agag jogged through it to keep up with the trotting horses. We answered with triumphant cries. Saul finally took pity on his former foe and let him up into the chariot as he returned to his tent.

That night, Saul held a lavish feast for his army beside the dead city of the Amalekites. We ate plundered livestock as firelight and shadows flickered against the mute, blackened stones. The king allowed Agag to sit at his feet, eating the same meat as Saul himself.

Men laughed and retold accounts of the fighting. Ahijah sent a sonorous prayer up to the heavens, honoring our dead. I felt sullen and questioned Yahweh in that moment. Half of my company—good and virile men whose names I knew—was gone. Men following my commands had died. Why had He not taken me too? Certainly the Amalekites had tried to kill me. I pondered my cup, swirling the wine around and staring at it, when I suddenly realized my name had been spoken. I looked up, startled, to find faces around the fire staring at me.

"Commander Beral, are you not listening to your king? Come up here and join me." Saul's smiling eyes met mine as he gestured to a seat at his left side.

I got to my feet and picked my way carefully through the seated men. When I approached the king, he rose and embraced me. All the fighters cheered behind me, and I recognized the voices of my soldiers among them.

Saul released me and turned to the glum Agag. "Here, Amalekite! Here is why you couldn't break us. Here is the man I stood with in the roadway—he and his crocodiles!"

The cheers rose again, and I blushed. Agag couldn't understand Saul's words, but he eyed my face in recognition.

Saul peered about into the rows of faces half hidden in the firelight. "Where are my two shield brethren? Where are Nissim and Yair?"

More shouts erupted as the two spearmen came forward, pushed along by comrades. They stood sheepishly before the king, shifting from side to side.

"Nissim, son of Hador. And Yair from the tribe of Ephraim. Never have I fought beside finer men! I have much to tell your fathers when we return. But tonight, I give you these." He slid a pair of golden armbands from his wrist.

The two former shepherds looked dumbstruck when he presented the baubles to them. They stammered their thanks and stumbled back to their seats amid the laughter of the assembled army.

I sat next to King Saul, but in the new flush of celebrating, my thoughts turned to his daughter. I imagined how her eyes would widen when she heard of my company's bravery. Her lips would part…

Jonathan sat down grinning beside me and squeezed my shoulder. "Beral," he whispered, "try not to daydream so much. We'll be home soon enough. She'll still be there."

⤙⬥⤚

The next morning, Saul stood high amid the ruins of Amalek in a position of respect, watching as his part-time farmer army marched away, each tribe carrying its own dead home for burial. Later, we in the standing army followed him to Carmel to spend the next full day stacking stones to build a monument to his victory. After a night's rest, we left the mountain and went down to Gilgal, still herding plundered Amalekite livestock before us. Nissim and Yair proudly sported their new armbands. Agag rode in the chariot with Saul. Spearmen grumbled about that in the ranks behind me.

Samuel found us at Gilgal the next day. I was sitting back against a large boulder, working the nicks out of my sword, when the old prophet swept by. As a Nazarite from birth, he had wild hair tumbling to his waist. He wore a severe expression and looked straight ahead as he stalked toward the king's quarters. A young boy with a goatskin sack trotted at his heels. Sensing something in the old man's demeanor, I set aside my honing stone and followed them through the camp.

Someone must have run ahead to tell Saul of Samuel's arrival. The king stood in front of his tent, arms held out in welcome.

"Greetings, Samuel. The Lord bless you! I have carried out the Lord's instructions." Saul's voice boomed with confidence.

The prophet answered harshly, "Tell me, Saul, did Yahweh not say to you to totally destroy the Amalekites and everything that belongs to

76

them—including cattle and sheep, camels and donkeys? What then is this bleating of sheep in my ears? What is this lowing of cattle that I hear?" He placed a hand to his ear in a mock gesture of listening.

Saul's face fell. He held his palms out and smiled uneasily. He swept his arms about the camp, gesturing at all of us. I noticed Jonathan had come to his father's tent. A crowd of soldiers gathered around.

"The soldiers brought them from the Amalekites," Saul said. "They spared the best of the sheep and cattle to sacrifice to the Lord your God, but we totally destroyed the rest." He finished, confidently shaking his head, his voice grown assured once more.

"Stop!" cried Samuel. "Let me tell you what the Lord said to me last night."

"Tell me," Saul replied.

"You, Saul, were once small in your own eyes, but didn't the Lord anoint you king over all the tribes of Israel?" The prophet turned and addressed all of us standing there. "And he sent you on a mission, saying, 'Go and completely destroy those wicked people, the Amalekites. Make war on them until you have wiped them out.'" He looked back at Saul. "Why did you not obey the Lord? Why did you pounce on the plunder and do evil in the eyes of the Lord?"

The king's face drained of color. "But I did obey the Lord," he said. "I went on the mission the Lord assigned me. I completely destroyed the Amalekites and brought back Agag their king." He pointed around the camp again. "The *soldiers* took sheep and cattle from the plunder, the best of what was devoted to God, in order to sacrifice them to the Lord your God here at Gilgal."

I felt embarrassed to see Saul shifting blame from himself. He was a better king than that.

"The Lord my God?" Samuel replied. His eyebrows rose. "*My* God?" He gazed at all of us surrounding the king and him. "Not *your* God but mine? And what is this I see dripping from the chins of your soldiers? Is it not grease from the fat of Amalekite cattle? Those same cattle and sheep to be sacrificed to the Lord *my* God?"

I think we were all overcome by the power of the words coming from that frail-looking old man as he raised his head and arms to heaven, but I didn't hear them all. I was watching the stunned face of my prince. As the man of God ranted against the sky, Jonathan's jaw tightened, and he looked down at his own feet. He closed his eyes. I felt anger at Samuel for the pain he caused my prince. Then my attention snapped back to the prophet at his last words.

"Because you have rejected the word of the Lord, he has rejected you as king."

A gasp shuddered through us who heard. Some of the men muttered fearfully. Saul looked stricken. His head bowed and his arms by his sides, he spoke so softly to Samuel that I could not hear, but it was clear that the king pleaded with him.

Samuel only shook his head. "I will not stay with you. I have already said that you have rejected the word of the Lord, and the Lord has rejected you as king over Israel." He wheeled to leave, and Saul grabbed at the threadbare robe the prophet wore. A piece tore away in the king's hands, and Samuel stopped. He stared at Saul with saddened eyes. "The kingdom of Israel is likewise torn from you today, to be given to one of your neighbors—one better than you. You may stay on the throne, but your seed will never inherit your kingdom. God, the Glory of Israel, does not lie or change His mind."

Saul dropped the fabric and covered his eyes with one hand while he reached out to Samuel with the other. His remorse clearly showed. "I have sinned. But please honor me before my people and before Israel. Stay with me so that I may worship the Lord God."

Samuel heaved a great sigh. He shook his head before laying a hand on Saul's shoulder. "Very well," he said. He turned and gestured to a commander. "Bring me Agag, king of the Amalekites."

Agag had been staying with Saul in the king's own tent, eating and sharing wine with him. Saul had treated the pagan as an equal for several days. That was probably why the Amalekite came forward so confidently, no doubt thinking that any danger to him had passed. He wiped crumbs from his lips as he walked out into the cleared area where Samuel awaited him.

The prophet took a sword from a nearby soldier. He waved it as he thundered. "As your sword has made women childless, so now your mother will be childless among women." Without pausing, he swung the sword in front of the Amalekite king's disbelieving eyes and spun completely around to bury it in his neck. Agag slumped to the ground, his head almost severed from his body. The men shouted their approval.

That afternoon, Samuel presided over the sacrifice of the Amalekite livestock. Saul worshipped alongside him. At dawn, Samuel and his young attendant left to return to Ramah. Saul led us back to Gibeah. Some of the men bantered and sang on the march, but Jonathan only frowned during that journey home.

I never saw Samuel visit or counsel King Saul again after that day.

CHAPTER THIRTEEN

David came to Saul and entered his service.

1 Samuel 16:21a NIV

KING SAUL CHANGED DRAMATICALLY AFTER that confrontation with Samuel. Severe headaches attacked him at all hours, but especially at night. He still held feasts for his officers, but they weren't cheerful occasions anymore. He brooded in silence at the head of every banquet, causing even his favorites to speak in hushed tones. Court attendants whispered that the Spirit of the Lord had abandoned him and that an evil one tormented him now.

All of Israel soon heard of the crocodile company's stand at the Amalek gate, so I didn't pay much heed to the king's moods. I found myself covered in the glory I had coveted. Were the fifty men who died following me worth that glory? I couldn't say. But one thing I did know: Michal looked at me openly during the banquets.

No matter how sullen her father appeared, Michal bubbled with gaiety at his table. She covered her mouth when she giggled as her eyes searched out mine, and I dared myself not to look away. Once, while she stared at me, the barest tip of her tongue slipped out and licked across her bottom lip. I had to shift my tunic. I vowed to speak to her, and one evening I did.

A winter banquet was coming to an end, and we commanders rose to take our leaves individually before the king's low table. I pressed a fist to my chest and bowed. "Good night, my king. Thank you for sharing your tables with me." My pulse raced as I stepped sideways and then said the words I had rehearsed over and over in my head. "And to you, gracious Princess Michal, thank you for your presence."

She tilted her head to one side and smiled at me, dimpled cheeks maddening in their beauty. "Commander Beral, I should thank you instead. Jonathan has told me about how you fought and protected my father against the Amalekites. I should like to someday hear the story from you as well."

No horde of screaming pagans had ever made my head spin as it did at that moment. I bowed, furious at myself for being so tongue-tied with nothing else rehearsed to say. "C-Certainly, Princess Michal. Whenever you wish," I finally stammered.

Saul looked up, not so morose and suddenly interested. His dark eyes darted from his daughter to me and back again. Jonathan stood behind him, deliberately cleaning out his ear and looking at the opposite wall.

"Yes, Beral," Saul said. "You must tell Merab and Michal about our stand together and how the crocodiles fought. Bring Zelig with you."

He looked at me with favor, but the message was plain. He had emphasized Merab, and my heart sank. Did he expect me to court the older sister, to reach for thorns instead of the rose?

I bowed again. "Of course, my king."

Outside, at the foot of the palace steps, I paused a long time in the darkness while other officers jostled past me, eager to get to their warm beds and wives. I looked up at a clear sky, my heart starting to settle at last as I took several deep breaths.

"Beral?" The voice came as soft as a dove from the entrance behind me.

Disbelieving, I spun around to see Michal outlined in the open doorway, more beautiful in starlight than I could have imagined. An attendant maiden waited discreetly behind her with folded hands. A pair of Ben-Ami's men came out and posted themselves on each side of the door. She tripped lightly down the steps to stand in front of me, close enough that I could pick up her scent. Sandalwood and flowers filled my nostrils.

"My princess?" I croaked.

She touched my forearm. "My father likes you, but he wants Merab to marry," she whispered. "You can wait?" Soft fingers caressed my arm.

"I will," I answered, timidly placing my hand over hers.

She glanced back at her attendant and the guards, all pretending not to notice my presence.

"Not here," she murmured, "and not now… but someday soon, Beral. I promise." She squeezed gently and brushed my arm as she turned to skip back up the steps.

The doors closed behind her, and I was left in the darkness with the guards. I walked to my barracks, stunned and happy. The stars had never looked crisper to me than on that night.

The king still suffered from headaches. He sat in darkened rooms with damp cloths on his forehead while his attendants fretted.

They pleaded with him. "Let us find someone to play the harp so that when the evil spirit from God comes upon you, you will feel better."

He threw platters and cups at them in reply. I was in the hall one evening, reporting to General Abner, and I heard the utensils clattering off the walls of his chambers.

And then one day, he agreed. "Yes, find someone who plays well and bring him to me."

Katriel, no longer commanding a fighting company, had become an aide to the king, eating at his table and growing fat. He suggested a certain youth. I was standing nearby and heard when he leaned his scented breath toward the king's ear.

"I have seen a son of Jesse of Bethlehem," he said. "He knows how to play the harp—a brave young man and a warrior. He speaks well and is a fine-looking man. The Lord is said to be with him."

Saul sent for him, so David, the son of Jesse, came to the king's household, bringing only a small harp, a donkey, and a goat. The king liked him immediately.

He was young with a fine appearance, his skin reddened from days spent tending his father's sheep. They summoned him to the king's chambers on his first evening in Gibeah. The king wrestled his evil spirits again that night and tossed about violently on sweat-soaked linens. David sat against the wall to strum his harp. Servants said that the boy's fingers moved lightly as petals over the strings while he sang psalms to Yahweh in a low voice, songs he had written himself. Saul eventually slept that night, and his mood improved greatly the next day.

After a week the palace staff buzzed with hope. Nightly sessions with the young shepherd brought peace to the king. Whatever demons tormented him stayed at bay when David played. With Saul calmed, all of Israel seemed joyous again.

Zelig and I received an invitation to spend an afternoon with Michal and her sister. Zelig was clearly uncomfortable about going into the presence of so much perfumed femininity.

"Why must I go, Commander?" he grumbled. "I've no interest in stealing touches from the king's daughter."

I smiled and shook my head. "Zelig, you have to go. If you don't, then I'll not get past the guards myself. Her father doesn't want *me* stealing touches either."

He grunted. "Very well, but her older sister better not graze a knee against mine. I have a good woman—one who's my age already."

"I know you do," I said. "Don't worry. Everyone knows your Jemima would take a rod to any other woman looking at you, even a princess. Just don't laugh today when I have to tell stories about my prowess and your valor."

"I'll go, Commander, but leave me out of your tales."

When we arrived in the great hall, the harpist, David, sat in a far corner, running his fingertips over the strings and singing softly. Both princesses were listening to him so intently they failed to notice us enter. Merab saw us first and nudged her younger sister.

"Oh, Beral, you've come," Michal exclaimed brightly. "And you are Zelig?" She stood and looked at the grizzled old warrior, her face frank with interest. "I've heard much about you too." Until that moment, I hadn't known Zelig was capable of blushing.

He didn't have to worry about Merab's intentions, though. She kept apart from us, silent and disdainful, uninterested in any sort of courtship. Servants puttered about, bringing us wine and dates. Michal, however, stayed fixed on me the entire visit. She wanted every detail I could recall of the fight against the Amalekites. I told her of our stand, our shield-to-shield retreat and circle. I emphasized the bravery of her father more than my own.

As she listened, her fists balled up into tight knots. "How valiant you were. Sometimes, I wish I were a man." She said it so vehemently it startled me into stopping the narrative.

"Yes, my princess, but I am grateful that you are not," I replied.

She giggled and clapped her hands once. "Beral, what a wonderful thing to say. Every maiden should get to hear those words." She flicked her gaze to me then dropped it to her lap. "Every maiden."

Behind her, Zelig rolled his eyes.

When my storytelling finished, Zelig and I took our leave, with no touches for me other than the hand Michal gave to Zelig as well. Yet, as we left the hall, I was sure I walked through green meadows, so lightly did my feet touch the stone floor.

"Commander Beral?"

I turned around to see who called.

David had followed us out the front entrance, carrying his harp slung loosely over one shoulder. The boy's eyes shone with intensity. "I listened to your story of the battle against the Amalekites. With your approval, sirs, I would like to compose a psalm about you and how Yahweh protects His people. I have some lines already." He unslung the harp and strummed it for a moment before he sang. He had a good, clear voice.

He sang, *"Beral and Zelig have said, 'If the Lord had not been on our side—when men attacked us, when their anger flared against us—they would have swallowed us alive.'"*

He stopped and lowered the instrument. "That's what I have so far. I have to add more." His eagerness reminded me of a pup.

"That will be a fine song, David," I said. "But leave our names out. Praise should not be diluted from Yahweh. Right, Zelig?"

The old veteran gave an elaborate shrug. "Certainly, Commander," he said.

David's face broke into a smile. "You're right, of course. I will finish it without your names. I'm glad you like it." He started back into the palace but halted halfway up the steps. "It will take me only a few days. Perhaps the princess Michal will help me. She enjoys music, and I'm sure she could compose better wordings than me." He said it with complete innocence and flashed another smile at us before he turned to go again.

I watched his back as he entered the palace. He was only a servant from a poor clan, but I didn't know whether I liked him or not.

Zelig was no comfort to me on our walk from the king's home. "Commander, I would be a happy man if you never ask me to do that again." He grunted. We walked along through the streets in silence for a few moments. Finally, he cleared his throat. "The king's daughter would be a prize for any young man. She is certainly a blossom to behold." He looked at a flock of sheep being herded down a side street. "But a beautiful mare can be a joy to handle, or she can be a trial to her master. I fear Princess Michal would be a difficult horse for anyone. A man should beware before he takes such a beauty home." He kept looking away from me.

"I think you trifle in my affairs a little beyond your place," I snapped. "And Princess Michal is not to be compared to a mare." I had never spoken sharply to Zelig before that moment, and I couldn't explain the uneasy feeling that had come over me.

Zelig stared ahead and didn't speak again.

CHAPTER FOURTEEN

*Now the Philistines gathered their forces for war
and assembled at Socoh in Judah.*

1 Samuel 17:1a NIV

THAT WINTER KING SAUL SENT a call throughout Israel for more stout twenty-year-old men to join his army. Many arrived individually and in small groups. To my surprise, most of them requested a place in my company.

"You need fifty men," Jonathan said to me. "Almost two hundred are gathered in Gibeah today. Since they all clamor to be called crocs, you can have your choice of them tomorrow."

Zelig and I walked to the training ground the next morning to make our selections. He had been offered Katriel's company to command but stubbornly refused it. I asked him why.

"I still prefer to kill heathens myself instead of having others do it for me," he muttered. "So long as you let me do that, Commander, I'll stay with you. We've already killed many together."

The men awaiting us looked far different from the surly, dispirited group I had faced months ago at that same spot. These were volunteers, wanting to serve under me. The fifty now-veteran soldiers left in the company stood tall in a line before them, staring hard at those who would join their ranks.

I looked at my proud spearmen. "Company, shields up!" I commanded.

Fifty bright new circular shields thumped together. Spears protruded forward. The crowd stirred and murmured.

After a pause, I shouted, "Advance! Zelig, call cadence."

The wall moved forward, stepping together to Zelig's shouted beat. Only eyes and spear tips showed above it. Some of the new volunteers moved hastily back to the rear of their group, and I took note of them as I began to winnow out the chaff. I halted the advance before it made contact.

"Spears down," I said.

The butts of fifty spears thudded into the ground as one sound. Climbing onto the mounting block between the two groups, I addressed the assembly of farmer and merchant youth.

"Do you see these soldiers? These men in front of you protected the king of Israel against twenty times their number of Amalekites. This company stood fast when others did not. Do any of you want to join them?"

The crowd responded enthusiastically. Every man would be a hero, a crocodile.

I held my arm up for silence and turned back to my company. "Shields up," I said.

Each man reached over his shoulder and removed a second shield slung across his back: war-weary, nicked, and battered shields. They held them aloft with two hands over their heads.

I waited a moment before I ordered, "Shields down." My crocs placed the grim relics down on the ground in front of them.

"Did you see those shields?" I asked softly.

Every man leaned forward to hear.

"Each one comes from a man killed in that defense of King Saul. Each one belonged to a friend and brother of these men standing before you. You would replace one of them?" I raised my voice. "If you join this company, you may be one of the next fifty to die in it. Who still wants to come forward?"

Men shuffled their feet and looked away. In the end, fewer than one hundred stayed to be tested by Zelig and me. The trials took hours, but we selected our fifty. We looked for strong men who could look me in the eye. I was also careful to pick from each tribe of Israel. This would be an Israelite company, not a tribal band. Those not selected went back to General Abner.

Our new recruits nervously waited for instructions.

"Pick up a shield and form two ranks," I directed.

They moved to gather the grounded shields. The crooked lines they formed almost sent Zelig into convulsions.

"Do you think you're pissing on a rock? Stop looking at your feet, goatherds!" He applied his switch vigorously to bare legs until the double lines had some semblance of straightness. The veteran spearmen formed a column beside them.

Finally, Zelig stood before me with his hand to his chest. "The men are ready, Commander," he reported.

I nodded and moved to the front. "Welcome to the crocodiles. Do you see that dung heap in the distance?"

These men learned faster, I think, because they had asked for this work and because this time I knew what they needed. Their drills went more easily with fifty experienced spearmen beside them. Within weeks, the newest members in our ranks could hold their own.

They would need to, for the sea people soon came surging back into Israel.

On a late spring afternoon, Judean tribesmen ran into Gibeah, breathlessly reporting that Philistine forces encamped along a hillside in the valley of Elah near Socoh. Within hours, Saul left his household behind and led the army southward to meet this new invasion. Runners went out to the other tribes to summon their clan militias and join us at Azekah.

My company marched at the head of Prince Jonathan's column. We believed we were the best of the standing army. I lengthened my stride to catch up to Jonathan as he walked with Herzi and aides.

"So, Beral, are you and your crocodiles ready for another fight?" he asked cheerily when I fell in alongside him.

My prince had been gloomy much of the time since his father's confrontation with Samuel. Today, though, the prospect of action made all of us step out lively, drinking in the sights and smells around us.

"Yes," I replied. "The new ones are anxious to prove themselves. The old ones are grim for their benefit. We are as ready as we were before Amalek."

"Good."

We walked several strides before I asked, "What is this I have heard about a new Philistine champion? Some giant?"

Jonathan pursed his lips. "I've heard that too. I suppose we'll see him when we get there."

After a march of several days, we arrived at the Elan valley late in the evening. Our camp set up hastily in the dark on the south side while Philistine cooking fires burned across the way at Ephes Dammim. Men went down to the tiny stream between the armies to get water and to cautiously watch for the enemy, but the night passed without incident.

At dawn, little gray birds twittered amidst the rocks as we stretched ourselves awake. Each unit formed ranks and faced toward the north side of the valley. My company took the center position before the king's tent. As the sun's first rays lit the Philistine camp, I surveyed their army. The heathens stirred from their tents and leisurely arrayed themselves against us but gave no indication of any further movement. Soldiers leaned on their spears to gaze back at us calmly. They greatly outnumbered us since our tribal soldiers hadn't arrived yet. I wondered if the enemy would attack before that happened. Then I saw Goliath.

King Saul stood a head above most men, but this giant loomed ribs and shoulders over the feathered helmets of the Philistine spearmen who parted for him. He paused long enough to let his armor bearer go before him. The man struggled to carry a large metal-rimmed shield while Goliath swaggered down the slope toward the trickle of water. I had never seen a man so big nor one as ugly. He walked like a lumbering bear, and I wondered if he had the bear's same latent quickness. In one hand he swung his bronze helmet that looked the size of a well bucket. Thick, matted hair stuck out all over his head, even down to his jutting brows. He yawned and flexed massive shoulders while he approached. We could hear the clinking of his huge polished scale-armor coat. His spear looked like a house beam.

The giant went to the edge of the rivulet at the bottom of the valley and hulked down to scoop water in his helmet. Upon straightening, he made a show of drinking from his headgear. He smacked his lips and drew an arm across his mouth, paying our army no heed. Then, with a comic twitch, he pretended to notice us for the first time. He gaped and covered his mouth in mock surprise before smiling broadly with gapped teeth.

"Hail, Hebrews, you sons of Moses," he shouted in our language. "Have you come here to our lands to visit? Why do you line up against us for battle?" He paused, holding his chin. "Perhaps you think you would fight us and drive us away? But surely you don't think that. Look at your puny army." He made an exaggerated show of thinking then raised his head as if a thought suddenly came to him. "Hebrews! Your king Saul would have you all perish in this valley. Surely you don't want to die here, do you? I can save you. Choose one amongst you to come and fight me. If that man should win, then we will become your subjects. If I win, Israel becomes subject to Philistine, as it should be."

He turned around to walk up the bank and stand beside the armor bearer. He faced us again and shouted, "I am Goliath! I defy your ranks, Israel. Give me a man to fight, and we will settle this. I wait here."

I stood silent in front of the company, glancing back at widened eyes and slackened jaws. Low mutterings sounded throughout our assembled force. No one man could beat this Goliath. I knew that, and so did every soldier standing behind me. King Saul and General Abner looked on at my side. Abner shook his head as they went back to the king's tent, but not before I saw a look of dismay on Saul's face.

Goliath continued to pace in the valley below us. He donned the huge shield, and from time to time, he shouted and waved his big spear. The Philistine army laughed with each insult he hurled at us. We could only stand mutely and watch. He went back to his lines at midday, but not before relieving himself in the small stream.

"Here, Israel. See what you grow if you don't cut it off?" He laughed.

That evening, we sat quietly around our fires. Men looked left and right, perhaps hoping to see someone else agree to face the giant. Saul summoned his officers at nightfall. Runners called for every brigade and company leader to attend. We gathered in a circle around his fire. Jonathan and Abner sat on each side of the king.

"Is there no champion we can send against that abomination?" Saul asked.

Our silence and glum expressions in the firelight were his answer.

The king swept his gaze over us. I thought he might select a champion himself, and my mouth went dry when his eye stopped briefly on me.

Instead, he blew his cheeks out and dismissed us. "We will wait for the rest of the army," he said.

Goliath railed every morning after that, even as more tribal and clan militias joined us. Eventually, we became almost equal in numbers to the Philistine army. But even then, we were dispirited by the giant's challenge. Each day, he devised new taunts.

One day, he pointed his spear directly at me. "You, Beral. Aren't you a crocodile?" he jeered. "Standing firm against Amalekites? Well, come stand against me! Show me the warrior you are. Show all of us."

My knees almost turned to water before my own soldiers. How could he know my name? I said nothing.

Abner set part-time soldiers from Judea in the line next to my company. Zelig and the squad leaders offered to show them some fighting skills. I watched them practice and became especially impressed with three of the Judeans. To my surprise, I learned all three were sons of Jesse—older brothers of David, the king's harpist and servant. The eldest, Eliab, stood tall enough to rival King Saul himself. I asked Zelig about the siblings.

He only shook his head in disgust. "Truly, Commander, they would be good fighting spearmen if they cared to be. They're quick and strong, but none of those three will join us."

"Won't they fight?" I asked.

He spat before he answered. "Oh, they'll fight when they have to, but they only want to finish this and go home to their flocks. A damned waste of manhood."

The standoff dragged on for weeks. We went through the same ritual each morning. Both armies took up battle positions and faced each other across the valley until Goliath strode down to the stream bank between us. The Philistines seemed content to wait idly by while he leered at us and chipped away at our morale. Rumors started that King Saul was offering great wealth and even his daughter's hand to any man who slew Goliath. That thought didn't excite me, for I knew, if the rumor were true, he meant Merab, not Michal.

One evening, reclining at a cooking fire with other commanders, I said to Jonathan, "My prince, I don't see any way to defeat the giant in single combat. He even towers over your father. Couldn't we rush my company to meet him? Or send a dozen archers forward?"

He formed a tight-lipped smile and shook his head. "Goliath could get back to his lines before any of us got close enough. Besides... it would work against us. He comes alone every day to stare us down. If we do anything but meet him in single combat as he demands, we only prove what he says to us—that we are cowards. No. We have to do it his way... except that we *can't* do it his way. It's certain death for any man to face him." He sat up and stirred the fire. We watched sparks rise into the night sky. "It seems our best hope is for Yahweh to help us again, but Ahijah's prayers aren't enough." He sighed then looked directly into my eyes across the firelight. "I find myself wishing that Samuel were here. I fear that, when he turned his face away from my father, he may have taken Yahweh with him."

Interrupting the long silence that followed, Jonathan abruptly stood up to yawn. He stretched his arms and slapped his thighs. "I suppose we could wait here until he dies someday. I've heard that giants die at an early age. It's certain he won't leave many offspring to replace him. Any woman foolhardy enough to lie once under that brute would never do it a second time. That must be why he's always in a foul mood."

Around the small fire, we laughed uproariously at that. But when Goliath walked out to taunt us the next day, it didn't seem as funny.

CHAPTER FIFTEEN

So David triumphed over the Philistine with a sling and a stone...

1 Sam 17:50a NIV

ONE MORNING, AS I SHRUGGED into my leather breastplate and gathered my armaments, I saw young David standing over with the Judean group. He carried a heavy bag on his back, probably grain and bread for his brothers. I supposed he would take the food to the supply keeper, a position Jonathan had established to ensure everyone ate equally. I forgot about the lad and moved the company to our battle position.

Goliath came as usual that morning, grinning and waving at us as a friend. "Ho, Hebrew boys," he yelled. "Have you found me a champion yet? You know, in my city of Gath, warriors will meet a challenge. Those that don't are called women. Is that what you are, Israel? Women?" He threw his head back and guffawed loudly. The shield bearer grinned and bobbed his own head like a simpleton. All the Philistines laughed. We accepted his jeers in silence as we always did while he ranted.

A disturbance erupted among the Judeans next to us. I looked over and saw David in their ranks arguing with his brothers. "Now what have I done?" he shouted. "Can't I even speak?"

Eliab, the eldest, shoved him away. "Why did you even come here? I know you just want to watch the battle!" he shouted in return. "Run back home to your sheep."

I couldn't allow undisciplined antics like that in front of the Philistines, so I sent Zelig over to quiet the disturbance.

He came back, shaking his head, and reported the argument to me. "Commander, it seems the shepherd boy is saying, 'Who is this uncircumcised Philistine defying the armies of the living God?' He's talking as if he would go slay the giant himself. He wonders why we haven't already done so." He squinted up at the sky. "I admire his spirit, but he knows nothing. His brothers are sending him home."

I chuckled at David's brash ignorance. We would all be better off without a harpist underfoot. In the valley below, Goliath kept up his braying. I heard a movement behind me and turned to see Abner approaching through my company's ranks.

"What is this I hear?" he asked. "Someone wants to challenge the giant?"

"Sire, it's only a shepherd lad coming from the desert to visit his brothers. He will be leaving soon," I replied.

Abner's face fell in disappointment. "A shepherd lad? A boy? Well, no matter. The king wants to see him." He shrugged. "Bring him to the tent. We'll trot him by his majesty, and then the young man can go."

"Yes, sire."

David's face brightened when I approached him in the Judean ranks. "Commander Beral!" he exclaimed. "I hoped I would see you here. I finished the psalm. Do you want to hear it?" My puzzlement must have showed. "The psalm I started that day with you and Zelig," he continued helpfully. "It's done now if you'd like to listen."

I scowled as I remembered. "Not now," I said gruffly. "King Saul wants to see you."

His eyes widened. "King Saul? Me?"

"Yes," I said. "You should be careful what you say in an army camp. The king wants to see the man who would kill Goliath."

I smiled to myself as I led David, now thoughtful, to Saul's tent, only a short walk behind our lines and close enough for the king to catch wind of talk about a potential champion. We approached Ben-Ami's guards standing in front of the closed tent. Ben-Ami stepped out. He put his hands on his hips and appraised David.

"Him?" He looked at me in disbelief. "This boy? Has he seen his seventeenth summer yet?"

I could only spread my hands in reply.

"Very well, then," he said. "This shouldn't take long." He raised the flap and held it aside while David and I ducked inside.

In the dim interior, Saul was sitting on an elevated stool near the back. General Abner and Jonathan stood beside him. Others had gathered inside as well, probably wanting to see our challenger. An audible groan arose when they saw only a youth. David, however, seemed not to be bothered by the disapproving crowd. He had eyes only for the king.

Saul beckoned him forward. "You are the one who says he would defeat the giant?" he asked softly.

"Yes, my king. No one should lose heart because of this Philistine. I am your servant, and I will go out and fight him."

The onlookers murmured to themselves. I heard a snicker and looked over to see Katriel covering his mouth. How did that self-satisfied hyena always manage to slink up so close to power? David stood quietly and met the king's eyes.

Saul studied him for a moment. "You can't go out against that Philistine. You are barely more than a boy. Goliath has been a fighting man all his life." He said it sadly, as if he tried not to mock David in front of these men, but David just stood taller when he answered.

"My king, your servant has protected his father's herds since he *was* truly a boy. I have chased down both lion and bear when they carried off a sheep. I have grabbed their hair and struck them and killed them to rescue the sheep. This uncircumcised Philistine will be no better than any one of them. He has defied the armies of the living God. Our same Lord who delivered me from the paw of the lion and the paw of the bear will also deliver me from this giant."

David certainly wasn't cowed. He spoke evenly, and the crowd fell silent at his confidence. He had a presence about him. I glanced at Jonathan, but he gazed at David, mesmerized by the young man's words. Saul leaned back in his seat and steepled his hands, never taking his eyes from David's face. After a long moment, he leaned forward. "Then go, and the Lord be with you," he said.

I was stunned, along with the onlookers. Men scattered from the tent like beetles from an overturned rock to carry the news of a challenger for Goliath. I stayed behind to watch David.

Saul turned and gestured to Nathon. "Get my armor and helmet. Dress this man with them."

The armor bearer's eyes narrowed in disapproval, but he nodded. "Yes, my lord." He moved efficiently though reluctantly, performing the task he normally did for Saul.

A tunic slid down over David's upraised arms. Nathon buckled the bronze breastplate fitted for the king. I could have put my fist between it and the smaller chest of its new wearer. The effect was almost comical with the helmet strapped on. The shepherd lad walked around the tent, trying to get used to the armor. Saul's sword clanked at his side and nearly dragged on the ground. He looked like a young son wearing his father's gear.

"I cannot wear this," David said. "I'm not used to it." He carefully slipped everything off and handed it back to a visibly relieved Nathon. Then he addressed the king. "With your permission, sire, I will fight as I always do."

Saul nodded, and the shepherd boy picked up his staff and walked out of the tent. An excited murmur traveled up and down the ranks of the army when he appeared. Spearmen craned their necks to see him. I stepped out into the sunlight behind the king and others as they followed him to the front line. Jonathan stood next to David.

"You don't have to do this," I heard him saying to the youth. "No one here can blame you if you decide against it."

David was half a head shorter. He looked up into Jonathan's face and said, "Don't be concerned for me, my lord. The Lord God will be with me."

Jonathan stepped back, and the lad started down the hillside. We watched in silence.

By that time, noon had nearly come. Goliath, swinging his big helmet, was already leaving. He and the shield bearer had almost climbed the slope to their camp before Philistine soldiers spotted David striding down. When they shouted, the giant turned around in disbelief. He shaded his eyes from the hot sun as he tried to make out the lone figure standing on the other side of the little stream. "What's this?" he roared. "The Hebrews have finally found a man amongst themselves? Come to me, then, Israelite, and we'll soon see the color of your blood." He spun his shield bearer around with a cuff on the shoulder, and the pair started back down toward where David calmly knelt at the edge of the water.

Saul watched his young champion. "Abner, whose son is that?"

"As surely as you live, O king, I don't know."

"What is he doing?" wondered Saul. "Is he praying?"

"No, I think he's picking up stones," Jonathan answered.

I could see David moving a hand under the water's surface, gathering small, smooth rocks. He abruptly stood up and dropped some of them into his pouch before he splashed across the creek. He carried his staff in the crook of his arm. I marveled at this boy's courage.

Goliath approached closer. When he could clearly see who faced him, he stopped. "What's this? They send a boy against me?" He raised his face to our lines. "Do you Hebrews think I am a dog that you would send a shepherd boy with a stick to fight me?" He dropped the helmet and shoved his shield bearer aside. He waved his spear as he stalked down, uncovered. "You little cat turd!" he bellowed. "Come here to me, pretty boy, and I'll give your guts to the vultures and your eyes to the jackals!"

David stopped too. He shouted back in a voice so clear we could hear every word, even at a distance behind him. "You come swinging your heavy spear, Goliath, but I come with the God of Israel beside me, the true God whom you have defied. The Lord gives you to me, and today your head will roll. Your whole army will become carcasses to feed birds and wild beasts."

I held my breath as I watched the youth drop the staff and start forward again. He swung an empty leather sling back and forth in one hand.

The two closed at a leisurely pace while David kept shouting. "Today the world will know of the true God of Israel, and they will know that it is not by sword or spear that He saves, for this battle is the Lord's, not man's!"

Goliath looked enraged. His face flushed a deep crimson, and he thrashed his spear from side to side furiously as he lengthened his stride. Suddenly, he broke into an awkward run, raising the spear and bellowing wordlessly. Incredibly, David started to run too. He flew up the slope like a rabbit toward Goliath. Without breaking stride, he took a stone out of his bag and placed it in the sling. He twirled it over his head. Once. Twice. At barely ten paces from Goliath, he flicked the sling with practiced grace. The stone flew straight and true into the giant's forehead. I heard the loud *clunk* as it broke through his skull.

Goliath's head jerked back. He stood openmouthed for an instant before slumping to his knees and then tumbling facedown into the dust. I was sure he died at that moment, for his body never quivered. The only movement in the entire valley was David, who ran to stand over the fallen giant. He jerked the huge sword out of the man's scabbard and swung it overhead with both hands down onto the giant's bare neck. The severed head rolled downhill on the beaten pathway, dribbling blood onto the dirt.

When the Philistines saw their hero dead, they ran. Colorful camp banners and tents collapsed in seconds as panicked men raced past in retreat.

I may have been the first commander to shout, but I can't be sure. "After them!" I yelled. We surged forward, screaming like diving hawks to run the Philistines down. David stood, grasping the bloody head by its hair and watching our soldiers bound by. I ran beside Jonathan, but we stopped at the corpse.

Jonathan looked at David. "That was a miracle. Yahweh is surely with you."

David dropped his eyes. "Yahweh is with all of us, my lord. He only chose to use me this day."

My company was pursuing routed men, and I wouldn't be needed to direct a shield wall that day. Zelig could lead them for this work. I decided to walk with Jonathan and David back to King Saul's tent. Abner met us to escort the young hero himself. David still carried the grisly head when he approached the tent, and this time both flaps were thrown open for him to enter erect.

The king sat upon the same elevated seat. He seemed puzzled as he stared at David. "Whose son are you, young man?"

"I am the son of your servant, Jesse of Bethlehem," answered David.

Saul sat back. "Ah yes. Jesse." He looked more closely at the youth in front of him. "I didn't recognize you now that you have the golden down of a duckling on your cheeks. You play the harp, don't you?"

CHAPTER SIXTEEN

...Jonathan became one in spirit with David, and he loved him as himself.

1 Samuel 18:1b NIV

I N THE MONTHS THAT FOLLOWED David's victory over Goliath, General Abner added another brigade of spearmen to the army, and I became its commander, leading my old company and nine more—a thousand men altogether.

Zelig grumbled when I once again made him my second in command. "Commander, you would take me away from my best service to Yahweh. I kill his enemies with my own hands. I don't send messenger boys to do it."

"So, Zelig," I replied, "will you command the crocodiles, then?"

He bristled and slammed his spear's butt into the sand. "Do you try to rid yourself of me so easily? Yair can have those spearmen. Let him lead and show them his gold armband. You'll need me more than ever now. I'll stay with you, Commander, if only to keep you from blundering through another battle."

I turned away to hide my smile from the grim old warrior. Neither of us would acknowledge our bond, not even to each other. "Very well." I sniffed. "We'll run all of them this afternoon."

My new status was announced at the next banquet. Soldiers and officers congratulated me, and I sat nearer the head of the table. Michal, however, seemed only polite when she took my hand. I squeezed hers a trifle while trying to hold her eye.

She looked aside and said, "Congratulations, Commander Beral. I am sure you deserve your promotion and will serve the king even better than before."

"Thank you, my princess. I will try."

Michal acted distracted throughout the meal, never resting her gaze on me, only flicking her eyes away without smiling.

King Saul had brought David into the feast, not as a harpist anymore, but as an honored guest. He sat near the king and next to Jonathan, with whom he appeared to be in deep conversation all evening. I noticed with a start that the youth wore one of Jonathan's own robes.

A month later, the king made David the commander of a hundred. I supposed he deserved it, although I didn't approve. The boy had no fighting experience except for his remarkable feat in slaying the Philistine giant, so it astonished me when David turned out to be an able commander. His men cheered him each morning when he arrived. The other officers in his brigade praised him too. They said his men could outrun even the crocodile company.

Perhaps they could, for David chose to arm his company lightly, with bucklers, bows, and light javelins instead of the heavy gear required for line spearmen. They never practiced the shield wall. Instead, he led them as skirmishers. He took them on short raids into Ammonite country, always coming back with plunder and weapons. Abner sent him westward on scouting patrols against the Philistines to prevent more surprise invasions, and David wore Jonathan's sword.

His successes started to gall me. The young man seemed to do nothing wrong. He stayed deferential to me when our paths crossed, yet I sensed something important slipping away. I couldn't say what or how badly until one fall afternoon when I allowed the brigade to finish training early because I wanted to hunt feral goats in the surrounding hillsides.

I went to Jonathan's quarters, hoping he would hunt with me as he usually did, but he wasn't at the palace. Simcha, his house attendant, greeted me. He thought his master had gone up onto a hillside overlooking the town "as he often does lately." I thought it puzzling that Jonathan would be routinely walking the hills without mentioning it to me.

I asked for his bow and quiver in case I came across him in time for a hunt. Then, with two bows over my shoulder, I set out for the path that snaked up the hill the servant indicated. I knew the route well. Jonathan and I used to sit on large boulders near the crest of this hill to talk. We had shared secrets there since our youth. I smiled a little, thinking he'd probably climbed there to be alone with his ponderings. *"And now here comes Beral, looking to shoot goats."* He would laugh, though, and we would climb over the rocks, competing for the first shot as boys again.

At the bottom of the hill, I craned my head back and shaded my eyes but didn't see him perched on any of the usual boulders. I shook my head and started the ascent. He would be at the other site we favored, at some distance over the peak. The day was beautiful without the heat of summer or the damp chill of winter. Dry grass whispered as it bent to the breeze. I took in deep breaths and enjoyed the light exercise. When I crested the hill, it surprised me to see a small cluster of people seated far below me, where I had expected only Jonathan. They sat in a rough circle with one person in the center. I counted ten people, two of them females covered modestly with robes and headscarves. One man stood and leaned on a staff.

The standing man saw me approaching and raised a hand in greeting. I realized he was Herzi, Jonathan's shield bearer. Others glanced at me and turned their attention back to the center speaker. My jaw tightened. I could see it was David.

Jonathan stood when I neared the group. "Beral, come join us. I should have thought to ask you sooner. Here, sit next to me." He eyed the second bow I carried but said nothing about it.

I sat on the rock beside him. Directly across the circle from me sat Michal with one of her maidservants beside her. She acknowledged my arrival with a nod. She had a sparkle in her eyes, but it wasn't for me. Her gaze returned to David.

The young company commander sat holding one of his harps and smiled, I think with genuine pleasure, at seeing me. "Commander Beral, I'm pleased you came. We are writing psalms to Yahweh," he said and strummed a chord. "Perhaps you would help?"

"I am only a soldier. I'll listen," I answered.

I sat quietly, although my face must have been flaming red, finally realizing that Michal had made another choice. I glanced sideways at Jonathan. His face was flushed as well. Looking around the circle, I saw many of the company commanders in Jonathan's brigade blushing uneasily and not meeting my stare. The only person there not aware of my desire for Michal appeared to be David, the very one now making her eyes glisten. She had forgotten my presence entirely, her knees folded to one side and holding a hand to her breast as she listened to the harpist sing. He let his voice wrap around all of us there on the hillside, and I fought the spell it cast. The harp sounded as if the breeze itself moved the strings. I hated the beauty of that moment.

"Give thanks to the Lord, for He is good, His love endures forever.

Who can proclaim the mighty acts of the Lord or fully declare His praise?"

David stopped and stilled the strings with his hand. "I've come this far with the psalm, and yet I can't find the right words to follow here." He stroked the strings again. "My princess, have you a suggestion?"

Michal clasped her hands and squeezed her eyes shut. "I think... I think... '*Blessed are they who serve their king, who constantly do what he directs...*'" She opened her eyes to look at David hopefully.

He idly struck a chord and looked at the sky. "Blessed are they... Something like that would work. Let me try it." The chord sounded again, and he sang.

"Blessed are they who maintain justice, who constantly do what is right."

He set the harp down on his knee. "Yes, that will be the next line." He smiled and nodded. "Blessed are they who maintain justice. That works very well."

I thought Michal would wet the rock she sat upon, her pleasure was so plain. After that, I watched as David took suggestions from anyone and acted as though each one were a gem before he then changed it around to his liking.

I forced myself to stay with them for another hour until everybody seemed satisfied with the progress of the damned psalm. Bitterly, I watched Michal mouthing the words as David sang them. When we finally stood to go, Jonathan laid a hand on my arm. He touched the extra bow over my shoulder. "Beral, if you still want to hunt—"

"No, my prince, it's getting too late in the day. I'll take your bow back." I quickly strode away from him and the group.

Michal's attendant shot me a look of sympathy as I hurried past. My eyes watered, for I knew Michal wasn't the only one who loved David this afternoon. The shepherd boy's psalms had snared Jonathan as well.

At the bottom of the hill, I quickened my steps to return Jonathan's bow and be away from his quarters before he returned. Afterward, I headed to my boarding room. My face must have mirrored the stone heart I carried inside me because, as I walked the narrow streets, people stepped aside without a greeting. I rounded the last corner, and there sat Zelig on the steps of the building where I lodged. He wore a household tunic and held a bulging wineskin and a cup.

"Good afternoon, Commander," he said.

"Zelig, what are you doing here?" Zelig never came to where I lived. I feared something was wrong.

"Nothing, Commander. I thought you might enjoy sharing this skin with me. It's very good wine and strong. It will make your face shine." Zelig reached out for my hand, and I reflexively pulled him to his feet.

I shook my head. "Thank you, but no, Zelig. I'm not in the mood for it today. Perhaps another time." I gestured as though I would go up the steps, but he made no move to step aside.

He nodded. "I know you're not, Commander, but I think maybe today we should drink this and talk a little." His voice rumbled as he laid a hand on my shoulder. "Please, Beral, walk with me for a little time." It was a gentle request, unlike anything the old soldier had ever done before.

He held his palm out to one side, and I reluctantly walked in the direction he indicated. Townspeople had avoided me earlier, but now they actually shrank away from us, a grim pair of King Saul's elite officers. Of course, Zelig always intimidated them.

We walked without speaking until we left the town's confines. The sun barely sat above the western hills, and we cast a long shadow when we finally reached a jumble of large boulders.

"We can sit here if it pleases you, Commander," Zelig said.

I grunted and sat down.

He slowly lowered himself onto another stone near me. "I'm getting old for a warrior," he said. "I should go to Abner and get a softer position." He uncorked the wineskin and poured a cupful. "Maybe I could count jars of olive oil in an army storehouse. No wait, I don't count very well. Have to do something else."

He offered me the cup. I took it but didn't drink. I looked at him as he watched night birds crossing the evening sky.

"What do you want, Zelig?" I asked.

He turned toward me and wagged his chin at my bow, still slung across my back. "How was the hunt?"

I took a sip. "I think you know already."

He sighed heavily. "Yes, I believe you didn't have a good afternoon." He looked over the top of the town at the hill I had climbed earlier. "They have been going up there every day for about two weeks now. You've been too busy to notice, but you had to see it eventually."

"So then, does everyone know that her nipples get hard when she looks at David? I must seem quite the fool to them."

He shrugged and shifted his feet. "There are a few who think so, I'm sure, Commander. There are always a few. And those few would relish your loss. You *do* have enemies at the king's court, you know." His eyes darted to me then away. "But the army supports you. As to the king's younger daughter..." He exhaled. "People know, but they side with you. The king's daughter is not popular with everyone, even though David is."

"David!" I groaned and clenched my fists. "I wish he had never come here."

Zelig reached for the cup, took it, and drained the remains before he spoke. "Oh, I wouldn't put all the blame on young David, Commander. Most people think he doesn't even notice her feelings for him. He only wants to sing psalms to Yahweh." He refilled the cup and handed it back to me.

"*Most* people! So this is all common knowledge to everyone— everyone but me!" I ran my fingers through my hair. "So how do you know of all this, Zelig?"

He chuckled without mirth. "There are not many secrets in the army and even fewer in the king's household. I hear things. I see things."

"But you didn't say anything to me?"

"Remember, Commander, I am not to trifle in your affairs, and so I didn't," he said.

"Until tonight."

"That's right, Commander. Until tonight."

I should have realized it would happen. All of Israel loved David, and the women of Israel especially adored him. When he returned as the young hero who slew Goliath, they danced and sang before him and King Saul in each village we passed through. The younger women showed their calves and knees when they twirled.

"Saul has slain his thousands, and David his tens of thousands."

That had annoyed me even then, for I myself had stood beside Saul when he'd fought and killed more than his share of enemy soldiers. No man ever matched him for valor, yet idle village chatter would make their king second to a boy. I remembered the looks Saul shot at David when the women started their singing. He hadn't liked it either.

Zelig and I stayed there at the rocks that night until a quarter moon rose. The wineskin emptied between us while over and over I absorbed the realization that Michal's affections had gone to another man, her fancy flitting away from me like a bird hopping from branch to branch. By the time we staggered back into Gibeah, the loss of the king's daughter didn't bother my heart so much. The true hurt was that Jonathan had known all along.

CHAPTER SEVENTEEN

And from that time on Saul kept a close eye on David.

1 Samuel 18:9 NIV

THE EVIL SPIRIT THAT TORTURED Saul returned, and once again, David played a harp in the king's chambers. Saul's blighted mood was evident to all his officers, for he no longer opened his banquet hall to us for feasts. Others worried about the king's temperament, but I only felt glad not to be attending alongside Michal and David.

One winter morning when I arrived at the training grounds to lead the brigade in a run, the men were buzzing with rumors. Something had happened in the king's quarters during the night, something involving David. No one knew exactly what had happened, only that Saul's household was still in turmoil. At the noontime meal, I went to the palace to see Ben-Ami. I found him sitting in his room, eating bread and fish, which he invited me to share with him.

"I suppose you also want to know about last night like all the others?" he said cheerily. "I have never been so well loved by visitors as I have been today." He wiped his mouth and pushed a platter toward me. "Here. Try this fish. The cooks brush it with olive oil before it's broiled. Very good." I sat down beside him and tried a bite. I could see the palace staff ate well.

"You've teased it out of me, old friend," I said while I chewed. "What did happen? I heard that the king went mad."

Ben-Ami wagged his head side to side as he poured each of us a cup of wine. "No, no. That's not quite true. You see, Beral, *that's* how wild tales get spread—tales that are far afield from what actually happens." He got up and looked out the doorway then returned and sat down again. "In truth, I wasn't in Saul's quarters when it happened, but Moshe was posted there. He's a good man and reliable."

"I heard Saul had a spear?" I prompted.

He chuckled. "Oh, yes. He was playing with a javelin like I've seen him do many times, batting it back and forth between his hands while he sat back. He had one of those foul headaches again. I've seen him that way too many times lately. The pain seems unbearable for him." He shook his head in a gesture of sympathy.

"What happened?" I asked.

Ben-Ami pushed the platter away and leaned back. "I can tell you what happened, but I can't tell you *why* it happened," he said. "Moshe tells me it was so fast that, at first, he couldn't believe what he had seen. He said Saul seemed to be recovering from his fight with the night demon. David's music usually works miracles for him. But then the king begins to rock back and forth. He starts speaking in another voice and another tongue. Moshe thinks he was prophesying to Yahweh, but who knows for sure? David stops playing, and the attendants just look at Saul." Ben-Ami stopped his narrative and stared at the far wall as if puzzled.

"And so what happened?"

He came back with a start. "Oh... That's when Saul snatches up the javelin he's been bouncing between his knees and throws it at David," he said. "Mind you, he's only this far from the boy"—he indicated the length of his room—"but David twists away"—Ben-Ami stood and pantomimed a violent jerk to the side—"and the point doesn't even snick him. The javelin sticks in the wall paneling while everyone just stands there. Moshe said David's mouth opened wide then snapped shut like a whore's tent flaps." He chuckled and retook his seat. "But then the king roars out some unspeakable sound and jumps for the javelin. He pulls it out and throws it again, but David ducks away again and runs out the door. The king just stands still, staring after him and heaving like a bellows."

I sat hushed and still, hardly able to believe the king's bodyguard, but I knew the story had to be true. "And then what?"

"Well, that's the oddest part of all," he answered. "King Saul sits back down on his bed. 'I believe I will sleep now,' he says. He lay back, and within a few moments, he's sleeping like a tired laborer." He wiped his hand over his face. "Moshe called for me, of course, and I left another man there to stand watch with him and the servants for the rest of the night, but the king never moved again. This morning, he was up and rested like nothing had ever happened. I'm not sure he even remembers it."

"What about David?"

Ben-Ami hitched one shoulder up in dismissal. "He's all right. I heard he was back with his company this morning, training as usual. I imagine he'll be a little wary from now on if he's called upon to play for the king."

I stayed silent for a moment, unsure how to ask the next question, but Ben-Ami asked it for me. "You want to know the same thing everyone else has asked me. Do I think the king is mad?" he said. He exhaled loudly. "No, I don't. This spirit or demon that comes upon him in the darkness has to be dealt with, yet I don't want to believe our king is insane. Saul is a strong man. He can overcome it by his will if Yahweh agrees." He reached for his helmet, signaling that our lunch was ending.

I got to my feet. "Thanks for the fish. It was very good."

"Think nothing of it, Beral." He lowered his voice conspiratorially as he strapped on his sword. "I'll tell you one other thing, though. Saul may or may not be insane, but David had still better watch himself. That young man is very popular, and the king has reason to be suspicious of him. If the spirit returns, I think he will try again."

But King Saul showed his displeasure with David in an odd way. Within a week of the incident with the spear, David was promoted to a brigade commander, equal in rank to me. Whatever pity I had felt toward him for suffering the king's disfavor evaporated at that news. I sat glumly when the announcement was made. That night, although the banquet hall opened to us again, I had no taste for the food.

Soon, however, I think I saw Saul's real intent. David's brigade was sent away repeatedly on difficult and dangerous campaigns while the rest of the army sat idling at Gibeah. He went deeper and deeper into Philistine and Ammonite territory. I believed he would surely be killed or at least eventually suffer a disgraceful defeat, but instead, the green commander succeeded in everything he tried.

Zelig and I stood along the roadway one afternoon when David and his men returned from one of the Philistine raids. Captured oxen pulled carts laden with grain and pillaged goods while a mob of dispirited captives walked behind. There appeared to be no Israelite casualties. People cheered throughout the city. Even my men joined in the choruses of praise for David.

He smiled brightly at me and raised a fist to his chest as he led his brigade past. "Greetings, Commander Beral," he shouted. "Yahweh has blessed us again." He still carried Jonathan's sword.

I raised my hand in return but said nothing. "What do you think, Zelig?" I said out of the corner of my mouth.

The old soldier moved his gaze up and down along the column of plunder. "I will be careful about my thoughts, Commander. It's evident that Yahweh does indeed favor that man."

"Yes," I said. "It seems so." I was becoming resigned to that fact.

Saul could not ignore that all the people of Israel and the men of the army loved David. In return for David's service, he offered Merab to him in marriage. My hopes flickered up for an instant when I heard that news but were dashed when David declined the proposal. Yet he did it so gracefully that the king could not take offense. The palace gossips went wild with the news, repeating his words over and over: "Who am I, and what is my family or my father's clan in Israel, that I should become the king's son-in-law?"

So Merab was finally given to Adriel of Mehoiah instead. A wealthy man from a distant village, he didn't know much of her temperament. Now Michal could be betrothed.

I had been, of course, the last one to be aware that Michal loved David—except for her father. It surely must have pleased the king when he finally did hear about his younger daughter's yearning. Nathon, still the king's armor bearer, was the little mouse who told me that Katriel had carried soft words to David—words that the king wanted planted in David's ear to further bind his loyalty.

Nathon heard Saul tell his aide, "Speak to David. Tell him, 'Look, the king is pleased with you, and I, Katriel, also like you. After all, I first recommended you to the king, didn't I? Now, why not become his son-in-law and please us all?'"

I groaned with the injustice of it. If only Saul would make that offer to me! "And what did David say to that?" I asked.

Nathon shook his head in wide-eyed bewilderment, not realizing how much his words caused me to grind my teeth. "The fool said no *again*!" He tapped at his forehead with his fingertips. "But the king knew how to deal with that this time. He said to Katriel, 'David is a stubborn man who feels he should not marry my daughter without a suitable dowry. Say to him that I want no other price for Michal than a hundred Philistine foreskins.'" Nathon smiled, pleased with the novel idea.

"David agreed?" I asked incredulously.

"Oh, yes! He marches out tomorrow with his brigade. He will probably raid westward through the sea people's towns until he collects his hundred tips." Nathon stopped and looked about, perhaps unwilling to be overheard. "Unless he's killed first."

I hoped fervently for that.

But David returned unharmed in ten days. I watched his men lope through Gibeah's streets, lean as hungry dogs, their eyes shifting side to side like scavengers' and still moving lightly after days in the field. Two men carried cloth sacks slung on a pole between them. The odor coming from the sacks caused townsmen to step back. David led the grinning bearers straight to Saul's palace while I followed at a fast walk. Ben-Ami waved them inside.

I took a place in the midst of court attendants standing at the rear of the large banquet hall. We watched as David approached the king's elevated chair. Saul shifted in his seat.

"Welcome back, David. Your mission was successful?"

"My king, I have done as you asked and more," David replied. He waved the team with the sacks forward.

They solemnly walked to the front and set their burdens down. David pointed to one, and a man upended that sack's contents. A collective gasp filled the room when a mass of sodden, stinking little lumps of flesh spilled onto the stone floor. Saul shrank back, but Jonathan, standing next to the throne, stepped forward to see. People held their noses.

"There are a hundred Philistine foreskins in this bag and the same number in the second bag," said David. "My king, would you like to count them?"

A babble of voices rose from all those who had crowded in to see. I stared in silence.

"No, Commander, your oath is enough." Saul looked vexed, though, as he stood. He glanced about until his gaze settled on Katriel. "See that this floor is cleaned."

"Yes, my king." The aide smiled weakly.

That was the only satisfaction I had that day, watching Katriel almost swoon at the thought of directing that odorous task.

Saul turned back to David. "It seems, then, that you have fulfilled my dowry request. Very well done, David." He held his arms out to address the room. "Bear witness to my words, all of you. Today, David has earned the right to become my son-in-law. He shall marry my daughter, Michal."

A delighted squeal sounded from the front, where Michal bounced up and down and clasped her hands together at her throat. The maidens around her chattered like birds in a fig tree while the crowd laughed and cheered. Jonathan came alongside David, and they embraced. Cries of "David, David" filled the room. David turned around to them, smiling and waving. I caught his eye, and his smile faltered at my grim face as he perhaps understood everything for the first time. I nodded to him.

Saul's expression also clouded when the palace rang with shouts for David. It must have troubled the king that Yahweh, the celebrating crowd, and even his own family loved the harpist so much. He couldn't even pretend to be pleased.

I hurried away from the king's hall, down the outside steps and past the spot where I'd once thought Michal had pledged herself to me on a winter night not so long before.

CHAPTER EIGHTEEN

All the days of Saul there was bitter war with the Philistines...

1 Samuel 14:52a NIV

T HE PHILISTINES, NO DOUBT PROVOKED by David's dowry
collection, carried out heavy raids across the border all summer.
Our entire army campaigned against them, each thousand-man
brigade operating separately along Israel's boundaries. We patrolled
for weeks, looking for enemy troops but rarely finding them. The only
heathens my men killed were those too drunk on looted wine to escape
when we approached. None of the other brigades had any better luck
except one—David's.

Once, as we returned to Gibeah, empty handed again, I saw David's
brigade just ahead of us carrying weapons and armor taken from dead
Philistines. "Damn him!"

"Be careful, Commander. Every bird that flies by has eyes and ears,"
Zelig said. "We don't know which bird has a tongue to talk about what
he sees." He rolled his own eyes at the townspeople gathering alongside
to measure our success.

Soon cries of "David!" filled the streets in front of us. I seethed quietly.

I grudgingly had to respect David's tactics. The light equipment his
men carried allowed them to pursue and catch Philistine units before
they escaped to their own lands. Truly, even my old crocodiles couldn't
match the pace of any of his companies. David never stood and fought
in a shield wall against the Philistines, but he harassed them and picked
at their flanks until the raiders broke and ran. Then he slaughtered

them. His brigade killed more of the enemy than all the rest of the army together.

Once afield, I kept the brigade moving, constantly searching for any incursion into Israel. Finally, a report came of raiders to the north, and we hurried in that direction. After a long forced march, I was met at Taanach by a village elder shaking his head at me.

"Where were you yesterday?" he demanded. "The Philistines came then, and we had to hide in the hills. Look what they have done here. Look!" He waved his arm around as if I hadn't already noticed the smoldering rubble that had been his town and the surrounding fields empty of livestock. We had pushed toward the column of smoke all morning. I eased my shield off and stood in shamed silence with sweat dripping off my nose. Once again, we were too late.

Standing there amid those ruins that day, I decided on a new approach, one similar to David's. The next morning, I took a hundred men—my old crocodile company that had been given to Yair—and ranged out in front of the rest of the brigade led by Zelig. We piled all our gear into carts except shields and weapons. Without baggage, greaves, and extra armor, we could run ahead farther and faster. If Yahweh favored us, we would overtake some Philistines, and since all their raiding bands outnumbered a single company, they would probably turn to fight us. I intended to use my beloved crocs as bait, toothed bait able to bite and hold until Zelig arrived.

We strode out at dawn while the brigade still loaded gear into oxcarts, and by noon, we were at least an hour ahead of the main body. A youth accompanied us on a mule to be a messenger back to Zelig if needed. Following a multitude of tracks in the dust of the highway, we traveled at a quick walk. As we moved through low, rocky hills, Yair suddenly stopped.

"Halt!" he ordered, his hand up. He put a finger to his lips. We stood in the roadway, breathing heavily. Just ahead of us, through a deep gorge and around a bend in the road, lay Megiddo, a village untouched by marauders so far.

"What is it, Yair?" I asked softly. I stepped up beside him but heard nothing.

"I thought there were voices, Commander," he replied.

Every man stood stock still, straining to listen.

"Perhaps it was nothing," he added.

Then we all heard it. A faraway scream pierced the still air before us, a sound carrying the agony of a woman in great distress.

"Forward," I called. "Strap your shields." The men slid shields off their backs and onto their arms as we trotted into the shaded gorge. It could have been an ambush had an enemy known we were coming, but instead, the rock walls hid us until we burst into view scarcely an arrow's flight from Megiddo. We could hear panicked shouts in the village from both men and women. I took in the scene quickly. Armored men in feathered helmets ran in and out of homes. They swarmed in the streets and onto rooftops, calling out and looking for plunder and women. I saw a youth thrown from a housetop. No fires burned yet. The raiders must have arrived only minutes before us.

"Yair, form a wall!" I barked.

He bawled orders, and quickly, two ranks of lightly armed spearmen stretched across the road.

"Back them to the shade. Set your flanks on the side walls."

Soon, the company stood at the mouth of the gorge with each end anchored against rock outcroppings. I stayed alone in front and watched the village.

The shouting and turmoil eased while the Philistines turned to confront our threat. Soldiers stopped pillaging to run forward and face us in a battle line on the roadway. They soon outnumbered our company with more still emerging from the village. Better disciplined than the Amalekites, they stood shoulder to shoulder and waited. One man, evidently their leader, climbed the outside stairs of a nearby house. From the rooftop, he stared at our position then looked at me, hands on his hips. Bushy black hair billowed out from under his helmet. His beard frizzled halfway down his chest. He conferred with an aide who had followed him onto the roof then turned to look at me again.

"Commander, shall I send the boy?" Yair shouted behind me.

"Of course you should send him. He should already be on his way," I replied over my shoulder. "Make sure he tells Zelig to hurry." Allowing time for the courier to reach the main body, I calculated that we would have to fight and delay these Philistines until nearly midafternoon.

114

Observing the hordes of enemy soldiers, I realized a flaw in these new tactics of mine. The raider band was much larger than I had expected. At least five hundred spearmen stood between us and Megiddo. I couldn't be sure we would even survive until help arrived. I heard the mule's hoofbeats receding behind us and prayed the boy would find the brigade quickly. The Philistine on the roof waved at me. I walked back to our lines.

"Yair, come with me," I said as I passed through the first rank.

"Yes, Commander. Nissim, take command. Call me if they move." Yair and I walked back along the road. I stopped at the shadowed, narrowest point of the ravine.

"When they come, we will pull back to here," I said.

The young commander studied the position and nodded. "That will be good. We can cover this gap here with forty shields." He craned his head back, looking up at the gorge on each side. "Commander Beral, may I suggest...?"

"Of course, but hurry. We don't have time."

I could hear the Philistines' taunts growing louder. Apparently, we all sported goat genitals. They would attack us very soon.

"Well, if we put a small number of men up there"—he pointed to the tops of the rock walls—"perhaps five men, they could pelt the pagans with stones when they come. I think it would disrupt them."

I looked up with new eyes. I should have seen this myself. The walls of the gorge were steep enough to keep attackers from scrambling around our flanks, but not so sheer that they couldn't be climbed. Yair's idea could help us.

"It's a good plan," I said. "Put five on each side. You know which ones can climb?"

"Of course, Commander, the ones who herded goats."

I laughed. Zelig had certainly called this company "goatherds" many times. Yair and I went back to the line. He talked to the squad leaders, and soon, ten picked men ran to the rear, looking for climbing paths up to the top.

The Philistines edged closer. We would be able to stop and blunt one or two charges, but not many more. Zelig might arrive here in an hour or so to find a hundred slain Israelite spearmen. We needed time. I pushed out from the shield wall and walked forward toward the Philistines, stopping halfway, about forty paces in front of our ranks.

The Philistine taunts rose louder. I understood well enough to know they meant us to die painful and ignoble deaths. Some threatened to come to me and carry out that threat, but their ranks held in place, checked by bull-throated squad leaders and captains. I pretended not to notice them, although I shook inside. Staring at the commander on the roof, I raised my spear high to him and then turned it around to drive the point into the hard ground beside me. I hoped he would interpret the gesture correctly.

He regarded me for a moment before he spoke aside to his aide, shoving the man's shoulder to send him running down the stairs. In a moment, the Philistine aide stepped through their lines. They quieted to a murmur.

He walked forward and stopped ten paces from me, crackling with nervous energy like a brush fire. "What is it you want before you die, Hebrew dog? Unless you are surrendering?" he asked in the language of the sea peoples. His hair shone black, and a youthful beard curled in wisps. He looked much younger than me, and I chanced a guess.

"What is the name of your father, the commander?" I asked in the same tongue, pointing with my chin at the man watching on the rooftop. "I would speak to him."

His eyes widened, and I knew I had guessed correctly. The son collected himself quickly to sneer at me. "My father is Achish, king of Gath and greatest of all battle leaders, and he will not speak to a Hebrew dog until that dog surrenders." He lifted himself, haughty as a young lion, chin raised to see the effect his insults would have. He was no fool, though. I saw his hand tighten on his spear.

I nodded slowly. "Achish. I've heard of your father. I would still speak to him. Tell him I am Beral of the tribe of Benjamin." In truth, I had heard of the king of Gath, but I doubted he would know of me.

The son laughed, a contemptuous snigger. "Prepare to die, Beral the whoreson." He turned to walk away from me.

I spoke to his back, loudly enough for all the Philistine line to hear. "If Achish is afraid, I understand. It is safer for him to send his little boy out to meet me. Yes, let him keep spearmen between himself and a single soldier of Israel."

My command of the sea peoples' language was limited, but the message hit squarely enough. The son spun around toward me again, his jaw working tightly.

I reached over and pulled my spear out of the dirt. "Please tell your father that I would speak to him. I will wait here."

The aide glared at me then turned to look up at his father, who watched with folded arms. I could sense the young man's turmoil. He wanted to kill me but dared not yet. Abruptly, he started back to his lines. Over his shoulder, he snarled, "You will die a slow death for this, Beral the whoreson."

Spearmen parted at his angry wave, and I was left alone between the two forces.

The menace in the Philistine ranks was palpable in the still air. They stared and muttered. Their lines stirred restlessly as we all waited. Amalekites or Moabites would have already attacked me. Beneath the hot sun, sweat ran down from under my helmet. My tunic was soaked at the armpits. I prayed to Yahweh with my eyes open. The aide climbed the stairs and began to talk excitedly to his father. He gestured toward me. I again raised my spear to Achish and shoved its point into the ground. He raised his own spear and started down the stairs.

Several more minutes passed before the Philistine king came out to me. When he finally walked through his battle line, he had on a fine red cloak and had changed his ordinary fighting helmet for one of polished bronze decorated with gold catlike figures. His son and an armor bearer followed closely behind. As Achish approached, he ran his gaze over our shield wall behind me. We faced each other at half the distance his son had chosen. Dark eyes sparked behind layers of black facial hair. His voice surprised me with its softness. He smiled, and perfect white teeth gleamed at me.

"You stand here very boldly, Hebrew dog, for someone with such a pitiful force behind him," he said. "I came to see why such a little dog would dare to request something of me. Speak quickly, Beral the Benjamite. My men are eager to kill you all."

I looked back at the company, poised and ready but few in number.

I turned to Achish. "A pitiful force? I think they will be enough," I said. "But I do have a proposal for you. Why lose so many of your men trying to defeat us? We cannot be beaten on our own land. Yahweh will protect us. You and I should fight instead. If you win, we will surrender to you. But when I prevail against you, your men surrender to us. I will give you time to prepare yourself for death, and then we will meet here again." I wasn't certain that the Philistine king even understood my halting speech.

He looked at me without expression for a long moment before his beard split in a grin. "So, Beral the Benjamite, you know this is your best chance to win here. You hope for a personal duel with me? Tell me, little dog, do you also have a young shepherd boy with a sling waiting? Do you think I am like that lumbering fool, Goliath?" His eyes slit with cunning. "No, little dog. You and I won't duel. I could kill you too easily, but I want my troops to have their way. And I want to give you to my son later. You've made him very angry today." The red cloak swirled as he spun around to leave.

"You are afraid to fight me, then?" I asked.

He stopped and shook his head, turning back to face me. "I am afraid of nothing, Hebrew, and I don't think you are either. Not yet. But now we are going to attack and kill everyone except you. *Then* you will fear. Now go and tell your men to pray to that god of yours that they can't see. You should pray most of all." He stalked back to the Philistine lines, followed by his son and armor bearer.

I stayed out in the roadway for a few moments more, not wanting to appear frightened. Enemy soldiers threw their taunts at me, but I ignored them again. Achish would allow me to get into my lines before he attacked. *Should I instruct Yair to kill me if I am about to be taken? No, it would demoralize the company. Better to fall on my own sword if that's needed.* I squinted up at the sun. The boy on the mule might have reached Zelig by now. I prayed the brigade was already hurrying to us as I walked back to the shield wall.

CHAPTER NINETEEN

The Philistine commanders continued to go out to battle...

1 Samuel 18:30a NIV

KING ACHISH CHOSE TO LEAD the attack himself. His soldiers chanted to their pagan gods and stomped their feet in unison. The sounds beat against us like ocean waves. At a signal I didn't see, they started forward in a controlled walk. Yair looked at me. I nodded and jerked a thumb to the rear. We had to fall back before the Philistines made contact. Men's stomachs turn to jelly at such moments, but my old crocs didn't show it. Yair moved them back in good order to the spot I had picked. Two ranks of forty with a ten-man reserve stood ready when the enemy appeared at the mouth of the gorge.

I hoped the narrow passage would throw them into confusion as they tried to squeeze in, but Achish halted them before they entered the smaller confines. The wide ranks re-formed into a large column, and they entered the narrow canyon at a run, charging us with a roar.

"Lock shields! Spears out!" yelled Yair.

Men braced themselves and leaned into their shields. When the enemy struck, their battering ram of infantry broke against our wall. Shields clacked together, and once more, our men stabbed to the side. The sounds of struggling men bounced back and forth between the rock walls. We threw them back, and they left dead and wounded in front of us. But that ram had hundreds of bodies pushing behind it. The tip pressed forward again. I positioned myself with the reserve as Yair directed the fighting men, *his* men. Nissim called a man forward to replace a downed one. If this became a battle of attrition, I would be up in the line soon.

Suddenly a loud *thunk* sounded in the Philistine mass, followed by another, then another. Stones the size of a man's head started falling on the heathens. The goatherds. They dropped rocks well away from us, but the barrage worked. Enemy soldiers fell with crushed skulls and broken shoulders. I saw one man's shield torn away, his shattered arm limp as he screamed.

The pagans looked up and shouted, "Back! Back!"

Stones chased them as they retreated from us to the gorge entrance. They backed away in good order. We had beaten them so far, but they weren't broken.

Yair sent two men forward to deal deathblows to enemy wounded, a practice I never liked yet a necessary one. An injured man could still crawl forward to thrust at your legs. A stunned man could revive. The Philistines clustering at the mouth howled in protest.

Achish kept his men in the gorge only close enough to watch us. I saw him in their lines, wearing his battle gear again. This time I waved at him. After the rock barrage, I felt that we could hold there long enough for Zelig to come. If only he would arrive soon...

"Putting men up at the top made the difference, Yair. It was a good plan," I said. "I will tell General Abner about it."

"Thank you, Commander Beral." He beamed, soaring at having successfully led the company in his first pitched fight as its commander.

I expected Achish to try again, but all his troops' rushes were feints. Their front ranks ran forward shouting, only to withdraw each time when the first rocks fell among them. They never reached our wall. I wondered that the barrage could have cowed them that much. Yair gave the command to rest, and the men relaxed where they stood, still wearing their shields.

The Philistines made yet another halfhearted effort toward us, this time slowing even before the first rock came. I puzzled at their behavior. They fell back, laughing and jeering as if they had just won a victory. Achish stood to one side, watching and not at all displeased with their efforts. His eyes scanned the tops of the tall rock walls above us on each side. A chill came over me.

I whirled to Yair. "Did the men up on top carry their weapons? Could they climb with them?"

He looked at me, puzzled. "I'm not sure, Commander. Probably not. It's a hard climb, even for goatherds. Why? Is it necessary?"

"Yes," I said. "We need to—"

A loud wail interrupted me. Every head jerked up to see an Israelite soldier flailing down from the cliff top, his scream cut short when he bounced on the hard ground before us. We stared in shocked silence at the body, and at that moment, the Philistines attacked in earnest. They poured into the gorge, howling and brandishing their weapons. Just before they struck us, another one of the rock throwers crashed down directly onto two of our men in the second rank. He never screamed because he was already dead.

My gut clenched. *I should have seen this.* Achish's sorties had distracted and kept us fixed in place while his scouting parties climbed around behind our soldiers at the top. I looked up to see Philistines. Two of them gripped another lifeless Israelite body by the ankles and wrists. They swung it out and dropped it in our midst. Another spearman in the line collapsed under its impact. Our goatherd climbers were probably all dead now, and more of their bodies would come tumbling down onto us. If we stayed here, stones would soon follow.

The pagans in front pressed us harder, driven by the weight of numbers behind them. We stabbed back, and many fell, but their attacks only retreated enough to be refilled by fresh men. Our position was becoming untenable. My crocodiles still fought well, jabbing and pushing at the Philistines, but some of them fell too. About ten lay dead or wounded. Feathered Philistine helmets teemed wall to wall in the gorge all the way to the mouth. Yair and I were the only reserves left. We should've been withdrawing, but the gorge widened behind us, and not enough crocs remained to lengthen the shield wall. Our choices were grim—retreat and be engulfed at the flanks or stand and be overrun. I wished Zelig were there.

"Commander Beral, the line won't hold!" yelled Yair. His eyes bulged.

"It *must* hold!" I shouted back. A spearman fell backward between us, thrust back by the spear lodged in his torso. Yair stepped up into the gap. He was right, though. Our shield wall had begun to crack.

The front line shuffled a step back involuntarily under the weight of overwhelming numbers. Soon it would buckle completely.

I looked into the Philistine mass and saw Achish shouldering his way to the front, looking for the collapse of our shield wall. In that brief flicker of time, I felt suddenly helpless. My mouth went dry, and if I could have made my legs move, I would have turned and fled, leaving the company to die where it stood. No one ever knew of the fear that clutched me in that moment—the chaos and noise of the fighting covered my weakness. But I myself would remember how I teetered ignobly at the brink of cowardice that day. And bravery didn't drag me back into the fight, only instinct and training. Another man went down, and I took his place in the first rank. The company became only two thin lines.

Immediately, a shield crashed into mine. The Philistine behind it snarled at me. He lost his helmet in the collision, and I made him pay for that by cracking him over the head with my spear shaft, something I had done many times behind Jonathan. The next foe stepped up over that man's crumpled form as I locked my shield with the men on each side. We struggled for footing to hold where we stood. I watched to the side, looking for the chance to jab at the man pounding on Nissim's shield next to me. A spearman in the second rank thrust over my shoulder into the mouth of a brutish soldier wielding an ax. That man gurgled blood and fell away.

Another Israelite body pounded into the roadway behind us from the heights above. A miss. One more direct hit would tear an opening in our line, and everything would be over. I stabbed to the right front into an unprotected armpit. Suddenly, I heard my name over the din of fighting.

"Beral the Benjamite! Look at me!"

I faced toward the man whose shield now fronted mine. Achish grinned back at me. He banged his spear tip against my shield and stepped back. "Well, Hebrew, you wanted a duel? So fight me now," he said. He gestured with his arms, motioning me forward. "Men of Philistia, stop your fighting and back away!" he roared. Commanders beside him repeated the order, and gradually, starting at the center where he and I stood, the clamor died away.

All around us, men on both sides separated, eyeing each other and panting. I stared at Achish in disbelief. "What's the matter, little dog?" he said. "Didn't you offer to fight me alone without some shepherd boy's sling? Can you not speak now, or don't you remember?"

"I remember. That was to be instead of this fighting," I said. "If we two fight, will you honor a promise to let my men go?"

Achish's chest heaved in silent laughter as he shook his head. "Ah, Beral the Benjamite, that is amusing. No, I will not spare them. Your men are already lost. I only want to kill you myself in front of them. Perhaps I can wound you enough to let my youngest son have you."

His son, the aide, stood behind him, glowering at me.

"So will you come out and fight me," Achish continued, "or will one of my soldiers be able to crow and say that *he* slaughtered Commander Beral the Benjamite instead of me? Would you deny me that pleasure?"

I took a deep breath. "You'll not spare my men?"

"I will not."

"Yet I will fight you."

The heathen mob shouted in glee. They quickly kicked bodies out of the way to form a half circle the width of the gorge.

I turned to Yair. "Complete the circle," I said loudly, indicating an arc with my hands. "And stay out of the way." I moved close to him and whispered, "I will take the fight to their side of the ring. When the Philistines are looking away from you and start to cheer, you and the company break and run. Run hard and fast back along the road until you meet Zelig. Tell your squad leaders to be ready."

Yair looked at me and shook his head. "Beral, if we run, they will kill you—"

"Do as I say," I hissed. I turned and walked into the circle.

Achish stood there, his arms folded. He smiled coldly at me.

"It's good that you might plot to save your command, Hebrew dog, but we will catch them if they run. I have plenty of fresh legs behind me."

"Perhaps," I replied. I pointed my spear tip at the armor bearer standing behind him. "Are there rules?"

"None."

"Then have him step back into the circle."

"Certainly. As you wish, Beral the Benjamite."

The Philistine king gestured grandly, and the bearer melted away into the mass of onlooking pagans. We began circling to the right.

Achish and I both carried spears and had short swords at our belts. My circular shield, heavy and solid, was probably better than his, but Philistines made breastplates of metal, while mine consisted of thick leather. He wore greaves on his legs and armored cuffs on his forearms. My extra armor was riding in an oxcart with Zelig's column. Achish dropped his eyes to my legs, and in that wink, I knew what he would do. He swung his spear around hard and low to the ground, meaning for its tip to pass under my shield and slash my shins or perhaps break a bone, but I thrust my own spear tip into the ground just ahead of his stroke. The impact of the two shafts jarred our grips.

Achish stepped back and looked at me. "You Hebrews are quick little dogs," he grunted.

In reply, I crouched behind my shield and charged into him. We clashed hard enough to drive him back a step. Before he recovered, I rammed him again, this time swinging the spear like a club at his head. He retreated with shield up, and we went around in a tight circle. The yelling that swelled around us from the heathen ranks was only noise to me, for Achish became my only focus. I stayed on the attack but couldn't harm him. He fought better than I had hoped. We maneuvered over to the Philistine side of our makeshift arena, and I stole a glance at Yair. He and the company hadn't moved. They watched and cheered me instead of running. I glared at Yair. *Run now!* Achish used that instant to repay me. He rammed shield and head into my body. I reeled backward into the Philistine ranks, dropping my spear. Instantly, arms and hands grasped me and held me spread out and helpless before my opponent.

"Here! Spear him, King Achish! Spear him!" The mob growled in delight as they waited for their king to deliver my death stroke. Achish only stood quietly. He locked eyes with me then turned around and walked to the center of our fighting circle.

"Let him go," he said. "I need no help with this Hebrew."

The disappointed soldiers released me and shoved me back into the circle without a spear. I drew my sword, the one taken from the Philistine captain at Micmash.

Achish's eyes narrowed as he looked at it in my hand. "I knew Anak, the owner of that sword," he said. "Did you take it from him yourself?"

"I did. I and my prince."

His head tilted to one side. "You were the one with Saul's son that day?"

"I was."

"Well... I might have misjudged you, Beral the Benjamite, but no matter. Expect no more mercy from me. I will kill you now and give that sword back to Anak's sons." He smiled grimly and started forward, drawing his own sword.

I have never fought anyone else as strong with a blade. His strokes hammered down on my shield, denting it and hacking chunks away each time. My parries barely deflected the attacks. I stumbled away from the onslaught. Unless he tired soon, I would lose this duel and die.

The Philistines' noise became deafening. I believed it would be the last sound I heard at my death. Then, abruptly, their shouting ceased, and a wail began. Achish heard the change and stopped. He moved away from me and looked about.

"What's happening?" he bellowed.

I stood mutely, too close to my own death to wonder at anything. Screams started in the pagan ranks, and I realized I was hearing the whistle of arrows. When I looked up, Israelite archers stood on the cliffs above us, shooting into the enemy mass. Shouts and the sounds of fighting echoed from the mouth of the gorge.

Zelig? How could he have arrived so swiftly, I wondered, and at the wrong end of the gorge?

Achish had no more time for me. He moved quickly into his army's middle, and I could hear him shouting orders as he worked his way through. "Form ranks! Push them back!" Suddenly he halted and turned back to me.

I hadn't moved.

He pointed his sword at me. "We'll finish this one day, Beral the Benjamite. Your god has saved you today," he yelled. Before long, he disappeared among the Philistines surging away from us with shields held overhead.

I didn't know it yet, but it was David, of course, who had come to our relief.

CHAPTER TWENTY

...David met with more success than the rest of Saul's officers, and his name became well known.

1 Samuel 18:30b

A FTER THE RAIDERS ABANDONED US, we stood in an eerie stillness for a minute, listening to the sounds of battle receding beyond the gorge entrance. "Yair, re-form the shield wall," I said. The company lined up and cautiously moved forward until we looked out in amazement toward Megiddo. The Philistines were leaving. I could see their backs beyond the village as they quickly marched away. Israelite archers jogged behind them and on their flanks like dogs harassing a retreating bear.

"Beral! I praise God you are alive! Are you wounded?" David ran to me in the roadway littered with enemy bodies. He grasped my forearms. "That was a brave stand your men took, but where is the rest of your brigade?"

I gaped at him. "What are you doing here?"

He released me to point at the low hills around us. "We have followed the Philistines since dawn this morning, trying not to be seen. I watched them enter Megiddo from that knoll there, and just as we were about to attack, you arrived and battled them instead." He shook his head in admiration, a gesture that surprised me. "I could not believe your bravery, fighting five times your number..."

"Zelig is coming behind me with the rest," I said. "We only meant to hold them until he arrived, but we were too far ahead." Now I shook my head. "Had you not come when you did... The company owes you their lives."

David's smile broadened to an oxbow. "Nonsense, Beral. You held. My companies can't hold a shield wall. That's why the Philistines broke through and escaped." He paused to gaze at the last faraway group of raiders disappearing into the hills. "We'll follow them and worry them all the way back, though."

"Your words are kind, David, but we were dead men back there before you came."

He nodded absently then turned back to me. "My archer scouts told me that you were fighting with Achish himself." He looked down. "I regret that they couldn't climb fast enough to save your men who were already up there."

"If your men watched, then they saw that Achish was about to kill me before they intervened."

"That doesn't matter. I know you were trying to save your company with that duel. They should have bolted when you gave them the chance, but they wouldn't leave you."

I answered with a lopsided grin. "Yes, and I am going to have words with Yair about his inability to follow my orders."

David laughed softly and took my forearms again. "Do as you see fit, Beral, but I would not be too harsh with your company commander. The men you lead are very loyal to you. You are a good man, Commander Beral, and I would like to be your friend."

"Of course," I replied without thinking. I believed David truly meant his words, but I couldn't be sure that I did.

David, however, seemed satisfied. He clapped me on the shoulder. "Come. Let's go into the village. We have to see what we can do for these people."

We walked along in silence for a moment before David cleared his throat. He looked down at the road as he spoke. "Beral, I should clear up an issue that pains me. I heard of your feelings for Michal only after she and I became betrothed. I promise you that I did not know before then. I hope your sentiments for her won't affect this friendship." He stopped abruptly and faced me. "Do you love her?"

I swallowed before I answered. Standing there looking into a face that showed no guile, I finally saw a truth I had not wanted to see. "I once thought so, but clearly she loves you now." I grunted. "I have no claim on her. I never did."

David stared into my eyes and nodded slowly. "Very well, Beral." Then he looked away at the village, rubbing his chin. "But are you sure? I can find a means to avoid this wedding—"

"No," I interjected. "Don't do that. I have seen the king throw a spear. He doesn't always miss."

He threw his head back and laughed. "Well said. Yes, thank you, Beral. Maybe, by that, you just saved my life today as well."

I held my palms out. "Just beware. You know she can be fickle. I can't save you from that."

We fastened our shields on our backs and went into Megiddo together. I found it hard not to like David, but he would always be a painful reminder to me of the fool I had been. Michal had wounded my pride more than my heart, yet the scar remained, and it itched.

Zelig arrived while we tended our wounded in the village. We clasped hands when he reached me.

"It looks like you dug a well for yourself almost too deep to climb out of." He cast a knowing eye toward some of David's men in the streets nearby. "Did someone throw you a rope?"

As I described the battle to him, Zelig looked over at David some distance away, overseeing the retrieval of his dead. "That man truly is under the blessing of Yahweh," he said thoughtfully. He turned his gaze on me. "And you were blessed today because of him. The rest of us certainly didn't save you."

David's archers returned the next day, reporting that Achish had taken his raiding party back to Philistine territory. We bundled our wounded onto oxcarts, hoisted the plundered gear, and marched home. Word raced ahead of us like a dust whirlwind along the roadway. When we reached Gibeah, people came out on rooftops and in the streets to cheer.

Once again, the familiar cries began. "David! David!" It was David the people celebrated. Always David.

The story of the fight at Megiddo was told and retold that night at a palace feast in our honor.

David praised me and the crocs. "I wish you all could have seen it," he exclaimed. "Commander Beral and one company—two ranks of spears—once again holding back an army of pagans. It was a miracle from Yahweh."

The listeners shouted their approval. Saul caught my eye and smiled, probably remembering our own desperate stand together at Amalek. Even Michal looked at me with favor. Still, it was David who received the loudest acclaim. His timely arrival, his cunning—he had brought victory out of a certain defeat. We all knew that.

He sat quietly, looking down at the table and flushing a deep red while court attendants praised him. Then my call came. "Beral, Beral!" they shouted. "Tell us the story. Tell how David saved you." I could not refuse. Jonathan looked at me expectantly as I rose to my feet. But David raised his eyes to me with a pleading look, shaking his head side to side. Was it mock humility? Or was David truly not looking for glory? I didn't know, but I told my tale of what happened. It *was* a noble stand, and I described it fully, trying to give glory to Yair and the crocs. Every eye watched as I told of the pursuit to Megiddo and our first stands there in the gorge. Eventually, though, I had to get to the rescue.

"Yair led the company bravely and well," I said. "The shield wall stretched taut as sailcloth but never gave way. And then, just as the sail might have ripped, arrows flew into the Philistine ranks—" The hall erupted in cheers and shouts. Commanders thumped cups on the low tables. Maidens and matrons alike trilled their admiration.

"Saul has killed his thousands! David has killed tens of thousands," the women sang.

I never completed my story of the battle. I finally sat down, only to notice King Saul staring at me thoughtfully. I felt like a wild deer that suddenly raises its head, sensing it's being stalked by a leopard.

Soon after that night, preparations began for the wedding of David and Michal. I had no desire to attend that joyous event, so when the day approached, I released the brigade for a week and went back to my home village of Lo Debar. More than a year had passed since I last visited my parents, and no one would notice my absence in Gibeah except possibly Jonathan. I traveled on a horse, followed by my own shield bearer riding a mule. Mazal, a sturdy lad of about sixteen, came from the tribe of Zebulon. I felt strange to have him dog my heels and watch over me as I had once done for Jonathan. When we arrived in the village, townspeople peered from their doorways. I waved at them, seeing familiar faces everywhere. Children ran ahead of us to my old home.

My father, Ammiel, met me at the doorway and kissed me on both cheeks. "My son, it is so blessed to see you again. I thank Yahweh that he has brought you safely through your service to the king. We have heard of your battles." His eyes gleamed with pride.

My mother stood back until she could contain herself no more. She stepped forward to wrap me in her tight embrace, and I was held again by the arms that had comforted me in childhood.

"Beral, my son," she cried as she rocked me side to side. "Why do you always stay gone so long?" She stepped back to take me by the hand. "Come in. Come in."

I allowed myself to be led inside. The front room of my old home seemed smaller, but the cooking smells brought back pleasant memories. Different rugs covered the walls and floor, and the wooden furniture was new. A room had been added onto one side of the house. An honest man but a shrewd trader, my father always prospered. He traveled for trade and kept large flocks of sheep nearby with the help of servants. My siblings and I had never been hungry under his roof.

"It is by the will of Yahweh," he would say whenever he profited from a transaction. As a boy, I accepted that, but as a man, I believed his eye for commerce contributed too.

Mazal waited outside with our mounts. My father stayed outside too, shooing away a crowd that began to gather.

"Begone, friends," he said. "My son, Beral, will stay with us several days. You can see him later. Today, he belongs to his family." He came inside, shaking his head.

"Father, what are all those people doing here? Has something happened?" I asked. I had recognized most of the faces outside, but none of them had come forward to speak to me. My father looked at me sharply for an instant then laughed, the uproarious laugh that meant he was greatly pleased.

"My son, don't you know? It is you they came to gawk at." He stepped up and grabbed me by the shoulders. "You left our village years ago as a boy, Beral. You left as a servant, a shield bearer to the prince. But now...

now you return as a commander of a thousand men. Your fame spreads across all of Israel. Everyone knows of your battles. Everyone knows how you saved our king at Amalek." He let go to look into my face. "I am proud to have you for my son. You have brought great honor to our family... and to this village."

I sat down, bewildered. Living in Gibeah, I'd never realized how much my deeds must have meant in the town where I had lived as a boy. I pushed hair back out of my face. "I only did what was necessary, Father," I said. "Many others could have done as well."

"Perhaps, son, but they didn't. It was you," my father replied. He patted me on the shoulder.

My mother spoke up. "That's enough of such talk for now. Here. Your brother and sisters want to see you." She beckoned to a side room, and my siblings came out. The two older ones had married and moved away, but a younger brother and two girls still lived there. I was amazed at how much they had changed. My sisters were maidens, not far from womanhood. They regarded me with the same wide-eyed awe the villagers had displayed until I stood and held out my arms.

"What is this? Not a hug for your brother?" I asked.

They smothered me like puppies, breathless with questions, mostly about life in the king's city, his palace, and the battles I had fought. Even there, though, I had a familiar rival for attention. My youngest sister, especially, wanted to hear stories about David and the king's court.

"What does King Saul's home look like?" she asked. "Is David really so ruddy and handsome as they say? I've heard he sings praises like a songbird and is very brave. Has he really killed his tens of thousands?"

I answered brusquely. "All our exploits get exaggerated, Bathsheba, even mine. Perhaps one day, you'll get to see and hear him. You can judge for yourself then."

Later, after an evening meal of lamb and barley, my father showed Mazal where to stable the horse and mule. He left the youth there and returned to the house, looking pleased. "So finally you have a shield bearer yourself. It befits you, my son," he said as he and I reclined at the table. Mother sat close by, hands in her lap. My brother and sisters had gone to their beds on the rooftop.

"Yes, Mazal is new but will be good, I think," I said. "He is somber and takes his duties very seriously."

My father nodded in satisfaction. "Good, good. A commander of your status should have at least one attendant."

"One is plenty for my wants, Father," I replied. "I have everything I need."

"Except a wife," Mother said.

"Annah! We agreed not to speak of that so quickly," my father grumbled at her.

"Speak of what? A wife for me?" I sputtered. "What have you been talking about
while I was away?"

My father held up his hand, and I fell silent. "My son, every commander in King Saul's army is married—except one." He looked pointedly at me. "It is time for you to betroth yourself to a suitable maiden, not one of those palace ladies with soft feet and hands and certainly not one of the servant girls you soldiers like so much."

My mother looked away from me.

"Father, I have no time to search Israel for a wife. I can only take a little time away from campaigning to even come to you," I said, exasperated.

"So tell me then, Beral. How do you enjoy the king's banquets?" My father's eyes bored into me. "There is time for that? You know, you'll not find what you seek there."

I blushed. What did my parents know about my life in Gibeah? Had word of my infatuation with Michal come to even *their* ears?

"Beral, we know of a suitable maiden, one fit to be the wife of a commander, and she has agreed," my mother said. "In truth, she is a wonderful young woman. She is a good and faithful daughter to her parents—"

"Not a young girl to set one suitor against another," interrupted my father.

Mother gave him a vexed look. "Please, Ammiel, that is no help." She moved to me and took my hands in hers. "Beral, you should marry a good woman pleasing to Yahweh. I fear your time at the king's palace has made you forget what things are important—"

"I have forgotten nothing," I exclaimed, jerking my hands away and standing up to pace the room. "Whatever you may have heard about me in Gibeah is of no consequence now. It is nothing to me now." I stopped and held my head. "Who is she?" I asked wearily. "Who is this 'wonderful young woman' you would have me wed?"

My parents glanced at each other.

Mother came to my side and held my arm. "Do you remember Reuven, son of Noam, your boyhood friend before you went into the king's service?"

I nodded glumly. "Mother, I'm not going to marry a man, even an old friend."

My father raised his chin in a warning look, and I instantly regretted speaking disrespectfully. I could see my sarcasm had wounded her.

"No, no, of course not!" she said rapidly. "But don't you recall Liora, his youngest sister? A sweet and peaceful girl."

"Liora?" I smacked my forehead. "Liora? She's only a child! Certainly I remember her. Reuven and I used to have to carry her because she couldn't keep up with us on her short legs when we climbed hills looking for lost sheep. I can't marry that child."

My father held his hand up. "My son, you left our village ten years ago. Liora is no longer a child. She is of age to be betrothed, and she is agreeable about this. I have dealt with her father on your behalf—"

"What!"

Her parents and mine settled it for me in the next few days without my participation. I stayed away by choice, not at all eager for marriage. However, before I left Lo Debar, my father and hers signed the *ketubbah*, and I became dutifully betrothed to the daughter of Noam, a maiden I had not seen since my boyhood. And because of that contract, I still would not know her face until our wedding night.

CHAPTER TWENTY-ONE

Saul told his son Jonathan and all the attendants to kill David.

1 Samuel 19:1a NIV

I HAD EXPECTED TO FIND GIBEAH still in celebration over the royal wedding of David and Michal, but instead, merchants and townsfolk shot anxious glances at me as I rode past them upon my return in the afternoon. The whole city seemed subdued. I was shocked to hear from Yair at the barracks that Saul had tried to kill David the night before by lunging at him with a spear. I soon found Zelig sitting alone on a stone block at the training site and sat down beside him to hear the whole story.

The old warrior fidgeted. "The king had wanted Prince Jonathan and others to kill David. I know because he sent for you too, Commander. He seemed disappointed you were gone." He looked at me strangely, no doubt wondering what I would have done had I been there.

I wondered, myself.

Zelig hitched his sword belt and shifted on his seat. "Jonathan talked him out of it and even got his father to swear an oath that he wouldn't have David put to death. Everything seemed fine until last night."

"Last night?"

"It's that damned spirit—that evil that comes up over Saul like a croc out of murky water." He slapped his knees. "David dodges the spearhead again and runs. Leaves his harp behind. That's all I know of it, Commander."

"Did David go back to his brigade today?"

"No, I suppose he's decided to stay out of sight in his house. Anything else he does now is likely to agitate the king."

"Yes. That would not be a wise thing to do." I paused, wondering how much time I had before my duties would consume me. "Have all the men returned from leave yet?"

"Most of them. Every company reports at least ninety so far. More trickle in every day. You gave them until tomorrow."

"Yes, that's right." I stood up. "We'll muster them here tomorrow an hour after dawn. No doubt they all need to be purged of the wine they've been drinking. A run around the dung heap will start the sweat flowing again."

Zelig peered up at me, his eyes narrowed. "You're going to the palace now?"

I nodded. "I am. I will see what else I can find out."

He reached up and grabbed my wrist. "Don't get mixed up in this business, Commander. There's an evil in the air. Madness rules us."

I shook off his hand. "You worry too much, Zelig. I never thought I would see you fret like this. I'm only going to ask Nathon what happened. I'll not get involved."

He stepped back and looked toward the hills. "There's more, Commander." Still looking away, he rubbed his mouth uneasily.

"Then tell me, Zelig." I put my hand on his shoulder. "There should be no secrets between us."

"I am uncomfortable with this, Commander," he replied, "yet it is better you hear this from me than from others." He stood and faced me. "Rumors have been coming out of Bethlehem."

"And since when have either of us cared about rumors from that miserable little village?"

"Bethlehem is David's home village."

"Go on," I said. "What could be so dire in his home village that you hesitate to tell me?"

"Men are saying that the prophet anointed David as Israel's next king. They say it happened even before he came here to play the harp."

"The prophet? *Samuel?*" I staggered back a step. "Samuel *anointed* David?" I shook my head. "How could this be?"

Zelig shrugged dourly. "Too many of Bethlehem's elders have agreed that it happened. It is probably true."

135

"But Yahweh *chose Saul!* Samuel anointed him as king," I exclaimed. "How could Samuel then turn to that shepherd boy?"

"I don't know, Commander." Zelig ran the stubs on his left hand through his beard. "But already Yahweh has turned away from Saul, and so has the prophet. Maybe this is part of Yahweh's will." He stared away toward the hills again.

"Never!" I shouted. *"Never!"* I turned to leave, but Zelig clutched my arm.

"Beral, don't go into that turmoil. No good can come from it. Let Yahweh see to these matters, and He will direct his affairs as He wishes." Zelig pleaded with me but released his grip.

"Saul is the king of Israel," I said evenly, "and Prince Jonathan will be the king after Saul. Do you agree with that?"

Zelig sighed and sat down heavily. He put his head in his hands and spoke. "Yes, Commander. It is only that—"

"It is only that *nothing!*" I interjected. "I am going to the king's house now to squash these rumors. I will find out who started them and squash him too."

"I fear it will not be that simple, Commander," Zelig answered softly, his face toward the ground.

"That will not be your concern," I replied. "See that the brigade is formed and ready to run tomorrow morning."

"Yes, Commander."

I spun around and walked away. When I looked back, Zelig still sat staring at the earth between his feet.

King Saul's palace looked unchanged in the evening dusk. I walked up the steps briskly, ignoring the fist salutes of the door guards. Inside, the banquet hall and throne area loomed empty and quiet, lit by only a few torches. A maid was there, sweeping ashes from the floor.

"Where is Nathon?" I snapped at the girl.

She whirled around, startled and clearly frightened at my tone. I had never spoken harshly to a servant before.

"Oh, my—my lord Beral," she gasped. Her voice squeaked with tension. "Please excuse me. I didn't hear you enter." She cast her eyes down, a servant's habit.

I remembered her name. "Be of good cheer, Miriam," I said. "I'm not angry at you. I only look for Nathon. Have you seen him?"

Her eyes closed, and her head dropped lower. "Yes, my lord. I think he is with the king in his chambers." She hesitated. "There are others too."

"Others? Is the king well?"

Miriam fidgeted with the broom, and her hand trembled. "Yes, my lord. I think so." She was still frightened of something. I didn't press her further.

"Thank you, Miriam. You may be about your chore now." I decided to leave the palace. Nathon would be alone another time.

I had almost reached the wide doors to exit the hall when the familiar voice of Ben-Ami hailed me.

"Commander Beral, I was coming to seek you. We heard you were back."

"Yes?" I said.

He strode across the hall toward me. "It's fortunate I found you so quickly. Come, the king wants to see you."

"Me?" I had been in King Saul's presence many times, but he had never summoned me before. Ben-Ami seemed in no mood to talk. I followed him to the rear of the palace. As we passed, Miriam met my glance with wide, fearful eyes before she looked away.

I entered the king's sleeping quarters for the first time and was surprised to see Katriel seated there and two of Ben-Ami's guards standing next to Nathon. The guards looked uncomfortable as Ben-Ami and I came in, and tension fouled the air of the chamber.

Saul sat on his bed in a sleeping robe. "Commander Beral, it pleases me that you have returned. Tell me. How is your father?" he inquired as I took a spot along the wall with the other standing men.

I saw a fresh gouge in the cedar panel beside me. "He is well, my king. Thank you. I shall tell him you asked about him," I answered.

"Yes, of course. Your father and I have known each other for a long time. He is a fellow Benjamite I have trusted for many years." He fixed me with a stare. "As I now choose to trust his son."

"Thank you, my king." I couldn't explain why, but a knot formed in my stomach. My heart raced.

The king rubbed his hands together then clapped them once. "Before you arrived, Beral, I was telling these loyal members of my household about a threat to the kingdom—a serious threat."

"A threat, my king?"

The others stared ahead silently, except for Katriel, who nodded along with the king's words.

"Yes, a threat that could destroy Israel. I think you could name him yourself, Commander." Saul leaned back. "He may have even wronged you." His eyes shone in the torchlight, and his hands jerked as he spoke excitedly. "It is David, of course. The usurper would have this throne for himself... just as he took my daughter for himself." He looked at me knowingly. "I realize now, Beral, that she should have been betrothed to you instead of that Judean, but he has the tongue of a serpent. He's fooled me and all of Israel with his words and his alleged 'mighty deeds.'" His hands balled into tight fists as he sat up. "But that stops tonight. You will correct this wrong—you, Beral, along with these other trusted men." He looked at me expectantly.

My throat constricted. I could barely speak. "My king, are you saying—"

"Kill him! Kill David!" he roared. "*That's* what I say. I command all of you to slay him and stop this attempt to end my dynasty—mine and Jonathan's."

A low, mumbled chorus answered, "Yes, my king. Yes, my lord." I truly didn't know if I responded at all.

"Katriel will lead you in this. Listen to him and do as he says," Saul continued. "He has a plan that I approve."

The fleshy aide wore a satisfied, tight-lipped smile as he looked us over with lidded eyes. "These men will be excellent for this task," he said. "You chose well, my king."

"Go, then," the king replied, waving his hand in dismissal. "Do as I have commanded and tell me it is done in the morning." He leaned back on the sleeping platform again. "Send the guard in. I will sleep now... without a harpist."

Katriel laughed. "Certainly, my king. You will not have to worry about a harpist after this night," he said.

We followed him back into the silent banquet hall, where Miriam still swept the floor.

"Begone, girl! Leave us!" Katriel shouted at her. "You should have already finished this."

"Yes, my lord. I'm sorry, my lord." She lifted a tightly woven basket filled with ashes and hurriedly left the room.

I gave her a nod, but she never looked up.

Katriel sat down at the head table. He leaned forward, hands on his widespread knees. This time he gazed at the four of us in obvious disapproval. "I suppose you will have to do," he said scornfully.

Ben-Ami and I shared a quick glance.

"Sit across from me." Katriel pointed to low seats directly in front of him across the table.

We moved woodenly and sat down.

He looked satisfied once more and put his fingertips together. "Now then, here is what we will do. Follow my directions, and you will succeed in carrying out King Saul's wishes." He paused and looked at each one of us carefully. "Success means you will have earned his gratitude, and I will see you are all amply rewarded." Silence lingered for a moment after he spoke.

I moved uncomfortably in my seat. One of the two guards sat next to me. I could smell the nervous sweat on him.

He blurted, "We are going to kill Commander David?"

Katriel fixed him with a serpent's stare. "What is your name?" he asked quietly.

"Kefir, my lord."

"Yes, of course. Kefir it is." The king's aide leaned farther across the table. "Do you serve the king, Kefir?"

"Yes, my lord. I serve him with my life if I must."

"That is good, Kefir. That is good," Katriel purred. Suddenly he yanked out a dagger hidden in the left sleeve of his robe and stuck the point on the tabletop, where it quivered upright before Kefir's frightened face. "But, Kefir, do not ever again question his commands to you or my orders to you. I would regret having to tell the king that one of his most trusted guards harbors a doubt about his duty. It would disappoint him very much. Do you see that, Kefir?"

"Y-Yes, my lord. I never meant to disrespect—"

"Of course you didn't, Kefir, but I sensed you may be less than eager about this task. You're not, are you? Tell me, Kefir." Katriel played the cat toying with a mouse.

"Yes—I mean no, my lord! No! I will do as you direct. I serve the king." He ran his tongue over his lips.

"Good, Kefir, good. I am glad that we settled that." Katriel sat straighter and eyed the rest of us, moving his gaze slowly across our faces, seeming to linger longest on me. "Do any of you have something to say?" He pulled the dagger out of the table and placed it back into his sleeve.

"Does Prince Jonathan know of this?" I asked.

Katriel turned his stare to me, a sly smile ugly on his round face. "Commander Beral, the prince's friend. I expected you to wonder about that. But no, the crown prince has no knowledge of his father's plan to save his throne for him. He will not be interfering." He settled his hands together on his wide belly. "King Saul knows how much his eldest loves David. It will take time before the son realizes how much his father has done for him—and how much we will do for him."

"I see."

"Do you, Commander Beral? Do you really? Have you any loyalties to David as well?" His eyes glinted like polished glass in the dim light. "Will you do as the king commands?"

I nodded.

"Say it aloud, Commander Beral. Say aloud that you will carry out my orders to kill David."

"I will do as you say," I replied.

CHAPTER TWENTY-TWO

"If you don't run for your life tonight, tomorrow you'll be killed."

1 Samuel 19:11b NIV

KATRIEL'S PLAN WAS SIMPLE. HE and Nathon would stay at the palace while the other four of us took turns watching David's house during the night. At daybreak, he would join us in front of its only door and strike down David when he came out. Katriel didn't assign the actual kill to anyone, so I assumed he wanted that honor for himself, but I truly doubted he had the courage to do it alone. One of us would have to step in.

I didn't want to be David's friend, but I wasn't his enemy. Even with the king to justify this assassination, my stomach churned with uncertainty, for I feared Saul was in the grip of his evil spirit again. And what would Jonathan think of me after I helped kill David?

We were to sleep in a palace storeroom while Kefir took the first watch at David's house. When Ben-Ami got up to relieve himself, I followed him outside. We stood side by side, urinating at the trench.

He sighed and looked up at the stars. "This isn't right."

"No, it isn't," I agreed.

"How did you and I draw this cast of the lot?"

I shook my head. "I don't know. King Saul trusts us, I suppose."

Ben-Ami chuckled, a bitter sound in the darkness. "That may be, but I don't trust Katriel. That talk about a 'reward' for us... You'll see. That smooth-skinned court politician will be the only beneficiary of all this." He let out a long breath. "And to kill David... I follow the king's orders, but I don't like it." He sighed again. "We'll do what we have to do."

We finished and hitched our tunics.

As we headed back inside, I said, "David is clever, and Yahweh seems to watch over him."

Ben-Ami stopped sharply and looked at me in the moonlight. "What do you mean?" he asked suspiciously.

"Nothing. Only that I have seen David come through many situations without a hair on his head damaged. He killed Goliath, after all."

"Goliath was one man, even though a giant," he scoffed. "David won't escape six men, even if one of us is a soft aide with no taste for battle."

"Perhaps you're right," I answered.

We entered a side door past one of Ben-Ami's guards. I took the next shift to watch the house. Standing in a darkened doorway opposite David's, I thought hard about what I was to do in a few hours, and I fought with myself. *How did I come to find myself in this place, set to murder an innocent man?* David had actually saved my life once. I could see lamplight flickering in an upper window of his house, and I made a decision.

After checking up and down the street, I crossed over and picked up a handful of pebbles from the ground. Taking careful aim, I tossed some of them up toward the lighted opening. They clattered on the sill and into the house. I waited a few breaths and did it again. A shadow passed across the window. I stepped to the door and waited, still not sure of what I would say. My heart hammered in my chest. Soon I heard a movement on the other side.

"David?" I whispered. "David?" I tapped lightly. "David, It's Beral. I have to talk to you. You're in danger."

I heard the inside bar being removed from the door, which then cracked open a hand's breadth.

"Beral?" Michal's soft voice—not David's or a servant's.

I couldn't speak. The door opened wider, and I could see her backlit by the lamp set behind her.

"Beral? What do you want?" She sounded frightened.

I stood in silence for several heartbeats. I hadn't expected her at the door. Tousled hair fell around her shoulders. She looked beautiful.

I can't describe the feelings that coursed through me at that moment before I found my tongue.

"I must speak to David," I whispered hastily.

"He's sleeping. I don't want to wake him."

"Michal, he is in great danger. I have to speak to him."

Her eyes widened. In the light of a new moon, they gleamed like moist stones. She reached for my arm and pulled me into the house before swinging the door shut and leaning against it. "It's my father, isn't it?" Her voice caught with concern.

I could only nod.

"What is he going to do?" she asked.

"In the morning, six men will meet David at this door to kill him. Katriel will lead them."

"Katriel! That sordid goat! I hate him!"

I took a deep breath. "I am to be one of the six."

"You? Oh, Beral, not you too!" she gasped. "Not you too." Michal put her hands to her face and started to cry quietly.

Without thinking, I put my hands on her shoulders. "But I came to warn him, Michal, not to murder him."

Suddenly, she came into my arms and clung to me. I felt a familiar stirring.

"Beral, oh, Beral. Dear Beral," she cried. Her tears wet the front of my tunic. "I've always loved you as much as David. It's so good of you to come."

I knew she felt my hardness. I had to push off gently or risk something I couldn't control, and I did so reluctantly.

She sniffed, wiping her nose and eyes with a scarf. "You're right, Beral," she murmured. "Best to stop this." She smiled timidly. We stood in silence, both of us regaining composure.

"My princess, David has to leave tonight. Your door is being watched by me at the moment, but my shift is almost up. He will have to leave another way." I paused. "I have to go. My relief will be outside shortly." I turned to leave. "I will be back in the morning with Katriel. Tell David." I reached for the door.

"Wait, Beral," she said. Before I could react, Michal stepped up and kissed me, an open-mouthed kiss that I melted into. She backed away. "Go. And thank you, Beral."

I reeled out the doorway and across the street, barely back at my doorway post before I heard the footsteps of the next watch arriving to relieve me.

"All is quiet," I whispered to Ben-Ami, who had the next watch.

We switched places, and I left. As I walked the night streets back to the palace, I pondered what I'd done. The moment I crossed over to David's house, I defied Katriel, and I defied my king. The penalty for that would be death if it were ever known. Yet a burden lifted from me, for I knew Jonathan would have approved.

I entered the dark storeroom where the other men tossed on their mats. I lay down and stared at the ceiling, recalling the press of Michal's whole body against mine for the first time. Her kiss had been passionate, but she'd done that while her husband of scarcely a week slept there under the same roof. I'd told David once as a weak jest that his bride would be fickle, never realizing how true those words would become. And how fickle was I? I had been betrothed barely two days myself. Yet my loins still groaned for Michal, and I rolled about in futile lust for the remainder of the night.

An hour before dawn, we assembled in the banquet hall again and sat at the same table.

Katriel had dark pouches under his eyes. He drummed his fingers on the table. "Here is what we will do. When we get to David's house, we line up, three on each side of the door with our backs to the wall. We fall upon him when he steps out shortly after sunrise. I have discovered that is when he goes to the training grounds."

I looked at the others. Ben-Ami wore a bemused grin. We were the soldiers. No one needed to tell us a commander's work habits. I fidgeted in my seat while Kefir chewed his lower lip.

Katriel spoke cheerily, not acknowledging how we loathed him. "Well then, let's be about our work."

We followed him in single file through the streets, trying to muffle the clank of our weapons as we walked. A woodcutter leading his string of donkeys out to get firewood in the hills looked at us curiously. Other early risers passed us, averting their eyes, knowing that armed men moving about in the darkness meant evil was at play.

The guard on the last watch met us at the house. "All's quiet," he reported to Katriel.

We placed ourselves against the sides of the house as directed. I had a spot nearest the doorway. Katriel took one of the farthest.

Townspeople walked the street in greater numbers as the sky lightened. From their expressions, I think many of them recognized us. Whether they suspected what we were there to do or not, they hurried past without speaking. The sun rose fully above the horizon, and long shadows stretched over the town.

Finally, Katriel stepped away from the wall. "This is taking too long. Nathon, knock on the door. Tell David that the king wants to see him."

The king's armor bearer rapped on the door. He cleared his throat and stepped back when it swung inward after several long moments.

"Yes?" I recognized Michal's voice.

Nathon bobbed his head. "I am sorry to disturb you, Princess Michal, but your father wants to see David immediately." He faltered and looked toward Katriel.

"I'm afraid that my husband is very sick today, Nathon. He won't be able to come," she replied, her voice never quivering.

Nathon, however, almost trembled. "Uh, very well, then, my princess. We'll be off, then."

The door shut, and I heard the bar slide into place.

Katriel was furious. "You dullard!" he hissed at Nathon. "You should have pushed your way in." He smacked the wall with his bare hand.

Nathon looked at his sandals, miserable and frightened.

"Come on," Katriel snarled. "We're leaving."

I shoved off the wall and strode briskly back to the palace, not slowing for Katriel's fleshy legs to catch up until I reached its steps.

Saul waited in his sleeping chamber. Katriel took a deep breath and squared his shoulders before he entered, his face set. I waited outside the doorway with the others, but we could all hear Saul roar his displeasure.

"You *failed*? He was *sick*? What sort of fools have I sent on a simple errand?"

Something crashed against the wall in the chamber. I heard Katriel's voice within, desperately trying to soothe our white-hot king. I heard him say Nathon's name.

"Don't blame your men, you fool!" Saul bellowed. "*You* were the one who assured me. *You* were the one saying it would be easy."

Out in the hallway, we eyed each other. The rage in Saul's words was frightening. I could imagine the spittle flying from his mouth.

Katriel murmured again. Then an ominous silence fell.

Suddenly, the door flew open, and Katriel stumbled out headfirst, shoved from behind. He fell and sprawled on the floor in a sad heap, his sword clattering on the stone.

King Saul towered over us in the open doorway. He gazed around at each man before he spoke. "Go back to his house. Find him and bring him to me in his sickbed. I'll kill him myself." He fixed his eyes down on Katriel. "Do not fail me again, little fat man."

Katriel's face went white. He struggled to his knees. "Y-Yes, my king," he stammered, but King Saul had already closed the door.

I waited in silence like the rest as Katriel got to his feet and rearranged his clothing with shaking hands.

"Come," he said. "We will do as the king commands." His voice cracked like a fourteen-year-old boy's.

He almost ran as he led the way back to David's house, not looking at us or speaking any further. This time, Katriel went forward and knocked. I stood behind him, beside Ben-Ami.

A servant girl opened the door. "Good morning, sirs. May I help you?" she asked.

"Tell your mistress that the king wants to see David," Katriel ordered, brave enough by then to face a young maiden.

"Oh, sirs, but my master is sick—"

"It's all right, Leah. Invite our guests in." Michal spoke from farther inside.

We stepped into the dim interior. Michal faced us with a forced smile, hands clasped tightly at her waist. Her hair was tied back and braided while jewelry glimmered on her neck and wrists. She stood proud as a queen, although nervousness showed. "Good morning, Katriel, Ben-Ami." She nodded to the rest of us, giving me no special notice. "I'm sorry, but did I not tell you that my husband is too sick to leave his bed?"

"Quite so, my princess, but your father insists. We will carry him in his bed to the palace." Katriel, once more the adroit speaker, gestured around at us and smiled obsequiously. "David will hardly be disturbed at all. Is he upstairs?" He moved past Michal toward the stairway. "Come along," he told us over his shoulder.

"But really, you mustn't—" Michal held up a hand then let it drop as we followed Katriel to the upper level of the house.

I looked straight ahead as I passed her. We went directly to the room where I had seen the flickering lamp during the night. A wide sleeping platform sat against one wall. I had a quick, uncomfortable image of David and Michal there in that bed, coupling as man and wife.

A figure lay there, covered in rumpled bedclothes. A shock went through me. *What was David doing lying here? Had Michal failed to tell him?* But then I noticed the hair seemed strange. The sleeping form under the covers wasn't right. Katriel saw it too. He reached down and snatched the bedclothes away. A carved wooden idol glared up at us from the bed, goat hair tied to its head with a band. It was one of the abominations captured by David's men in their raids against the pagans. Michal had followed us up the stairs and stood in the doorway.

"He's not here! Where is he?" Katriel blustered. He whirled to Michal. "What did you do? He's not sick, is he? Where is David hiding?"

She didn't answer but only hugged her elbows.

"Search this place! Find him!" he shouted at us. He bent quickly and flipped the bed over, scattering spare bedclothes across the room. "Well, go on, you brainless sheep! Start searching." He pushed past Michal onto the staircase. When I followed him out of the sleeping chamber, Michal's eyes flicked to mine for an instant as I brushed by. I hoped no one else noticed.

Ben-Ami found a coiled rope next to an upper rear window in another room. It had been securely tied to a beam and, if thrown through the waist-high opening, would trail down to an alleyway behind the house—a place unseen from the street in front. When he showed it to Katriel, the aide puffed with indignation.

"Here is how he escaped," he sputtered. He turned to me. "And it was while all of you were keeping watch. This is not my fault."

"My lord," said Nathon, "he may have had help." He indicated the rope.

"Help?" Katriel looked confused as he looked at the neatly stacked coils. His eyebrows shot up. "Of course! Someone had to pull the rope up. Someone coiled it." He spun around to Michal, who still followed us. "How do you explain this?"

Her mouth quivered. "My lord, I had no choice. He said he would *kill* me if I didn't help him." Hands to her face, her shoulders shook like a winnowing screen. It was a remarkable performance. Katriel looked shocked then smiled blandly at her. The blame would not lie with him, and his relief was plainly visible.

"Don't worry, Princess Michal," he purred as if calming a skittish horse. "Come back with us to your father and tell him what David has done to you."

"Yes, yes, I will do that. I must tell him," she agreed.

Shortly after, as we went back to the palace, people openly stared at the sight of the king's daughter walking in the street with her maidservant and an armed escort.

The king sat waiting in the main hall. He scowled when we entered without a litter. "What is this?" he asked suspiciously. "Why have you brought my daughter to me and not David?"

Katriel paused and murmured to Michal, "My princess, it would be better if you yourself approached your father and told him about David's threats to you. I should not interfere." The portly aide stepped back and bowed. Katriel would claim no part of the failure. That lay on us who stood guard during the night and on Michal herself.

Michal went forward and threw herself down on the shallow steps in front of Saul's throne. She had always been his favorite, denied nothing while she lived in his household, but here she trembled fearfully as she looked at Saul through tears. "My father, David is gone. He made me lower him on a rope to escape unseen. He put a false idol in his bed to confuse anyone who came for him."

The last words wailed from her, and she lowered her head and sobbed. I marveled to myself at how easily she lied.

Saul balled his fists to slam them on the arms of his throne. "Why did you deceive me like this? Because of you, my enemy gets away!" He stood up to his full height, his eyes menacing.

"But, my father!" she cried. "He said he would kill me! He said, 'Let me get away, or I'll kill you too.' What could I do?" On her knees, she reached arms out to him, pleading for his mercy. I had once seen Saul willing to kill Jonathan, and I held my breath, not knowing what he would do this time.

The king picked up his javelin and swung it against the stone floor with both hands, cracking the shaft and sending the bronze point clattering across the hall, barely missing his daughter. Michal shuddered, her face down to the floor.

Saul sat back heavily on the throne. "Get out of my sight. Go away, and don't show yourself to me again until your husband is dead."

CHAPTER TWENTY-THREE

Then David... went to Jonathan and asked, "...How have I wronged your father that he is trying to take my life?"

1 Samuel 20:1 NIV

I N A FEW DAYS, SPIES reported that David had gone to Samuel at Naioth. The king dispatched men to capture him there, without any of us six he first sent to David's house. Saul no longer trusted us completely. I don't believe he trusted anyone.

The detachments sent to take David all came back confused and unable to explain what happened. They said Yahweh intervened in some way, turning them all into babbling, prophesying priests. It vexed Saul so much that he declared he would go to Naioth himself.

"Why am I surrounded by fools?" he fumed openly. "Am I the only hand of God in my kingdom?" But when he too returned without David, he said nothing more.

Ben-Ami told me what happened, saying that the Spirit of God had come over the king as he traveled on the road. Saul stripped naked in front of Samuel to speak of Yahweh in a loud and continuous stream of ecstasy.

"I've never seen my king do anything like that," Ben-Ami said. "And I don't think he wanted to, either. It looked like Yahweh forced him. He lay there in his own piss a day and a night before he got up, bathed, and came back."

After that, Saul no longer tried to capture David. Word spread that the king would even welcome David back at court. I wouldn't have trusted that rumor myself, and David must not have either, for he did not return to Gibeah. Weeks passed, and I wondered if we had seen the last of David the harpist. During that time, Saul's countenance menaced everyone like a looming thundercloud, lightning flashes hiding within his blackness. Servants avoided his stare when he walked about the palace. Troops feared his temper in the field.

A month later, my brigade was practicing its response to an arrow attack. Mazal followed me to a rooftop where I watched as a body of archers loosed volleys of blunted shafts into the massed companies. Commanders shouted at men to "cover" as the ranks crouched low behind their shields. Zelig walked in the midst of them, daring any archer to aim at him. His switch flicked out and swatted the backside of any spearman he caught peeking around his shield. They learned quickly, and I was pleased with them. Then Mazal coughed softly behind me. I turned to see Jonathan standing next to him on the roof while Herzi waited farther back at the stairway.

"My lord," I said. "Welcome. Have you come to see how we pull our heads in like turtles?"

"Yes, Beral, your brigade looks good. It is still the best in our army." He stepped up beside me and looked out over the rows of kneeling men, Zelig the only one actually visible, cropping up out of the huddled shields like a cedar post as he moved about, bawling and switching. "This exercise is a good idea, Commander. I think I will have all the brigades do this... except David's, of course." He looked sideways at me with his hands held behind him. "They're too light."

"Of course, my prince."

Jonathan glanced at my armor bearer. "Mazal, go and talk to Herzi."

"Yes, my lord." The youth walked back to where Herzi stood out of earshot. No doubt, the pair could compare stories about the eccentricities of their masters.

Jonathan leaned his hands on the rooftop's parapet. "I've needed to talk to you, Beral."

"Yes, my prince."

"Do you remember, Beral, years ago when we were young? How we used to talk about anything we pleased? Women, hunting, fighting, even some of our fears? I have missed our talks."

"As have I, my prince. We were brothers then."

151

He smiled ruefully. "Yes, and then we became men. Men with burdens to carry." He shook his head. "I should never have promoted you, Beral—not that you didn't deserve it and warrant it." He placed a hand on my shoulder. "But I lost a friend that day—a true friend."

"No, sire! I am still your friend," I cried.

Mazal and Herzi swung their heads around toward us.

I continued in an undertone, "I will always be a friend to you."

"Yes, I know that, Beral. I would still trust my life to you as I have already many times in the past," Jonathan said. "But now our friendship is strained." He waved a hand around. "Changes at the palace, in our status, in us ourselves. We move apart. I feel there is no one to confide in anymore," he said.

"There is David."

"Ah yes... David." He turned to me. "My friendship with David has bothered you, hasn't it?"

I stared away from Jonathan and looked down at Zelig. The brigade had finished its training below us. Zelig had formed the men up for a last run around the far dung heap. I waved him on when he looked up. I would not be running with them today.

"Yes, a little," I replied to Jonathan.

He nodded. "Beral, my closeness with David does not affect my love for you. Both of you are my friends." He stopped to watch the brigade jog away—a thousand men running in unison—always an impressive sight. He spoke in a thoughtful voice. "David has a gift, a spiritual gift from God because David is truly in God's hand. He loves Yahweh as surely as he loves me or anyone else." Jonathan rested one hip on top of the parapet. "But you, Beral, you are my oldest friend. I can talk to you of things that even David doesn't know. And Beral"—he put a hand beside his mouth to whisper—"even I sometimes tire of always talking about the goodness of Yahweh. David *can* be boring."

The corners of my mouth turned up. I laughed while he and I clasped elbows.

Jonathan turned somber as we let go. "My sister told me what you did for David," he said, looking me in the eye. "It was a noble and brave thing to warn him—to go against my father as you did."

I looked at my feet. "I only did what I felt was right. Ben-Ami felt the same way."

"Perhaps he did, but only you *acted*, Beral, and Yahweh guided your actions. It does little good to think about deeds if you do not do them."

I blushed, remembering again how Prince Jonathan always listened for Yahweh's voice. I also knew my actions with Michal had not been directed by Yahweh. Apparently, she had not told her brother about that part.

"Thank you, my lord," I mumbled.

He leaned back against the low rampart. "Actually, I have a request of you—one you could deny if you wished. I would think no less of you."

"Certainly, my prince. Name it, and I will do it. You should know that." I bristled a little that Jonathan would have any doubt about me.

He smiled and held up a hand. "Caution, Beral, you should hear the request first before you grasp it with both hands. Every sack may look alike, but sometimes one contains an asp. Hold it carefully," he said. "I don't need you to do anything. I only want you to accept something—something that is very important to me."

At times, my prince could talk in riddles. "Accept something?" I asked.

"Yes." Jonathan took a breath. "I have made a covenant with David—a covenant I hope you will honor as well."

"A covenant? My prince, what could your covenant with David have to do with me?"

"David and I have sworn an oath to each other—an oath of love and loyalty. He will protect me as long as I live and never cease his kindness to my family."

I clutched my tunic with a fist. Jonathan had never made such a covenant with me. "Why should you even need an oath from him?" I asked. "You, the crown prince of Israel... I am still here to protect you and your family, and no harm will come to you while I draw a breath." I looked outward at the hills.

Jonathan placed a hand on my shoulder, and I tensed at the touch. "Here is the asp in the sack, Beral. These things of Yahweh's are not always easy for us to see until they are untied and shaken out. And that is when some people are bitten."

"I don't understand your words," I answered. "Things of Yahweh's?" I turned to face him. "What is it you want of me, my lord? How do I honor this covenant that has nothing to do with me?"

"I only want you to accept this, Beral. And understand that David and I are not enemies over the throne. This is all in the hands of Yahweh."

"The hands of Yahweh." I grimaced. "And so what do you promise him, my prince? What do you pledge in return to David for his unfailing kindness?"

Jonathan looked away. "I will try to protect him from my father."

"Your father? Surely the king won't try to harm David again." Even as I spoke, I knew my words rang hollow.

Jonathan froze me with a stare. "And surely you know my father is oftentimes in the grip of a spirit from the evil one—probably the same spirit that took Eve. As it drove her and Adam from the garden, it may drive my father's house from the throne."

"But, my lord," I sputtered. "Your father is king, and David is not of his blood. You're not saying that he—"

Jonathan cut me off with a gesture. "There is nothing more to say, Beral. My covenant with David is made, and I hope you someday give him the same devotion you have given my family."

"I will do as you say, my lord, but I do not believe this to be necessary, and I do not understand why you, the next king of Israel, say these things. No one else is more fit for the throne than you, and Yahweh will place you there. Any other talk is foolishness." I turned my back and walked away from him—a provocative gesture, considering my words. Any other man would have received a lashing for such disrespect. "Come, Mazal," I said over my shoulder as I hurried down the stairs.

That night, King Saul held a meal for the festival of the new moon, a rare occasion for him in those days. He barely picked at his food but sat hunched over as though his stomach pained him, not speaking, only staring at the empty seat across from him next to Jonathan. It was David's place at the table. Saul no longer allowed music in the hall, and the meal was solemn. Jonathan sat quietly, also eating little, deep in his thoughts with a finger alongside his nose.

Finally, Saul spoke to him. "Why hasn't the son of Jesse come to eat with us? He wasn't here yesterday either."

The hall went silent. I paused, a wine cup halfway up to my mouth. Saul's eyes burned, showing intensity behind the soft question.

Jonathan looked up and smiled. "Oh, of course, my father. I'm sorry I forgot to tell you. David asked me for permission to go to Bethlehem for the festival. His family is observing a sacrifice, and he wanted to see his brothers. That's why he is not here at the king's table."

Everyone in the hall knew Jonathan lied.

Saul's nostrils flared as he silently stared across the table at his son. "Liar!" he thundered. "You son of a perverse and rebellious woman! You think I don't know how you've sided with the son of Jesse? Shame! Don't you know as long as David lives, you will never be king of Israel?" He stood and pointed at Jonathan. "Now go and get him. Bring him here, for he has to die!"

Jonathan choked with emotion. "But why should he die, my father? What has he done?" he cried.

Saul responded by snatching up the javelin always resting by his chair and hurling it at Jonathan. I and all the guests leaped to our feet, overturning the table. Jonathan tumbled to the side, and the short spear missed him by a hand's breath. It clunked, quivering, into the wood behind his upended seat while meals slid onto the floor. It barely missed Herzi, standing beside the chair. His face suddenly drained of color, Jonathan got to his feet and stood before his father. Both men's beards trembled with anger. Then my prince turned on his heel and walked from the hall without a word.

The feast ended at that point. Attendants followed Saul to his chambers as guests hurried to leave. Servants scurried about, clearing spilled piles of uneaten meat and bread. Miriam was working frantically when I looked back from a wide doorway before I stepped outside.

I would have killed Saul without thinking if he had harmed my prince. That realization struck me like lightning, and the thought of what would have happened afterward made me shake. The other guests hurried past me while I caught my breath in the night air. I stopped for a moment to wrap my cloak tighter against a chill fall breeze.

"Beral?"

Michal stood in the shadowed darkness next to a wall beside the route I would take to my quarters. Wrapped as she was against the night with her head covered, I would not have known her except for the voice that thrilled me even in that charged moment.

"My princess?" I said, moving cautiously toward her. "What are you doing here? Where is your maidservant?"

"Leah is at home. I left her there."

"But why? You should not be out here alone. Gibeah is not safe even for you at night. No city is safe for a woman."

"I needed to see you."

My heart jumped, sensing dangerous ground. Still, I stepped forward. "To see me?" Her eyes were visible under the headscarf, and they looked back at me, bold in the muted light of the new moon.

"Yes." She moved closer to me. "David has been gone for weeks. Have you seen him or perhaps heard anything of him since that night?"

That night. "No, Michal, I have not." I shuddered inside, for I'd called her by her name, though she seemed not to notice. "Though I think your brother has seen him recently."

"Jonathan?" She tossed her chin up and to the side. "He loves David more than himself—a poor trait for a king. I know he would tell me nothing." She came still nearer and touched her fingertips to my arm. "But you would tell me, Beral. You would tell me where he is and if he is returning, would you not?" She stood close enough that she had to raise her face to see mine.

Once again, I drank in her sweet scent. "Yes, my princess, I would tell you anything I know."

"I knew I could trust you," she whispered. She sidled next to me. "Walk me to my house. As you said, these streets are not safe for a woman at night."

We walked the dark streets of Gibeah without speaking, but I felt Michal's hand on my arm. I stepped back when we reached her doorway. She turned around to face me. "Thank you, Beral, for watching over me."

"Gladly, my princess," I replied, my voice husky.

She rapped lightly on the door and looked at me as it swung inward. "Are you going to come in?" she asked.

156

I reluctantly shook my head. "Not tonight, my princess." I smiled weakly.

"Very well, noble Beral. Not tonight." She stepped through the door and faced me again. "Come back if you hear of anything about David—or if you don't."

The door slowly closed between us. I walked away in anguish. Michal pulled me toward a precipice whose abyss I did not want to look into. *Why had I said "not tonight" and not a simple "no"?* I was betrothed, but I still struggled against desire, and not for my own honor nor David's, but for Jonathan's.

CHAPTER TWENTY-FOUR

*...Jonathan called out after him, "Isn't the arrow
beyond you?... Hurry! Go quickly! Don't stop!"*

1 Samuel 20:37b-38a NIV

I WENT TO SEE JONATHAN AT dawn the next morning, hurrying
because I could scarcely take in the events of the day before—his
covenant with David, the king's violent madness, Michal. Sleep had
eluded me most of the night. I only knew that David must lie behind
everything. Even Michal's subtle offer came because of David's actions
or, rather, his absence, but I couldn't mention *that* muddled problem to
her brother.

Simcha met me at the door. "Good morning, Commander Beral," he
said. "Do you seek Prince Jonathan?"

"Yes. Has he breakfasted?"

"Oh, yes, my lord. He has already eaten and gone to practice his
bow. My son, Idan, went with him to fetch arrows." Simcha hitched his
chin a trifle, his pride evident that his youngest boy could serve Prince
Jonathan too.

"Idan is growing fast, is he not?" I replied. "I will go and join them.
The prince practices at the stone Ezel as usual?"

"I believe so, my lord, but he didn't say."

I walked through the sunrise to the faraway field where, years before,
Jonathan and I used to practice archery together, though Jonathan never
shot that early with me alongside him. Puzzled, I smelled a dead ox in
the well.

When I reached the outskirts of Gibeah, I left the beaten path to the
archery field and took a parallel goat trail, slipping along out of sight

until I could crawl up on a boulder overlooking the area. Peering around the top, I could see Jonathan and Simcha's young son standing in the distance by the natural stone pillar, Ezel. Jonathan bent low to talk to the boy then took an arrow from his quiver. Pulling a bow that few other men could, he aimed high for distance with no target anywhere. He loosed the arrow to fly upward until it became a speck in the early light before falling out of sight in the rocks past the far edge of the field.

Jonathan pulled two more arrows and spoke to Idan again. The lad scampered away even as Jonathan shot them over him, both of them landing near the first one.

"Beyond you," Jonathan shouted. "The arrows are far beyond you. Keep going."

The boy disappeared into the rocks for a short while before he emerged, clutching the three arrows. He ran back to the prince in triumph. Jonathan tousled the boy's hair before he unstrung the bow and handed it to him along with his quiver. The boy nodded then turned to go back to Gibeah. I ducked behind my rock as he pattered by below me. My prince stayed behind beside Ezel, facing away from me.

I eased up to my knees, intending to call to Jonathan, when suddenly, a figure appeared on the opposite hillside to the south. It was David, looking like a shepherd again. His beard and hair were unruly, his clothing worn and dirty. With a shout, he ran down the slope, leaping from rock to rock like a mountain ram. I settled back to watch as Jonathan went to greet him.

They embraced for a moment, slapping each other on the shoulders. David kissed my prince on the cheek and bowed to the ground three times before Jonathan lifted him to his feet. I could see that both men cried as they talked. After several minutes, they embraced again before David spun around and loped away, going up the far hillside almost as rapidly as he had come down. Jonathan raised a hand in farewell and watched until David disappeared over the crest.

I climbed down from my hiding place and leaned against a tall boulder next to the main path with my arms folded. After a long while, Jonathan appeared, walking slowly with his head bowed. He didn't see me until I spoke.

"My lord."

He stepped back and unsheathed his sword before he recognized me. "Beral? It's you?" He glanced around as if just becoming aware of his surroundings. "What are you doing here?" Then he straightened up and lowered the sword. "How long have you been here?"

"Long enough, my lord," I said. "I saw David."

His eyes widened. "You saw David?" He looked down the pathway behind me. "Are you alone? Did anyone else see?"

"No, sire, I am alone. Idan did not see me either." I pushed away from the rock I leaned on and stood straight before him. "My lord, will you tell me about what is taking place here? I do not want to interfere with your affairs or those of the king's, but if you trust me, I would still be your friend."

Jonathan dropped his eyes to the pathway. He sheathed his sword and nodded to himself. "You're right, Beral. You usually are. I should have talked more clearly to you months ago. I wanted to, yesterday on the rooftop, but I stumbled over my words, and you bolted away." His eyes crinkled as he flashed a grin at me. "Here. Let's sit up there, and I will tell you about David."

We moved off the well-trodden path until we could seat ourselves above it unseen by the curious. Jonathan heard my stomach rumble. He took a flatbread from his pouch and handed it to me. He took another for himself.

"How many times, Beral, have we eaten together in the field like this?" he asked.

"Many times, my lord. And we usually ate from the same bag then too."

He chuckled. "Yes, we did. You've always been a good man and a good companion. I regret not having had the wisdom before this to tell you of what's been in my mind and heart for many months."

"Then tell me now, my lord."

"It will disturb you, Beral."

"Please."

"Very well, then." Jonathan drew a deep breath and held it for several heartbeats before he spoke. "I will not be the next king of Israel," he said.

"My lord?" He could not have stunned me more if he had struck me with the flat of his blade. I felt my face drain of blood as suddenly everything became clear. Jonathan had been trying to say this to me for months, but I had refused to hear him. Now, I could not deny the signs or his words any longer. I was the husband coming home to find his wife lying in the arms of his neighbor. The flatbread dropped, uneaten, into my lap.

"It is not the will of God that I should be crowned king," he continued. "That honor will go to another man." His calm demeanor contrasted sharply with my agitated state. I gritted my teeth, for I knew whom he meant.

"David," I said evenly.

"David."

"But, my prince, that cannot be! Your father was ordained by God to be king. You are his firstborn—"

"My father has lost the throne. He has displeased Yahweh, and so his house, including me, will have no part of the future of Israel." Jonathan spoke quietly with no trace of bitterness or even regret. I could not accept his words so easily.

"And where does this come from? Samuel? That old man is well past his usefulness in the kingdom. No one listens to him anymore, my lord."

Jonathan drove a fist into his thigh. "No, Beral. Never say that again. Samuel is God's prophet. He speaks for Yahweh, and his words are truth." He lowered his head. "And it is not only Samuel. Yahweh has made this known to me as well."

"But how, my lord?"

"I have had visions, Beral. Visions and dreams—always the same. My father disobeyed God too many times to be allowed to rule God's people. Yahweh will have a king who loves Him with a contrite heart. My father does not."

"And so *David* is that man? Why not you, my prince? I know you follow Yahweh faithfully and with your whole heart too, regardless of your father's faults." Prince Jonathan was the noblest man in Israel. How could God not choose him? "It is not right," I said softly.

Jonathan only wagged his head. "We can't worry about that, Beral. Yahweh's ways are above our ways." He pointed to the ground beside my sandal. "See those ants there? They will never know our ways, and we will never know Yahweh's. I don't try to anymore. I only accept it."

"It's not right," I repeated. We sat in silence for several moments.

161

"So what is going to happen, my lord? How is David to become king? And when?"

He shook his head again. "Now *that* I don't know. David has been chosen and anointed by Yahweh. I suppose it will happen when His will allows it. Though there is one thing I know—David will not strike down my father, the king. He has sworn this to me. In his eyes, my father is anointed by Yahweh, so only Yahweh can remove him." He looked at me and placed a hand on my shoulder. "This is what I wanted to tell you yesterday. David and I have sworn oaths to each other. He will not harm me or my family when he is king. And I, in turn, will serve him when that happens. Can you accept this?"

I stared at the flatbread in my lap. "If I must, my lord."

He clapped my shoulder. "David likes you, Beral. He knows you don't fully trust him, but he truly wants to be your friend. He has told me so many times."

I shrugged glumly. "Very well," I said.

"Do try to give him your favor. David is God's anointed." He stood up and stretched. "He will stay away now, though. I was warning him when you saw us because my father will kill him if he ever comes back to Gibeah again." He chuckled to himself. "The king would kill God's chosen and ordained before he would ever bend his own neck to him. But he was right last night. I will never be king while David lives." He reached down and pulled me to my feet. "And that's the will of God."

We went back to the pathway and started toward Gibeah. I scuffed my sandals in the dust. "Does Michal know of all this?" I asked.

Jonathan glanced at me as he continued to walk. "My sister is a shallow woman, Beral. She knows nothing, nor is she interested in the ways of Yahweh. It is a weakness in her, although it pains me to say this about my own blood. That idol you found in David's house? It was her personal one." He looked sideways at me. "She can be dangerous too, in her way. You were fortunate after all not to be betrothed to her. And now you should stay away from her. Resist her."

I blushed and nibbled at my bread. How much did Jonathan guess? Thoughts and a single kiss had been my only sins thus far. I vowed to myself that I would speak no more with Michal. My betrothal would stand. We went back the rest of the way in silence. Both of us finished our flatbread by the time we reached town.

CHAPTER TWENTY-FIVE

But the king said, "You will surely die, Ahimelech,
you and your whole family."

1 Samuel 22:16 NIV

A YOUNG MAN CAME TO MY quarters the next evening with a message from my father. The wedding between Liora and myself had been arranged to take place in my home village in one month. I responded that I would arrive three days in advance for the festivities unless I were called to military duty at that time. I think I hoped for a Philistine invasion.

As the messenger left, I donned a cloak against the cool air and walked out to General Abner's home to tell him of my impending plans.

He laughed heartily at the news. "So, Beral, you are finally to be wed, eh? That is good. I was beginning to wonder about you." He made a foppish gesture with his wrist and laughed again. "The king would not want one of his favorite commanders more fond of boys than women." He laughed again and clapped me on the back. "Tell me, then, who is she? She must be a beauty if she lures you to her bed. She is beautiful?" Clearly, Abner had already been heavily into his wine cup at the evening meal.

"She is Liora, daughter of Noam from my home village of Lo Debar, my lord. I hear that she is comely."

"You *hear*? You haven't seen her, then? Ha! That is good. I actually envy you, Beral."

"Yes, my lord."

He took me by the arm. "Come in, Commander. Come in and

have wine with me. We will celebrate your wedding to this Liora." I reluctantly entered his house to be feted by the general and his wife, both of whom were more excited about my coming marriage than I. After an hour, I excused myself, pleading an early-morning run the next day. Abner followed me outside, his mood turning sober.

"Commander, there is to be a council with the king in the afternoon tomorrow. He wants us to gather on the hillside where the tamarisk tree stands. I sense that he is troubled." He rubbed his forehead. "Maybe that's why I drink too much wine tonight." He shook his head, trying to clear his thoughts. "At any rate, my congratulations, Beral. And may God give you many sons and daughters with your new wife."

I went to bed that night wondering why the king would call a council. Abner had never been a man to fret or to be wine sotted. Something worried him.

I also pondered marriage as I lay there. I tried to remember what I could of Liora, daughter of Noam, from years before, but nothing new came to me. She had been a round-faced child with curly hair spilling out of her headdress when she played. I knew Reuven well then, but I never paid much attention to his youngest sister. I guessed that would have to change in one month. Abner's drunken words about finding an old pleasure in a new wrapping caused me to smile, yet it was Michal I thought about before I fell asleep.

The next afternoon, at about the ninth hour, dozens of men milled around a lone tamarisk tree high above Gibeah. Commanders and attendants had climbed the hill to wait for the king, murmuring to each other while they hitched their sword belts. Zelig and I waited in their midst without speaking, and Mazal leaned on his staff behind us. General Abner stood silently in the tree's shade, gazing down at the town's buildings. I think I was the only one there who suspected his half-lidded stare came from a pounding headache begun the night before.

Saul's chariot appeared at the bottom of the hill—the same Amalek chariot captured from Agag. Two mules struggled to haul it up the rocky slope, bouncing and jolting its occupants. Ben-Ami and eight of his guards easily jogged alongside. The chatter stopped as we watched its tedious progress. Jonathan did not come, but we could see Katriel standing in the chariot next to the king. He constantly reminded me that an animal's dried dung could float in any water where gold and silver sank. A body of priests snaked out of Gibeah behind them and began their own laborious walk up to our position. There looked to be nearly a hundred of them, wearing the linen ephod of their calling.

A chair had been brought up for the king, and he sat down next to where General Abner stood. Katriel bowed and left his side. Saul swept his glare around at the rows of commanders and officials arrayed before him. "Listen to me, you men of Benjamin. Do you think the son of Jesse will give you fields and vineyards as I have? He would make you commanders of hundreds and of thousands? Is that why you have all conspired against me?" He shifted forward in the chair. "None of you would tell me when my own son made a covenant with David. None of you! No one tells me that my son urges David to lie in wait for me as he is doing this very day."

I shifted my feet, uncomfortable with the king's vehemence. I had recently received my own fields from him. Others stared at the ground in silence. I wondered how he had found out about their covenant.

"My king?" Katriel's voice came out of the ranks behind me.

I looked over my shoulder to see him coaxing another man forward. I recognized Doeg, an Edomite who shepherded the king's flocks.

"Go ahead," said Katriel to him. "Tell the king what you have seen."

"Yes, Doeg my servant, tell me what you know," said Saul. He smiled like a benevolent father at the shrewd-looking little man and held an arm up with his palm turned up in welcome.

The Edomite bowed low in front of King Saul's chair. "My beloved king, your humble servant would tell you what he has seen happening in your own kingdom."

"Stand then to tell me," said the king.

Doeg straightened. His eyes glittered with the attention he commanded here. "My king, I saw David, the son of Jesse, come alone to Ahimelech, the priest and son of Ahitub, at the village of Nob. Ahimelech prayed for David. He gave David bread and the sword of Goliath before he released him on his way."

Saul's eyebrows went up in a mock display of disbelief. "Ahimelech did this? Are you sure it was the son of Ahitub?" he asked.

I realized then that Saul had already known what Doeg would say. This was a staged performance.

"Yes, my king, it was Ahimelech, and there he approaches even now." Doeg turned and pointed behind us. The contingent of priests was now arriving at our site. I recognized the chief priest of Nob at its head, his puzzled expression showing he had no idea why he had been summoned there. Ahimelech had always been gracious to me and my commands when we chanced to travel through his village, supplying us with as many provisions as he could spare. I thought him a good man.

Saul called out to him. "Ahimelech, son of Ahitub, come here before me."

"Yes, my lord," the priest answered. He walked forward, sweating from the climb, to bow in front of the king.

Saul said, "Tell me why you have conspired against me. You blessed David, the son of Jesse, and gave him provisions and a sword. David has rebelled against me, and now so have you!" The king stood as he spoke the last.

Ahimelech stepped back, his mouth open in shock. "But my lord, who is more loyal to you than David, your own son-in-law, and who is more highly respected? I have prayed for him many times in the past. Please don't accuse your servant of betraying you." He sank to his knees in utter bewilderment. "I know nothing at all about this whole affair," he moaned.

"Be silent before me!" Saul thundered. "Ahimelech, you will surely die, you and your whole family!" He looked about for Ben-Ami. "These priests of the Lord have sided with David. They knew he was fleeing from me, yet they aided him and did not tell me. Strike them all and kill them!"

But Ben-Ami and his guards only bowed their heads. None of the commanders moved. My heart raced. Katriel had a hand to his mouth, perhaps thinking this punishment had gone beyond his intention. Not one of us wanted to be noticed, and the silence made that moment seem an eternity.

"Just as I thought. All of you conspire against me," Saul growled. He glowered at his officers.

Abner spoke, "My king, we are loyal to you. It is only that these are priests of Yahweh—"

"Silence! If none of you can carry out my wishes, then I still have one here who can." He pointed to Doeg. "You! Go and strike down the priests."

"Yes, my king." The Edomite's grin was sheer evil. He pulled a curved sword from beneath his robes, obviously expecting to be called upon. He quickly went to Ahimelech's side and delivered a two-handed blow to his neck even as the old priest stared at Saul in disbelief. Blood spurted far enough to stain the king's robe. With a grunt, Doeg swung again and beheaded Nob's chief priest.

Immediately, a chorus of wails rose from the other priests. Doeg slithered toward them and began the slaughter, wielding his sword with both hands on one after another. His loud exhalation with each impact on a bowed neck was the only sound except for their diminishing cries. I did not see a single priest try to resist or flee. Some called out to us with outstretched hands. "Save us, you men of Israel! We are Yahweh's priests!"

None of us had moved to kill the priests, but none of us moved to save them either. We were sworn to obey the king's commands. He had been anointed by God's prophet after all, so could anything he ordered actually be evil? Somehow I knew that this was, yet I could not take a step to interfere. Fear for my own life and my family's gripped my sandals and held them fast to the rocky soil, where I stood in shocked silence. If I had intervened, would that have stopped the killing? Would others have sided with me? Was everyone else afraid too? I wanted to retch. No battlefield slaughter ever affected me this way.

At last, only one young priest remained. He stood and looked directly at Saul while Doeg paused for breath behind him. "You murdering abomination!" he shouted. "You are no better than a heathen. To think that you should rule God's people. You will be repaid for this! You and your family."

"Silence him, Doeg," said the king.

The Edomite swung his blade, and the priest fell. The hillside settled into complete stillness for a moment. Bodies, some of them headless, lay clumped around Doeg's feet, and blood soaked the ground. He bent to wipe his sword on a linen ephod, a last indignity to Yahweh.

I started down the hill. All of Saul's officers shuffled beside me in silence. I looked back at Mazal and saw tears streaking his face. He wasn't much younger than that last priest. I reached and took his hand. The youth had never experienced murders such as those. Neither had I, and my eyes watered too. No battlefield ever looked like this hillside littered with Yahweh's priests.

"A bad business," muttered Zelig.

"Yes," I replied.

That afternoon, Saul sent Doeg to Nob at the head of sixty foreign toughs who claimed allegiance to the king. They slaughtered the entire village, including the women and children, even its animals. One son of Ahimelech escaped. I slumped in dismay when I heard of the massacre. King Saul's mad vendetta against David was bringing sorrow throughout Israel. Like every small village, Nob had kinship ties all over our nation. I considered Jonathan's words and now realized the truth in them. His father actually could lose the kingdom because he had lost Yahweh's favor. I wondered if, for Jonathan's sake, anyone would mourn that besides myself.

After the killing of the priests, men began to quit King Saul's army—not the terrified, undisciplined farmers who deserted at Micmash, but our regular soldiers, men who had stood shield to shield with me and other commanders against Philistines and Amalekites. They left to join David. Most were Judeans from David's brigade, but even Benjamites, Saul's own tribesmen, crept out in the night. Their families, fearing reprisals from the king, went with them. Throughout Israel, many who felt wronged by Saul sought out David in the desert. He took his own parents to safety with the king of Moab, supposedly because Jesse's grandmother had been a Moabite named Ruth. Eventually, a force of four to six hundred fighters and their households followed David.

Saul raged against them, particularly the soldiers who walked away. He led expeditions after David, following the rumors that came in about him. David was seen in Keilah, then in the desert of Ziph, then the desert of Naon, then En Gedi. Everywhere the king's forces went, they arrived too late to catch him. I thanked Yahweh that my brigade had not been called upon yet in the fruitless search. Saul only chose those with no loyalty to David to search for him, and my closeness to Jonathan probably made me suspect in his eyes. His doubts were justified, for I truly did not know where my heart lay. The king slipped further into madness each day, but I could not turn against Jonathan.

David's elusiveness made all his exploits the stuff of legends to the people of Israel. Incredible tales sprang up about him. It was said he could see and hear things no one else even sensed. He moved unseen in the night like a shadow. He killed thousands of Israel's foes. I knew those were exaggerations, but the one about his stealthiness had a ring of truth. David actually got close enough to cut off a corner of the king's robe while Saul relieved himself against the wall of a cave in En Gedi. He spared the king's life when he could easily have killed him. I heard from commanders who had been there that David then swore an oath he would never harm Saul or his family. Saul returned to Gibeah, visibly shaken. David faded back into the wilderness.

CHAPTER TWENTY-SIX

So David and his men, about six hundred in number,
left Keilah and kept moving from place to place.

1 Samuel 23:13a NIV

M Y WEDDING DATE APPROACHED. ZELIG accompanied me on
horseback while Mazal followed on a mule as I rode again
to Lo Debar. Children ran before us in the streets, dropping
palm leaves and flowers in our path. My father was especially pleased to
meet Zelig.

"Welcome, Commander Zelig. We have heard of your service. My
son speaks very highly of you and credits you with much of his own
success." He talked rapidly, excited to finally greet the mighty warrior,
well-spoken of in all of Israel.

"Thank you, my lord Ammiel. Your son, Beral, is the only commander
I would choose to serve under," answered Zelig. He flushed to the roots
of his beard. I had never heard him say that before, and it embarrassed
both of us. My parents immediately loved him.

Lo Debar feted me for two nights, each feast as elaborate as the
village could afford. Liora and her family did not attend. Though I
wanted to finally see my bride, my mother would not hear of violating
the custom of us staying apart until the night of our *chuppah*. Zelig sat
at my right hand, an honored guest in my father's home. I suspect Mazal
even found a willing maiden. The youth wore a silly grin each time a
certain serving girl entered our house to assist my mother and sisters
with the preparations. I knew I wouldn't stop the inevitable, but I tried
anyway by setting him to cleaning and polishing my gear and Zelig's
whenever she came in.

"And see that you stay out of robes not your own." I lightly cuffed his ear. "Else you will spoil her virgin dowry."

"Yes, my lord." Mazal bobbed his head and carried my sword and shield away to work on them.

I shook my head ruefully when I saw him give the servant girl a sidelong glance before going out. She smiled back with an expression that would swell any young man's blood. Had I been any less susceptible as a youth?

On the second day, I greeted Reuven, my childhood friend and future brother-in-law. We embraced awkwardly.

"How are you, Reuven?" I asked. "I hear that Yahweh has blessed you exceedingly well."

"Yes, my lord," he answered. "I have married, and my firstborn is a son." He spoke with the manner of a shy child meeting a stranger, looking down and fidgeting.

"'My lord'? Reuven, do you remember Beral, the boy you always bested when we raced? Look up. It is still me, standing here before you."

He raised his head enough to look at me beneath his eyebrows. "I do remember that boy. He couldn't cast a sling as far as me either."

I laughed, and we embraced again, this time pounding each other's back. "Well said, Reuven!" I declared. "Well said. I have never mastered the sling to this day."

We walked through the village together while I looked at scenes little changed from my boyhood. Reuven proudly showed me his house, built with the help of his family. I met his wife and saw his baby son before I finally asked about what burned inside me.

"Reuven, I have not seen your sister since our boyhood. What is Liora like now? Does she still have trouble finding sheep?"

He stopped to cock his head, eyes looking far away as if he listened to distant music. "How long has it been, my friend? More than ten years?" He wore a little grin. "I think you will find my chubby little sister of your memory has changed. You will recognize Liora, but you will be surprised too."

"Surprised? How will I be surprised?" I asked.

His grin grew broader. "Ah, Beral, if I were to tell you, then you wouldn't be surprised." He took me by the elbow. "Come. Let me show you our village's new well."

I could not get another comment out of him about my wife.

The day of the *chuppah* came at midweek, as accustomed. I sat that morning with Zelig, watching the preparations for the bridegroom's feast. Women and girls stepped over and around our sprawled legs until, at noon, my mother bustled us out of the house.

"Go," she said. "Get out of the way, my son. Go exercise your horses or something. Just you be back here at sunset."

Zelig and I looked at each other and shrugged. "Commander, a wise soldier knows when it's time to follow orders," he said. We got up and went to saddle our mounts. I decided to trot them a bit along the roadway.

The fall afternoon had turned out crisp, a fine day to be out, but I rode in silence, looking at my horse's ears and thinking about the upcoming change in my status. I also thought about Michal. My head was too full to pay heed to my surroundings, so I didn't see the others until Zelig spoke.

"Commander. The road ahead…"

We reined up. In the road a mile in front of us marched about forty armed men in a column of twos. Two mounted men rode at their head. Sunlight glinted off polished shields, spear points, and helmets. Laden donkeys followed behind the soldiers. I leaned forward to study them.

"Philistines?" asked Zelig, admitting my younger eyes served better than his own.

"No, not Philistines," I answered. "They look like Israelites. It could be a patrol, but why would Abner send one here?"

"Should we warn the village?"

"No, I can see them better now. They are from our army." I shaded my eyes and squinted. "I think I recognize Ben-Ami on one horse and"—my eyes widened—"and Prince Jonathan!"

I kicked my heels into my horse's sides to canter out to them. Jonathan also urged his mount faster toward me. When we met in the center of the roadway, I pulled up so quickly I almost tumbled over my horse's head.

"Be careful, Beral." Jonathan laughed. "All that pounding will bruise your testicles—something you don't want today on your *chuppah*."

Ben-Ami trotted up to us, guffawing as well. "Yes, you don't want your virgin bride's first look to be at a pair of blue balls, do you?" He and Jonathan roared at their own humor.

I stared at them in slack-jawed wonder. "What are you doing here?"

Ben-Ami answered. "It's a beautiful time of the year, is it not? Prince Jonathan and I thought we'd journey around to see how God blesses Israel. And these men"—he gestured behind him at the approaching column—"all volunteered to accompany us."

"Volunteered?" I looked at the spearmen and recognized commanders and soldiers of my brigade, holding their spears aloft and grinning. I turned to Jonathan in confusion.

"Beral," he said, "did you think that I would not come to the wedding of my oldest friend and companion? Did you really think Ben-Ami wouldn't want to be here either? Many more from your command desired to come with us, but we could only bring this number. They drew lots except for Yair and Nissim. Those two insisted on their right to attend."

I looked behind me at Zelig.

He raised both hands in a gesture of surrender. "What else can we do, Commander? Courtesy requires that we invite these weary travelers to be our guests." He smiled at my prince and the spearmen crowding around us like flocks at a watering hole. "Welcome, Prince Jonathan and men of Israel. Come now, let us lead you into Lo Debar, where tonight we celebrate a *chuppah*!" A roar of approval went up from the forty.

I looked at Jonathan. "Thank you, my lord," I said.

He grasped my forearm while our horses danced side by side. "Don't thank me, Beral. You know I love you more than my own brothers."

I rode back to the village in a daze, but not so much that I didn't hear the ribald comments from the footmen about my approaching wedding. Jonathan rode beside me. I think he said some things too.

Our entrance into Lo Debar caused a sensation. Children, the elderly, everyone ran to see when the cry of "Prince Jonathan" rang through the streets. People stared openmouthed. Ben-Ami's quick calls had the ranks in step and precise as they escorted us to my father's house, and that was the only time I ever saw my father overwhelmed.

His mouth opened and closed like a fish's before he bent down on one knee and bowed his head to Jonathan. "Prince Jonathan, son of King Saul, you do me and my household a great honor to come here. Please, get down and rest here. My house will offer you its best, humble as it is."

The prince dismounted to stand before my father. "Arise, Ammiel. You have already given me the best of your house—the friendship and service of your son, Beral, the bravest and most able of my commanders."

My father could have wept with joy. My mother shrank back in the darkened doorway, her eyes round as silver coins. "And don't concern yourself with feeding us tonight," Jonathan continued. "We have brought with us two fatted calves, sweets, and some of our best wine."

Excitement rippled through the gathering crowd. Soldiers brought up a pair of red heifers and pack animals laden with foodstuffs and wineskins. Town matrons accepted the gifts and quickly led the calves away to slaughter. The village had the crown prince of Israel along with more than forty men to feed and only a short time to enlarge the feast for them.

A watching stranger would have thought Prince Jonathan owned my parents' house, so graciously did he become the host to my awed mother and siblings. "Please go about your preparations as before. Herzi will attend me," he said. "I only need a place to rest and get ready."

"Certainly, my lord," answered my father. "Annah! Wife, stop staring at our prince and show him the side room. Clean it out."

My mother, still standing in shock, suddenly jerked into movement. She snatched my two sisters by the elbows and pulled them to the low doorway of the adjacent room used for storage and sleeping in poor weather. "Quickly! Move these things out of here," she ordered. "The prince must have more space than this. Bring a lamp."

The girls began dragging out jars and sacks, stacking them along a wall. While they hurried to roll down a rug and prepare a sleeping mat, Herzi carried a large bundle into the house.

"Here it is, my lord," he told Jonathan.

"Good." Jonathan peeked into the little room. "This will do nicely, young maidens. You work as well as your brother." He smiled, and I thought they would swoon right there. "Come, Beral," he said. "Will you join me for a moment?" He took the bundle from Herzi and, ducking his head, went into the side chamber.

I followed without having to lower my own head. When the heavy curtain dropped over the doorway, the small room dimmed even with the lamplight.

Jonathan squatted to unroll the bundle on the sleeping mat. He held up something made of cloth. "Here, this is for you."

"For me, sire?" I reached out and took a robe made of the finest, softest white linen I had ever touched. As I held it up, I saw the hem and neck had been lined with dark blue. A red sash completed it. It was the clothing of a wealthy man. "I cannot take this, my prince," I said.

"Of course you can," he replied. "This is the night of your wedding. Here…" He felt around in the folds of the bundle. "Take this too." He dangled a long silken wrap in one hand as he got up from the mat. "It's to be your loincloth. See, I had the seamstress cut a long slit in it, in case you didn't want to take the time to unwind it." His cocked eyebrow and crooked grin made him look the part of a lecher.

I had to smile in spite of myself. "Thank you, my lord. This is generous of you."

"No, it is not generous. You saved my life how many times? And for that I give you scraps of cloth? Now go and let me lie down for an hour. Leave the robe here, and when you come back, we will dress here together."

"Certainly, my prince." I walked out of the chamber into the main room, where a dozen people stared at me. I put a finger to my lips. "Shhh," I whispered, pointing behind me toward the curtained doorway.

Heads nodded as I walked outside to look up at the lowering sun. My *chuppah* was two hours away.

I wondered what Michal did at that very moment, but only idly. Soon, I would see Liora, and now that the time was near, I found myself eager to do so.

CHAPTER TWENTY-SEVEN

You have stolen my heart, my sister, my bride; you have stolen my heart with one glance of your eyes, with one jewel of your necklace.

Song of Solomon 4:9 NIV

"SO THERE YOU ARE. I thought you might have just kept walking." Prince Jonathan laughed softly as I stepped into his room an hour later. In the dim light I could see him lying with his hands behind his head. He shifted and sat up. "That would be comical. Commander Beral ben Ammiel—afraid to complete his wedding."

I fidgeted for a second. "I suppose people would laugh at that, but they shouldn't worry, my prince. I am here." I wore what I hoped was a confident smile, but my eyes stayed downcast.

Jonathan stood and looked at me solemnly. "Beral, my friend, understand that few of us get to marry whom we might desire. Certainly not me. And perhaps not you either. In the days before I betrothed to Reina, there were other maidens, as you well know. I could have wed any of them. Yet that choice was made for me just as yours was made for you. I smile at you now because I find myself satisfied—very satisfied—with the wife I did not choose myself. A loyal woman who gives you children is always God's blessing, whether or not she is your first choice." He cupped a hand to his mouth and affected a whisper. "Even if she can be a she-dog at times, like Reina."

I smiled at that. "Thank you, my lord." Had I detected a slight emphasis on the word *loyal*?

He clapped my shoulder and stepped over to draw back the curtain.

"Send Herzi and Mazal in. We need to get prepared." He turned back to me. "Abner told me you haven't seen your bride yet. Is that true?"

"It is true, sire."

"Well then…" He punched my shoulder. "Don't worry, my friend. I have already checked for you, and what I heard made me think about taking another wife, but Liora, daughter of Noam, is already signed to a marriage *ketubbah*."

Wondering why we were laughing so heartily, our shield bearers crowded into the chamber. Prince Jonathan and I undressed in the low light. He put on formal attire while I allowed myself to be anointed with scented oil. Mazal's clumsy hands fumbled through the task. He tugged the new robe over me, trying to straighten its folds and smooth the wrinkles. A comb ran through my hair and beard. The two bearers and even Jonathan acted like schoolboys released for the afternoon. They practically giggled as we finished dressing. I tried to maintain some measure of dignity and refused to arrange the silken loincloth with the opening in front, as Jonathan kept insisting.

"Oh come, Beral," he said. "You will want to be quick once you see your bride. Don't delay it by stopping to unwrap yourself."

"Thank you, sire, but I will contain myself."

The two shield bearers bit their lips to keep from laughing. Finally, they strapped our sword belts around us, polished metal gleaming in the soft lamplight.

We raised the curtain and entered the larger main room. A collective gasp sounded from the waiting women, and the men nodded in approval. I felt a little foolish in such finery yet pleased too at their reaction. I looked well dressed, but Prince Jonathan was resplendent in a purple court robe trimmed everywhere with crimson. Golden threads formed intricate embroidered patterns around the shoulders and torso. A simple gold circlet served as his headdress. His scabbard shone with silver insets.

He moved aside to let me take the lead. "Go in front, Beral. This is your night."

My mother came to me and took my face in her hands. Her eyes glistened. "My son, I am so pleased for you. So pleased." She ran her hands over the fabric of my robe. "You are so handsome tonight. Did the prince gift this to you?" She turned to him and bowed. "Thank you, Prince Jonathan. This is such an unexpected and generous act."

He inclined his head and said nothing.

"It is time, my son." My father swept an arm toward the door.

I walked out between two rows of spearmen, standing at attention in the dusk. Ben-Ami barked an order, and they fell in step behind me. Prince Jonathan walked next to me, smiling and nodding at the townspeople who lined the street, and Mazal carried my burnished shield behind me. My family followed the soldiers. I looked straight ahead as I led the procession to the house of Noam, where I knocked at the doorpost.

"Welcome. Please come in," came the invitation from within. That domicile was smaller than my father's, and when I entered, I found the front room crowded with Noam's relatives and friends. He stood apart in the center, pride evident in his bearing. All eyes turned to Jonathan, prince of Israel, when he squeezed in behind me. That is, all eyes except mine. I stared at a figure dressed in white. Standing behind her father and to one side, she quickly looked down at the floor, her hands clasped before her. A linen headdress and veil covered her face so that only eyes and hands were visible. Those eyes flicked up to meet mine for an instant before they searched out the floor again.

Noam stepped forward to embrace me. "Welcome, my son-in-law," he said.

"Thank you, my father," I replied.

I remembered Noam well from years before. Reuven's father had treated me even then like one of his sons, and I revered him as a boy. He took a step back and turned to the silent figure behind him. Taking a hand, he led her to me and placed it in mine. It trembled slightly.

"Daughter, behold your husband," he said, his tone formal.

She raised her eyes to me and held the gaze that time. My parents must have come into the house by that time, but I never knew it, not while I looked into Liora's eyes.

By unspoken assent, people in the stifling room shuffled about until a path opened to a side door with an ornate rug hung to cover it. I felt a gentle push on my back from Jonathan. Still holding my bride's hand, I walked past smiling family members and raised the heavy covering, only to find a second carpet hanging on the inside wall of the doorway. I pushed through both curtains, having to release my grip on Liora. When the coverings dropped behind me, we stood on opposite sides. I hastily lifted the carpets again, feeling foolish as I reached for her hand once more. She followed me into the chamber without a word. The outside sounds died away when the coverings dropped into place. We were alone and facing each other.

The room had been decorated as lavishly as Noam could afford. A dozen candles brightened the small space while sweet, aromatic oil burned in a lamp set in a niche. The odor of the scented candles permeated the air. A sleeping mat lay in the corner, covered with pillows and soft lambskins. My head almost brushed the ceiling.

I knew the etiquette. The maidens and servant girls I had bedded before weren't chaste and never pretended to be. Those hurried encounters were kept discreet for the most part. But tonight, I would openly lie with my bride for the first time. I had made it a point of honor to stay untainted since agreeing to our *ketubbah* months before, so the first stirrings were already beginning in me.

I took both her hands in mine before raising one to tilt her chin up. Her eyes widened slightly, and they were moist. Was she crying?

"Liora?"

"My lord." She looked down again.

"Call me 'husband' or 'Beral.'"

"Yes... Husband," she whispered.

"Please. Remove your veil for me now."

She reached up and slowly undid the fastenings until the veil fell aside and her face became visible to me.

I sucked in my breath. "You are beautiful," I breathed. "I did not remember." She looked away from me toward the wall.

"Thank you... my husband." Her voice rasped, and she cleared her throat.

I carefully unwound the rest of her headdress. When it fell to the floor, raven-black curls tumbled around her shoulders and down her back. I stepped back. Liora *was* beautiful. The hair framed an oval face that carried liquid brown eyes set above a regal, arched nose. She looked at me openly, parted lips revealing a tiny gap between her front teeth. I leaned in. Her breath was cinnamon. I set my hands on her shoulders, intending to slide her robe away. She quickly placed her own hands over mine to stop me.

"No, my husband. Let me undress you first." She whispered it so softly I wasn't sure I heard her correctly over the murmurs filtering through the closed doorway. Her hands shook as they fumbled with my clasps. I unbuckled my sword belt. When I turned away to lean it against a corner of the room, her hands ran over my shoulders, pulling down my linen robe from behind. Facing her again, I saw her eyes widen as she took in my scars.

"Oh my husband... Beral, you have so many wounds." She placed fingers lightly against my chest, and the touch thrilled through me.

"I am a soldier, Liora. This is what happens to us."

Her eyes fluttered. "From this time forward, I shall pray every day for your safety, my husband," she said.

Only the silken loincloth covered me now, the ludicrous opening safely tucked out of sight.

"Don't think of that now," I whispered.

I reached again for her shoulders, and she let me, her hands working a fastening at the back of her neck. Suddenly the robe piled at her feet, and Liora stepped out of it, wearing nothing before me but a polished red stone on a cord. Her entire body flushed in the low light, but she looked back at me with bold eyes.

My stare dropped to her breasts, firm and high with large nipples already beginning to thicken. Further down, thick pubic hair hid what lay beneath. Wide shoulders and lean arms looked strong while firm, rounded thighs and buttocks completed a beauty I had not expected. I undid my loincloth. She demurely cast her gaze away, but I knew she looked first.

"Liora, how long has it been since you and I searched for your family's sheep?"

She tilted her head to one side. "It has been many years, my husband. I sometimes still climb the hills looking for my father's strays, but why do you mention that?"

"I only thought that, when you rode on my back as a child, I never imagined then that one day we would gaze at each other this way as husband and wife."

She smiled at me, and it made her face even more beautiful. "I never doubted this day would come, my husband. I have always prayed to marry you." She dropped her glance to my maleness. "Have you thought of me?"

"Not as much as I should have."

"I will try to change that," she said, her voice growing husky. She raised her chin. "You will find me a virgin."

"I am sure."

"How do you wish to consummate, my husband?" she asked, her voice so low I barely heard it.

"Wha—?"

Liora knelt in front of me next to the sleeping mat. "I have watched how rams and stallions mount," she said. Her voice faltered as she slid forward onto her elbows. "Is this pleasing to you?" She stared ahead at the mat as she spoke. I almost lost control at the scent of her.

"Not this time, my wife. Lie down on your back," I said.

"Yes." She felt under a pillow and pulled out the virginity cloth, her name stitched along one border of the white square. She laid it out carefully in the middle of the pad before she rolled onto her back atop it. Her hands and forearms were darkened by the sun and her face lightly tanned, but her body shone as fair as alabaster in the candlelight.

I knelt beside her. Lowering myself to an elbow, I carefully coaxed her legs apart with my free hand and ever so softly spread my fingers up the inside of her thigh. We both shivered. Her breasts rose. Her eyes never left me while I maneuvered myself between her knees.

I wanted to be gentle. Liora rolled her thighs open further as I found her with my fingers. The soft moistness aroused me so that I couldn't pause, and I lowered myself to enter her with more force than I intended. She yelped at the first stroke, but then... but then in seconds, her back arched and we began the rhythm as old as Adam. Her breath hissed in and out while we rocked together, her face buried in my neck, her hard body feeling wonderful. I drank in the sweet smell of her thick hair.

Too quickly, I had to spasm. Liora moved rapidly under me when I shuddered and moaned aloud. I collapsed over her, gulping air in great gasps. Outside the chamber, we could hear joyous whoops throughout the house as our listening attendants realized the marriage had been consummated pleasurably, at least for me.

I raised myself on my arms to look at her, and she stared back with half-lidded eyes. Tears ran down the sides of her face.

"Liora, are you hurt?" I asked, startled. I started to withdraw, but she held me tightly.

"No, no, I am fine, my husband." She studied my face with a solemn expression. "I was speaking the truth, you know. I *have* prayed to be betrothed to Beral, son of Ammiel, ever since we were children," she whispered. "Yahweh is good to His humble daughter." She wrapped her arms around my neck to draw me down to her.

We lay that way for several moments and listened to the singing outside our room. Never before had a maiden ever waited and longed for me as Liora had just confessed to doing. I hugged her tightly.

Finally I rose up on my knees. "We should greet our families. The guests will be waiting for the feast."

She smiled. "Let me dress you, my husband."

We stood together in the candlelight next to a clay bowl with water and towels. We cleaned ourselves and re-dressed each other. Liora admired the fabric and feel of my robe. I showed her the opening in my loincloth, and she blushed.

"Prince Jonathan sported with you about this?"

I shrugged. "The prince and I have been friends for a long time."

She turned even darker. "I will not be able to face him, thinking of this," she said softly.

"Yes, you will. You will meet him tonight, and you will surely love him as he will surely love you." I hugged her briefly, and we turned to the doorway.

"Wait!" she exclaimed. "I mustn't forget." She bent to pick up the virginity cloth and held it out for me to inspect. A bright-red stain was still damp on its whiteness. "For my father," she murmured.

We went through the hanging carpets to the rousing cheers of those gathered in the house. I presented the proof of his daughter's virginity to Noam, and he beamed with pride as he held it aloft to the guests, showing his family's honor remained intact. Women trilled and clapped. Liora blushed as men cheered again.

She and I led the wedding party back through the streets to my father's house. Ben-Ami's soldiers carried torches and shouted joyfully for townspeople to make way. Tables and benches had been set up in front of the house for guests, but we bypassed them to enter the house. Prince Jonathan followed us inside to meet Liora.

He bowed, taking her hand and never letting his gaze leave her face. "Ah, so this is the bride of my friend, Beral," he said. "I do not believe I have ever seen a more beautiful young woman—certainly not at my father's court." He laughed and took her by the elbow. "Come. Let me sit beside you and your husband. I'm sure you would like to hear some stories about him, and I have many." Liora's eyes opened in wonder as she took a place between the crown prince and me.

Our wedding feast lasted far into the night. No one went hungry. Jonathan regaled the party with battle stories in which I was always heroic. Zelig nodded at every tale. My prince charmed the whole room, including Liora.

"He truly likes you," she whispered to me once when he left to relieve himself.

"No man ever had a better friend," I replied softly.

The last of the village guests returned to their homes after midnight. Ben-Ami and his group went to board in a stable. Before they left, I clasped the forearm of each man who had come with him. I embraced Yair and Nissim, both wearing the armbands King Saul had presented to them long before at Amalek.

Jonathan insisted on bedding down with the detachment of soldiers. "Don't worry, Beral. It will be far better bedding than some places you and I have both shared. Take the room your father would give to me. Tonight, it should be yours."

Liora and I did take the private room, and we consummated our marriage again without a wedding party listening on the other side of the doorway. I started more slowly, and she dug her nails into my buttocks that time when I spent myself and then again as I kept moving until she cried out for herself seconds later. Afterward, I awoke during the night and lay there in darkness, listening to my wife breathe. I pondered the wisdom of my parents. Liora's purity charmed me. Why had I ever wanted Michal?

CHAPTER TWENTY-EIGHT

But Saul had given his daughter Michal, David's wife,
to Paltiel son of Laish, who was from Gallim.

1 Samuel 25:44 NIV

WE RETURNED TO GIBEAH THE next day. Liora rode an animal for the first time as Mazal walked beside the patient mule. Prince Jonathan, Ben-Ami, and the spearmen accompanied us. Whenever I glanced back, my wife's gaze was on me. *My wife.* I rolled that thought in my head, an unfamiliar but increasingly pleasant thought.

Late-afternoon sun cast long, soft shadows as we entered King Saul's home city. Townspeople waved and shouted congratulations. I smiled in return. I had never felt more content with my lot.

I slowed to ride alongside the mule. "King Saul has deeded me a vineyard outside of the city, but we will live here near the palace at first," I said to Liora. She nodded once, her eyes sliding side to side, taking in the sights of a strange city far larger than Lo Debar. "We will have to stay in my quarters until I find a satisfactory domicile for us," I continued.

"Anyplace we can be together will be satisfactory, my husband."

I looked sideways at her. I thought I knew what "be together" meant, and a hot flush coursed through me. Liora eyed me back for a second before she dropped her attention to the mule's ears.

I reined up to address our escort. "A man is truly blessed to have such comrades. Now, go to your homes while I go to mine," I said.

Zelig put a fist to his chest. Ben-Ami winked, and the footmen cheered as they split away. Jonathan stayed behind.

He leaned over in his saddle and took Liora's hand while he addressed me. "Congratulations again, Beral, on marrying such a woman as this. Surely, her heart will warm your household and your life together."

"Thank you, sire," I said. "And thank you for your gift of the robe. I have never worn anything finer."

He waved a hand. "Think nothing of it, friend. I suspect it is in good condition still, since you didn't wear it very long last night." He laughed and turned his horse to trot away with Herzi following close behind.

Liora and I looked at each other. Without a word, I squeezed my own horse to start toward my private barracks quarters. Suddenly wanting to hurry, I urged him to quicken his step. Mazal trotted gamely alongside, leading the mule to keep up.

I stayed away from my training duties for two weeks while we set up our household. My bride proved to be a pleasant companion in the cramped room where we lodged until I procured a nearby house with more space and stairs to its roof. I also received permission to hire the girl, Miriam, from the king's household. Liora, the youngest daughter of Noam from Lo Debar, became a married lady with a servant.

My company commanders made a great display of feigned surprise when I appeared for a morning run after my long absence.

"Commander Beral, are you sure you want to go with us today?" asked Nissim.

"Yes, aren't you fatigued?" added Yair. "Maybe you should rest after your, uh... travels."

Zelig's voice rasped. "Watch your tongues, commanders." He turned to me with a straight face and said, "They are only worried about how soon you can recover your stamina, sire. I already told them that, of course, Commander Beral would save some strength for training. Being newly married wouldn't drain you of all your life's juices."

I regarded them in silence for a moment. "Have the men put on all their gear and carry shields and spears. I will start behind all of you. Any man I pass will get the flat of my sword blade."

"Yes, Commander," they chorused, all of them grinning.

As they went to form their companies, I regretted the bold words, for in truth, I *was* tired. Lying in the arms of Liora or kneeling behind her every night did take its toll. I passed not a single man on our run to the dung heap and back. Even Zelig smiled upon seeing how far behind I lagged. I exercised with them all that day, using my sword and spear. That was the first night I did not lie with Liora for sex. She hummed softly to me as I rested my head on her breast before I fell into an exhausted sleep.

A few days later, shofars blew from the palace in the afternoon, and I left the training grounds to answer the summons.

"The prophet Samuel has died," announced King Saul to his assembled commanders.

I stirred uneasily and glanced around the hall. Some men cried silent tears. Jonathan's face looked stricken as he stood behind his father's shoulder, leaning against the back wall for support. My prince had revered Samuel for as long as I could remember, and while the old man's death could hardly be a surprise to anyone, the news must have greatly troubled him.

"See to your companies," said Saul. "Prepare them to march to Ramah. We will go there tomorrow to bury him."

As we filed out of the room, I approached Jonathan and saw his reddened eyes. "You are greatly grieved, sire," I said.

"Yes," he answered. "Samuel was a great prophet of Yahweh, and I will never have the benefit of his wisdom now." He drew in a shuddering breath. "And I fear that his death is the start of events we have no control over."

"Events?"

"Yes." Jonathan glanced around before he stared me in the eye. "Remember, I will not be the next king." He patted me heavily on the shoulder and turned to walk to his quarters, his head bowed.

Most of the army marched for Ramah the next day, where all of Israel mourned Samuel. The gathering crowds were impressive, but the king said nothing to them, instead choosing to let the priests handle the entire burial ceremony. Even I felt some sense of loss there as I watched thousands of my countrymen weep for the old man of God. However, by the time we started back to Gibeah, I had dismissed the prophet from my mind. I thought rather of Liora and how she moved under me.

Training soon resumed in earnest. The Philistines had increased their activities along our border, and Saul was still restless to catch

David. I pushed the brigade hard each day, sensing that Jonathan might be right about events beyond our control. Storm clouds were forming over Israel, and not all of them came from without. Whatever happened, I didn't want us to be caught unprepared.

The winter sun was starting to set earlier, and I often didn't return to my house until nightfall. One evening, as I walked home through the streets of Gibeah, I heard a familiar voice.

"Beral."

My heart sank. Michal was standing in the same manner as she had been when we last met, alone and covered. I stopped and looked about. No one else appeared.

"My princess," I said.

She came forward to place her hand on my arm. "I've needed to talk to you again." She also looked up and down the street. "Come. Let's move out of here. I have a place." She tugged at my tunic. I followed her reluctantly down a narrow side lane until we came to a recessed door set in a high wall. It opened silently when she pushed on it. We stepped through into a wealthy man's tiled plaza. I realized this house and garden belonged to Katriel. Michal closed and bolted the door behind us. We were alone in the dimly lit garden. With her back to me, she slipped off the head covering. The hair on the back of my neck rose.

"Did you have something to tell me, my princess?"

She turned and almost jumped into my arms, wrapping her own around my neck and kissing me with an intensity I tried to resist, yet our open mouths found each other. Michal pulled herself up off the ground to envelop me with her legs. Her robe rode up, and I found myself cupping her bare buttocks. How many times had I dreamed of that moment? But I closed my eyes and saw Liora. Slowly, I loosened my hands to let Michal slide back down.

She stayed tight against me, the side of her head pressed to my chest. "Oh, Beral. Oh, Beral," she moaned.

I became aware of my own sweat smell and the dirt and grime on me that would soil her fine clothing. Placing a hand on each shoulder, I gently pushed her away, even as my loins throbbed for her. Saul's daughter knew what that gesture meant, and her eyes flashed in the darkness.

"You could marry me, Beral! Are you a fool?" She came to me again, clasping me around the waist and leaning back to look up into my face. "Do you know what David has done?" The harsh whisper came through clenched teeth.

"No, I do not," I said, acutely aware of her hips grinding on me.

"He has *married* again!" she hissed. "Married that whore, Abigail." Her mouth contorted into a picture of rage, lips drawn back in a snarl. She let go of me and put both hands to her face. "He has left me and married a whore from Maon," she sobbed.

I shook my head, bewildered. "Abigail of Maon? But she is married to Nabal." I remembered Abigail, a good-looking woman but married to a mean-spirited man. Nabal always overcharged my men for provisions whenever we passed through his holdings near Carmel.

Michal uncovered her face and glared at me. "Are you really such a fool, Beral? You don't know? Nabal is dead. David went there and killed him so he could marry his whore wife." She sniffed and wiped her nose on the back of her hand. "My father is annulling my marriage to David." She raised her head. "Do you see it now, Beral? We can marry, you and I. I should have been betrothed to you all along. My father was the one who wanted me to marry David."

"I am already married, my princess," I said, ignoring the lie about the reason for her marriage.

She snorted. "A village twat? I heard about it. You can divorce her easily enough. My father will get the priests to allow it. Think of it, Beral. Now you and I can be married!" She reached for my hand and smiled coyly at the ground. "We could start here."

"I don't want to divorce Liora," I said.

"Liora? I forgot that was her name. Well, you may keep Liora. She can be one of my attendants if you like. I'll even let you go in to her during the days when I'm unclean." She squeezed my hand.

I released it. "I'm sorry, my princess. I only need one wife, and I will not divorce Liora." I said it over my shoulder as I headed toward the doorway to the lane. I heard her gasp. Then feet pattered on the stone flooring behind me. I turned around barely in time to catch her wrists before she struck me. "I'm sorry, Michal."

"Beral, you *must* marry me," Michal wailed. "My father plans to betroth me to Paltiel of Gallim." She dropped onto the floor in a heap.

"I can't go to live in Gallim, not with that disgusting old man." Her hands went to her face again. "I just can't!"

I unbolted the door. "I'm sorry," I said again, keeping my gaze away from her.

Suddenly, she was up and leaping at me. This time, her fists pounded my back while she screeched. "I hate you, you simple, stinking boy! You should have stayed a shield bearer. I hope you die in your next battle. I hope you *die*!"

I slipped through the door and shut it behind me, thankful that Michal didn't try to follow. Out in the lane, I could still hear her raging. Another voice joined hers on the other side of the wall, a man's voice, low and soothing. Katriel. I couldn't understand what he said, but I understood her.

"No, he wouldn't agree to it!" she cried. "I hope he dies." Then, raising her voice, she called, "I hope you die, Beral. I know you can hear me. I hope you die!"

I took a deep breath. So somehow Katriel had gotten involved in this matter of Michal's betrothal. Apparently, I could make powerful enemies with little effort. I straightened my shoulders and hurried home.

Liora was waiting for me at our doorway. Her face brightened when she spied me striding to her out of the darkness in the street. She rose on her toes to place her cheek against my beard. Then she stepped back, looking at me strangely, sniffing and wrinkling her nose. I knew she smelled sandalwood, Michal's scent. Her pained eyes carried a question.

Before she uttered a word, I took both her hands in mine. "Liora, there is no other, and there will never be another," I said. "Do you believe me?"

She stared at me intently for a heartbeat. "Yes, I do," she breathed.

We embraced. I could hear Miriam bustling about at the meal table in the next room while I savored that moment with my wife.

Michal married Paltiel, son of Laish, less than a month later. The portly groom's face shone with wine the night of his wedding feast after their *chuppah*. Michal looked hard and bitter. She stared at the table and never glanced in my direction. When their entourage left for Gallim the next morning, King Saul ordered the army formed up in ranks to honor his departing daughter. Relief washed over me as I watched them go.

Zelig stood at my right shoulder. "A mare that muddies your spring water will do the same for a new owner," he grunted.

I looked sidelong at him. His face remained impassive.

"What does that mean, Zelig?"

"Nothing, Commander. Just thinking aloud."

"I see." I couldn't help smiling. Michal would not muddy my life after that day.

CHAPTER TWENTY-NINE

So Saul went down to the Desert of Ziph, with his three
thousand chosen men of Israel, to search there for David.

1 Samuel 26:2 NIV

I N EARLY SPRING, SOME ZIPHITES came to the king's court and
reported that David was living among them on the hill of Hakilah.
Immediately, Saul readied three brigades, including mine, to
march for the desert in pursuit. For the first time, I would be chasing
David myself.

Liora sensed that something bothered me. The night before the
brigade left, she cradled my head as we lay on our bed. "What troubles
you, Beral?" she said in my ear.

"Nothing." I shifted my weight, taking comfort in the feel of
her breasts.

She combed fingers through my hair then sat up. "Tell me what it is
that has you restless as a foaling mare," she said. "You haven't been still
all evening. You didn't eat much of the broiled lamb Miriam prepared
for you this night. She noticed too. What concerns you, my husband?"

I sighed. In a very short time I had learned that Liora was a perceptive
woman. "It's this hunt for David."

"You don't agree with it, do you?"

I arched an eyebrow at her. "No, I don't, but it would be best if
you didn't mention those sentiments to anyone else." I sat up beside
her. "I don't know exactly how I feel about David. I don't entirely trust
him myself, yet I feel the king's hatred for him may be misplaced." I
shrugged. "And he saved my life once."

"Yes, I know, and I am grateful to him for that, my husband." She paused and ran a forefinger down my arm. "There are also rumors... Some say David should be king."

I stiffened and stared at her. "And where do you hear such rumors?" I asked.

"In the market square. I was talking to Jemima."

"Zelig's wife?" I put a hand over my eyes. "Liora, you must not speak to her or anyone about these matters. It's not safe."

"Jemima isn't the only one talking about it. It is discussed all over the market," she said. "Is it true, Beral? David will be king of Israel?" she asked. "What about Jonathan?"

I stood up and started to pace in our sleeping chamber. "I don't know. The prince himself believes that the will of Yahweh is for David to take the throne." I stopped. "That may even be so, but you must never say it. King Saul still has followers, and he would be ruthless against those he suspects of disloyalty."

"Yes, my husband." She looked down at her lap. "And so will you really hunt for David? Or would you let him escape again?"

I exhaled and sat down beside her again. "I will do as I am told. The rest is in the hands of Yahweh," I said.

"Yes."

She blew out the lamp, and we both lay back on the mat. I stared at the ceiling with my hands behind my head.

"Will you be gone long?" Liora's voice came like a soft breeze in the darkness.

"I don't know. Probably only a couple of weeks."

She rolled to her side, facing me. Her small hand touched my chest. "Lie still," she whispered. "I will do this."

Silently, she rose to straddle me, pulling her sleeping gown up over her head. As she rose and fell on top of me, I cupped her breasts and forgot about David and the king and everything else. Such was Liora's spell.

The next morning, King Saul rode at the head of the force that left for the Desert of Ziph. I chose to walk in front of the men I commanded. We stopped next to the road along the shoulder of Hakilah, the massive hill where David had reportedly settled. At the evening meal, commanders met in the center of the camp at Saul's sleeping site. He sat on a stool and listened as Abner spoke.

"Tomorrow, we'll start from here," the general said. "There are wadis and caves all about this hill. Tell your men to search out every little hole and cleft."

One commander of a hundred said, "Sire, David has six hundred men, and they couldn't hide in any of these little coney holes. We can search faster if we only look in the larger caves. Why don't we do that?" No doubt he expected a commendation for his cleverness.

"Because we are not searching for six hundred men!" Saul jumped to his feet, knocking over the stool. "We look for *David. David!* Take him, and the six hundred will crawl back to us." He glared around, daring anyone to disagree with him. The abashed young commander retreated into the rear ranks, away from the firelight.

Zelig and I walked back to where our men would sleep. We had to pick our way in the gathering darkness through thousands of spearmen settling down for the night. Curses ripped the air whenever we stepped on someone. "Mind your tongue, man!" Zelig barked each time. "This is Beral's foot that steps on you." In an aside to me, he said, "We are packed in too closely here. They are afraid of a raid by David's men."

"Afraid? Of six hundred men?"

"It's not the six hundred. Our men fear David himself. They know that Yahweh guides him." Zelig said it as truth, and I did not dispute him.

We prepared sleeping sites next to each other, sweeping away the little rocks before spreading out our blankets. I rolled up in my cover with my spear stuck upright in the ground at my head, and I stared at the starry sky.

"Zelig," I said, "our wives should be cautious in what they say to each other. Unwise talk brings down trouble upon both speaker and listener. I have spoken to Liora about it."

In response, I only heard the rise and fall of Zelig's chest and wondered if he'd already gone to sleep.

After a long pause, he rolled to his side, facing me. "I understand, Commander," he said quietly.

That day's march had not been hard. My stamina had come back as good as it had ever been. Yet I felt heavily fatigued, and I fell into a deep sleep. We all did.

"Abner! Abner!"

The voice, coming from a great distance, penetrated my consciousness. I sat up groggily to unwind my covers. The sun already peeped over the horizon as I stood and jerked my spear out of the rocky soil. Zelig got up as well, rubbing his eyes. We had not intended to sleep that late. Where were the night watchmen, I wondered. All around us, men were only just awakening.

"Abner, son of Ner! Aren't you going to answer me?" The call came again.

Two men, easily visible in the early rays of the sun, stood on a far hill facing Hakilah. I couldn't recognize either one.

"Who are you? Who calls to the king?" bellowed Abner. He rose next to Saul's sleeping position, holding a sword and fumbling his helmet on.

One of the figures on the other hill cupped his hands to shout back at the general in a familiar voice. "Aren't you supposed to guard the lord your king, Abner? Then why did you not? Your guards fell asleep. Don't you know that you and your whole army deserve to die for this? You didn't protect the Lord's anointed."

"What are you talking about? Who are you?" Abner shouted.

"Look around you, General Abner. Where are the king's spear and water jug that were near his head?"

Abner's head whipped about, looking down at the ground where Saul staggered to his feet, and Ben-Ami got up on the other side.

Saul stared at the two men in the distance. "Is that your voice, David my son?" he called.

"Yes, it is, my lord," answered David. "Why are you pursuing me? What am I guilty of? I am only a flea that you hunt. Has the Lord incited you against me? Or have men done this? Why do I have to be driven from the Lord's inheritance? Do they want me to serve other gods far away from the presence of the Lord?" David held a spear aloft. "Here is the king's own spear," he shouted. "Have one of your men come over

194

and take it. The Lord delivered you into my hands last night, but I did not lay a hand on you, the Lord's anointed. As I valued your life today, may the Lord value mine and deliver me from these troubles."

Saul dropped his head then raised it to reply. "I have sinned. Come back, David my son. I will not try to harm you again. I have acted as a fool. I have erred greatly." Tears ran down his cheeks as he called out again. "May you be blessed, David my son. You will do great things and surely triumph."

The entire camp listened to the exchange. Bewildered men looked at each other. How had David come in amongst us to take that spear and water jug lying next to Saul's head between Abner and Ben-Ami? No one saw him? Was the king going to call off the pursuit? Voices buzzed throughout the encampment.

I looked at Zelig, but he stared intently toward the two men.

"I'm going to get the spear back," I said.

He regarded me suddenly as if he had been startled out of a dream. Then he inclined his head in agreement. "Yes, it should be you," he said.

I lay down my spear and walked through the muttering troops without my sword and helmet. Men grew silent and stepped aside, some of them nodding as I passed.

Outside of camp, I stopped to urinate against a boulder, wondering the whole time why I was going and why everyone seemed to expect this of me. I went down into the shallow valley between the army and David's hill. The rocks were still cool from the night. I crossed a wadi and started up the opposite slope, aware that three thousand pairs of eyes watched behind me and two pairs watched before me. I made sure not to stumble.

As I approached David, I saw the man beside him was Abishai, a Judean spearman who had deserted from my old crocodile company. David leaned on Saul's spear, clean and groomed. As I neared them, he smiled in welcome. "Beral, it is good to see you, my friend."

I nodded once. "David." I stared at Abishai without a word. He darkened but didn't look away. David watched the silent exchange between us, and his smile faded.

"Don't be angry at him, Beral. We all only follow our hearts as Yahweh sees fit to guide us. You do the same, don't you?" David asked.

I turned to him. "Is that why you lead a rebellion against your king, the father of your friend, Jonathan?" I pointed at the mass of soldiers across the way on Hakilah. "We are all assembled here because you follow your heart?"

David shook his head slowly. "I lead no rebellion. Have I attacked anywhere? Have I killed even one soldier of the king?" He swept an arm over the range of hills behind him. "We come here to be left alone. We mean no harm to Saul. He is God's anointed king of Israel, and I will never raise a hand against him."

"There are people saying that you would be king instead."

He looked at the ground, shaking his head again. "I know what they are saying. It's true that Samuel anointed me once, but it's also true that I have sworn my loyalty to Saul and Jonathan. Whatever happens will be in the hands of Yahweh. It will not be at my hand," he said.

I looked out at the hills and wadis. Six hundred of David's armed men and their families hid somewhere nearby. Probably, a number of them watched us at that moment.

I took a deep breath and turned to Abishai. "You are well, Abishai? Your son, Malach, has recovered from his illness?"

The spearman looked shocked that I addressed him. "Y-Yes, Commander, we are well. Malach is weak still, but his fevers have gone."

"I will pray to Yahweh tonight for his good health."

"Thank you, Commander. I will tell him so." He darted a glance at David, who never took his eyes from me.

"Abishai, would you leave us for a moment?" I said.

The spearman looked anxiously at David then back at me, apparently worried that I planned to attack his leader. David only stared at me.

"It will be all right, Abishai," he said. "Beral is a friend. Wait and watch from there." He pointed down the back slope.

Abishai still looked doubtful. "Are you sure, my lord?" he asked.

David turned to him sharply. "Beral is an honorable man!" he snapped. "You of all my followers should know that. Didn't he lead you at Amalek when you stood with King Saul?"

Abishai looked down, embarrassed. "Yes, my lord," he answered. He met my eyes. "I apologize, Commander. I do not suspect you of treachery."

"Thank you, Abishai. I bear you no ill will."

Abishai set his spear over his shoulder and descended the hill, kicking loose stones down ahead of him. David and I watched him go then looked at each other.

"It *is* good to see you again, Beral. I hear you have taken a wife," David said. He reached forward to clasp my shoulder, but I shifted away out of his reach. He dropped his hand and appeared puzzled.

"They mustn't see you touch me, David," I said. "I cannot be mistaken as your friend."

"Oh... Yes. I suppose it has come to that." He rubbed his chin. "But you can touch this." He extended Saul's spear. I took it and set its point in the ground next to the water jug.

"I understand that you are married again also," I said.

David smiled ruefully and shrugged. "Yes. I'm told Michal didn't take that news very well. Is that true?"

Then I smiled. "Very true," I said. "Did you know the king has given her to Paltiel?"

His eyebrows rose. "Paltiel? Of Gallim? No, I didn't know that." He paused. "Well, you did tell me once that she could be fickle."

"It wasn't her idea," I replied.

"Fat old Gallim. No, I'd guess he would not be her choice." David chuckled. "But he will treat her well if he is smart." He straightened his shoulders. "You wanted to speak to me alone, Beral?"

"Yes." I leaned forward on the spear but stared down and away from David. "Prince Jonathan believes that you will indeed become the next king of Israel," I said. "He says that is the will of Yahweh." I exhaled loudly. "I do not approve of Yahweh's plan, but..." I looked up at him. "I want there to be no animosity between you and me or between our two houses. I say this because I fear that my prince may be right. You may be the next king."

David folded his arms across his chest, his expression unreadable. "There is more, isn't there?"

"Yes," I replied. "You understand that I serve King Saul. I also serve Prince Jonathan."

David nodded, and I continued.

"I hope I never have to raise my hand against you, David, but if I must, I will, and if my prince is right, I would fall—"

"You have nothing to worry about," David interrupted. He looked at me with knitted brows. "It is done. I make the same promise to you that I made to Jonathan. No harm will come to your family or your wife's." He bent to pick up the jug and handed it to me. "In truth, Beral, I have a hope that you would see fit to serve with me one day. You need not fall fighting me."

"I will not leave their service. If you are king, then that means Jonathan is dead. I cannot serve you if that happens, even if I yet live. My only wish is to serve him."

David met my eye as he spoke. "Beral, your life is precious to me. If you ever die in battle, it will not be at my hand."

"Why don't you return with me to Saul's camp? He has invited you back and promised no harm will come to you."

He cocked his head to one side and grinned sadly. "Tell me, Beral, if you were me, would you return to the king's court?"

My mouth opened with nothing to say. I shrugged helplessly.

"There is my answer." David laughed. "You would not place your life in the king's hands either if he feared you as he does me. The spirit that torments him could come back at any time. I have seen it enough already."

I could not disagree with him. I lowered my head for a moment before turning to go back to Saul's camp.

As I walked away, David called to me, "Beral, what of Jonathan? He is well?"

I stopped and looked back. "He is well. The king does not allow him to come with the army when it searches for you."

"Probably a wise decision." He smiled. "Tell Jonathan I wish him good health."

"I will, my lord." I raised the spear in farewell and continued down the slope. When I neared the bottom, a thought shook me. *Had I just called David "my lord"?*

CHAPTER THIRTY

The Philistines assembled and came and set up camp at Shunem,
while Saul gathered all the Israelites and set up camp at Gilboa.

1 Samuel 28:4 NIV

D AVID HAD BEEN RIGHT. SAUL'S amnesty toward him lasted
barely a month until the evil spirit visited the king again.
Then he railed against the son of Jesse.

"I should never have let him slip away from me!" he ranted. "He will
not fool me again. David must die for the sake of Israel!"

The army went out over and over, searching for the fugitive. My
brigade spent countless days tramping like oxen from one reported
sighting to the next, always knowing we would not catch him. A year
passed that way without any further sightings of David.

Otherwise, that year proved to be the happiest of my life. I moved
Liora again to a house next to the vineyard Saul had deeded me. Miriam
came with us, and the two of them discussed things that only women
understand about managing a household, a task that I completely
avoided. Together, they prepared meals better than any I ate at the
king's table.

And the nights... Never before had I lain with a woman who was
willing to love me, and before my Liora, I had not even known that such
a love could happen to a soldier. Yahweh did not bless us with a child
yet, but I felt certain it would happen, because we surely did as much as
we could as often as we could.

Eventually, word came that David had done the unthinkable. Foreign
travelers reported that he and his six hundred were settled at Gath in

Philistine territory and in the service of King Achish, my old foe at the village of Megiddo. They said he led raids against Achish's enemies, but never once did he mount an attack on Israel. The news that David had fled safely out of his reach seemed to dispirit Saul, and he sat on the throne, brooding for hours at a time, no longer caring to send us out on fruitless searches. We later heard that David moved to Ziklag, still a vassal of Achish.

The Philistines themselves were another matter. In late summer of that next year, they swarmed across our borders again, coming up in large numbers from Aphek to the plains of Jezrel at Shunem. Saul gathered up all of Israel's fighting men and went to check the Philistines' advance. He told Jonathan to bring his younger brothers, Abinadab and Malki-Shua, to give them an actual taste of battle. We camped on the forested slopes of Mount Gilboa, close enough to see and be seen.

My blood went weak when I saw the large gathering of enemy forces. Their flanks stretched toward the horizon on each side of us. Hundreds of pennants fluttered in the fitful breeze. They drilled constantly, and drums pounded in their camp as companies of infantry paraded back and forth across our smaller front. Chariots rumbled beyond their camp, the dust rising high into the sky over us. I and other senior commanders met with General Abner at the center of our lines. Saul and Nathon strode up as I arrived. Abner set his mouth in a grim line, but the king turned pale when he looked upon this latest Philistine invasion for the first time.

"What's this? Have they brought their every man and boy to attack us? Who can be left in Gath?" His voice cracked.

"My father, we can defeat the sea people yet again with Yahweh's help," said Jonathan. He stepped forward and thumped his spear butt on the ground. "The pagans cannot stand before Him."

Saul stared at his son. "So do you try to sound like David, son of Jesse, now? Has he addled your mind?" He snorted. "Look at them! Can you even count all of them?" Holding a spear in one hand, the king spread his arms wide to encompass the entire Philistine horde. "We can't be victorious against this many."

I stole a glance at Jonathan. My prince wore the same sober air as Abner. All around me, other commanders looked at each other in dismay. If King Saul, the bravest of Israel, had no heart for this battle, how could we hope to win? Jonathan tapped his spear on the rocks again. "Father, you must ask Yahweh for guidance," he pleaded. "He has saved us before. Surely God will not abandon His people now to die before heathens."

Saul stroked his beard and looked at his oldest son. "Do you think me an impious fool? Of course I will ask Yahweh for victory, and perhaps He will hear me this time, but I doubt it." He spun on his heel to return to his tent behind our lines in the shade of a tall cedar tree. Ben-Ami and Nathon went with him. I could hear him talking to Ben-Ami. "Send the priests to my tent. Get Ahijah."

Ahijah the priest—still in the king's service since Micmash, even after the slaying of Ahimelech and the priests from Nob—came and entered the king's tent as the sun set. A dozen other priests followed. I heard prayers being lifted up during most of the night while the low fire inside the tent cast vague silhouettes on its walls. Figures inside paced and raised their arms to the heavens.

Outside, a little higher up the slope, Zelig and I reclined on our elbows, staring into a small, crackling fire barely kept alive with handfuls of dry twigs and brambles. We listened to the murmurs below us in the tent. From that site, we could see hundreds of Philistine campfires stretching away in the distance.

I sat up and crossed my legs in front of me. "Zelig, how many nights have we spent like this, looking across a valley at enemy campfires?"

Zelig pushed himself up and stared at the Philistine fires for a moment before he answered. "Commander, when I was a younger man, I used to number the battles I fought in and the men I killed." He cleared his throat and spat to one side. "But I lost count somewhere years ago, and now I don't bother to tally them. Truly, I don't know how many times you and I have sat looking at the fires of men meaning to kill us. Philistines? Moabites? Amalekites? It never matters. The number of times never matters either. You and I just fight Israel's enemies whenever we're told to and trust Yahweh for the rest."

"Well said, Zelig. Well said." Jonathan stepped into the firelight with a bundle of sticks. He knelt to place them with our dwindling supply of fuel and then settled cross-legged next to me. He gestured back toward the king's tent. "Is any of that groaning I hear in there going to have an effect on Yahweh?" he asked.

His attitude shocked me. "Of course, sire. You said it yourself. Yahweh doesn't want to abandon Israel. We are His people." Zelig only stared into the fire.

Jonathan smiled sadly and tapped my knee. "That isn't what I asked you. Do you think Yahweh hears my father's prayers?"

"Of course, sire. King Saul is the ruler of Israel. Surely Yahweh listens to him," I said. My voice sounded shrill even to my own ears, and I felt like a young boy caught stealing figs from a neighbor's tree.

"No, Beral," Jonathan answered. "Yahweh listens to a contrite and humble heart. I fear my father has neither."

"Then why did you ask him to pray for guidance?"

He sighed and looked up through tree branches at the night sky. "As a son, I had hoped." He shrugged. "But he said himself that he doubts God will listen. With such an attitude as that, Yahweh will surely turn His face away."

"Are you saying that we will lose this battle, my lord?"

He slapped his knees and rose to his feet. "No. In truth, I don't know what I'm saying. I can only agree with Zelig's words. We fight Israel's enemies and trust Yahweh for the rest." He started to walk away but stopped. "I think we will know by morning if my father is going to get an answer. Rest well tonight." Prince Jonathan left and gradually disappeared in the darkness.

I fell asleep to the sounds of prayer still softly rising from the king's tent.

The priests filed out at dawn, haggard and hollow-eyed. Apparently, Yahweh hadn't responded to Saul's requests during the night, and Ahijah couldn't hide his dejection.

Jonathan approached them to ask, "Did you receive guidance from Yahweh?"

"No, sire. Even the Urim would not give us an answer we could understand," Ahijah mumbled. "God does not hear us today."

My prince's shoulders slumped. He dropped his gaze to the ground. "Very well," he said. He took a deep breath and looked up to see me watching. "It seems we will fight the Philistines alone at first until Yahweh moves to help us."

Those were brave words, but I knew Prince Jonathan, and I heard the uncertainty in his voice.

We readied ourselves for battle while the enemy called out and paraded below us. I inspected each of my companies, searching for any man fearful of what lay ahead. They all met my eyes, some with misgivings, but every one standing firm. When I completed those rounds, I climbed up on a rock outcropping to survey the enemy horde below us.

"The men trust you," said Zelig. He had been at my side while I walked through the ranks and now waited behind me at the base of the rock. "They know that if Commander Beral leads them, they can survive this fight and defeat the Philistines."

I turned to look down at him. "They believe that?" I asked.

"No, Commander, they *know* it."

<hr />

The Philistines chose not to attack just yet. Our spies said that they waited on more chariots coming from other cities besides Gath. Late in the evening, a huge dust cloud from the west closed with their camp. Those chariots had arrived.

The commanders met as usual after dark. General Abner stood at the fire while Katriel loitered at his shoulder. Neither the king nor Jonathan appeared. I wondered what had happened. King Saul had not left his tent all day since the priests had departed in the morning, and I stayed too occupied to notice who came and went there. I also wondered if David camped somewhere below in the midst of the enemy fires.

"The Philistines have been reinforced with two hundred more chariots today," said Abner. "They will surely attack in the morning. Deploy your ranks before dawn to be ready. We will stay up on these slopes. The hill and rocks will keep their horses from closing with us."

We took this in silence. The real danger from chariot forces came from their archers, not from being run down. Abner assigned positions in the line. My brigade, usually in the center, would take the far left side in the morning, a decision I agreed with. We could defilade back better than any other unit if we had to counter an attempt to sweep around our flank. As the war council ended, I slipped my helmet on and started to leave.

"Commander Beral," General Abner called to me.

I stopped and turned back. The general waited for me, wide legged and solid in the firelight, stroking his beard and watching me approach.

I brought a fist to my chest. "You wanted to see me, sire?" I asked.

"No, I don't. King Saul does," he answered. "Come with me."

I followed uneasily. Meetings with the king never boded well for me. Abner stopped at the tent's entrance and let me enter alone. I heard the door flap close behind me.

Low light came from a burning brazier, but it lit the interior enough to show the two people standing there with the king—Ben-Ami and Katriel.

"Come in, Beral," said Saul. He extended his hands to me, palms up in a gesture of friendship.

I crossed the inside space to take his hands in my own and bowed slightly. "Good evening, my king," I said. Smoke made my eyes water.

Saul smiled at my discomfort. "Don't worry, my son. There will be no attempt against David tonight, but I do have another special task for you—you and Ben-Ami." He looked at the guard commander, who appeared confused.

Only Katriel seemed to know what was happening. The aide's jowls rippled as he nodded in agreement with his king.

"Certainly, my king. What is the task?" I asked.

Katriel stepped forward to answer. "Don't worry about that at the moment, but go at once and find some commoner's clothing to wear over your tunics. When you return, hide your swords beneath the cloaks and don't carry spear or shield. You must not look like soldiers tonight."

Ben-Ami and I looked at each other.

"Yes, my lord," I said, directing my gaze back at the king. I hurried out of the smoky tent, followed closely by Ben-Ami.

"What is this about?" he asked, bewilderment evident in his voice as we walked away in the darkness.

"I don't know. Perhaps he wants us to act as spies," I answered. "Do you have an old robe?"

"I think so. You?"

"I can get one. Zelig will know where to find one," I answered. "Let's meet here outside the tent and go in together. I don't want to stay in there alone with the king and Katriel."

He laughed softly. "Yes, my brother, I understand. Katriel is a toothed worm who would eat the insides of men better than himself—a parasite that works best in the dark." He slapped the trunk of a cedar as we passed. "We will meet here at this tree and then go in to face him together."

"A parasite. That is a good likeness." I paused while we continued to walk. "I have a fear that the worm may have already infected our king's mind." I stopped talking, fearful I had already said too much.

A long silence followed, punctuated only by our footsteps before Ben-Ami sighed. "I fear so too, Beral."

We separated to find our apparel, and I looked for Zelig. He sat at a low fire with some of the company commanders, all of them gnawing on the charred remains of a young goat. I took him aside and explained that I needed a common robe or cloak.

"Why is that, Commander?" he asked, scratching his beard.

"The king wants Ben-Ami and me to wear them over our own clothing and to cover our swords. I think he is sending us somewhere tonight."

Zelig tilted his head to the side. "In disguise? Now, why would he want that?" He grunted, a sharp, cynical sound. "I'd wager Katriel is involved in this somehow."

"He is."

"Thought so. Very well, Commander. Take my old laborer's robe. It's dirty and a little foul, but no one would think you an Israelite officer if you wore it."

I went with him to our sleeping site, where he unrolled his pack and shook out a rough woolen garment.

"Try this on," he said.

I couldn't see it clearly in the dark, but Zelig proved only too correct about its odor. It seemed his armpits enveloped me as I slid it over my head.

I coughed. "You will have to air this out when I return," I said. "Do you ever let Jemima wash it?"

"I didn't tell you it was frankincense, did I?" He grinned but then clasped my upper arm and sobered. "Be cautious, Beral. Something smells here besides my old clothing, and I don't trust anything that Katriel has his hand upon."

"Nor do I." I hitched the garment over my sword belt. "You know where to deploy the brigade if I don't get back by morning."

"Yes." Zelig bit his lip, something I had never seen him do before.

I met Ben-Ami back at the cedar tree. He wrinkled his nose as I neared him.

"It's Zelig's," I said.

"Zelig's? I thought it belonged to a wild boar—a dead wild boar."

We entered the king's tent together, and I welcomed the smoky interior, which covered my odor. Saul stood as we lowered the flap behind us. He had on a commoner's robe similar to the ones Ben-Ami and I wore.

"You're back," he said. "Now we can get started."

CHAPTER THIRTY-ONE

*Saul then said to his attendants, "Find me a woman who
is a medium, so I may go and inquire of her."*

1 Samuel 28:7 NIV

NOTHER PERSON WAITED BEHIND SAUL, alongside Katriel. He
came forward when the king beckoned to him.

"This is Tal," Saul said, "our guide tonight."

Tal appeared to be a youth of about fourteen. He had a shrewd look
about him, his cunning eyes taking me in as I studied him. The unruly
hair tangled about his face hadn't seen a grooming comb for a long time,
if ever. He wore a filthy tunic and no sandals.

"Where are we going, sire?" asked Ben-Ami.

"To Endor," replied the king. "I am to meet someone there."

Endor? The small town lay more than an hour's hard walk to the
north. I slid my eyes over to Ben-Ami. He returned my look with a
gesture of helplessness.

"There are horses waiting for all of you outside," said Katriel,
stepping up to Saul's side.

"Excuse me, my lord, but I won't need a horse. I can run." The boy
had a confident air, reminding me of a young David.

I didn't trust him.

The king raised his eyebrows. "Are you sure, lad? I understand it is
a long way."

"Not that far, sire. We will stop well south of the village."

"Very good, then. Lead on, Tal."

We stepped out into cooler fresh air, and Katriel showed us to the
horses. "May Yahweh guide your steps safely back, my king," he said.

I gritted my teeth at his obsequiousness, but King Saul didn't see the fat aide the same way I did.

"Thank you, Katriel," he replied. "We will be back before dawn."

We left Katriel and led the horses quietly outside the encampment before mounting. True to his word, the boy stayed on foot, trotting ahead of us at an amazing pace as the horses followed with a fast, jarring walk. Ben-Ami rode a short distance behind our guide, then the king, and then me. We traveled in starlight, and the others appeared to me as shadows in the night. Clumping hooves became the only sound except for the cries of night creatures. I missed my own horse. The one I rode was infamous among the king's couriers for its especially rough gait, and the severe jolting shook away my curiosity about our errand or its secrecy.

An hour passed before we stopped abruptly. When Tal came back to hold the bridle of the king's horse, I drew alongside to listen.

The boy pointed up the slope of a tall hill on our left and whispered, "She is up there near the top, my king. The way starts there." He pointed out a dim pathway that snaked up the incline. "You will not miss it." He reached out for my bridle too.

I dismounted heavily, grateful to be off that torturous beast. Apparently, Tal would tie the horses while we took the trail upward.

Saul led our ascent. Ben-Ami shrugged at me behind the king's back. Saul didn't speak, and neither his guard commander nor I had any idea what we were doing. *Did King Saul bring us out here with him so he could tryst with a woman?* I didn't like this. I felt for my sword hilt under the robe.

Saul stopped where the ground leveled a bit. He turned around to face us and spoke so softly I strained to hear him. "Soon I am going to consult a medium here. Katriel has assured me this one will be able to do what I ask." He paused, looking about. "Say nothing to me or to her while we are in her presence. This woman must not know who I am."

My jaw dropped, and I stepped back involuntarily before I spoke. "A medium? Sire, Moses outlawed those people who would speak to the dead! Did you not expel them from Israel yourself? A witch should not even be here in our land." My whisper sounded harsh in the quiet night.

Saul straightened and raised his chin. "Apparently this one stayed, and since Yahweh is not answering me, I will consult whomever I choose. Perhaps this will be Yahweh's way to speak." His expression was shrouded in the night, but anger simmered in his voice.

"Are you certain about this, my king?" asked Ben-Ami, much calmer than me. "Moses did say such a practice would defile our people."

"I am king of Israel!" Saul hissed. "I will do what I do. Say no more about this, but just follow me. She can't be much farther." He spun on his heel and started up the winding path again.

Ben-Ami lowered his head to follow. I stood in silence for a moment before I too fell in behind the king. I would have felt better if that climb actually were a sexual visit for him.

Soon I could see tiny lights ahead of us. As we neared, I gradually made out a crude stone hut, built against the slope of the hillside and looking like a pile of rocks covered with a roof. The lights came through small cracks in the chinking.

Saul put his hand out to stop us. "This must be her home," he whispered. "Remember… say nothing." He went to the doorway set into the facing rock wall and rapped on the rough wood.

After a long moment, I heard a scraping step inside as someone labored to the door.

"Who is there?" called an old woman, her voice watery with phlegm. "You had best beware if you mean me harm. I have power here."

"We will not bring you trouble, woman. I only need to consult with you. I have silver for your payment," answered Saul, his head close to the door.

The woman paused before she lifted the bar on the inside. The door sagged in wearily. I gripped my sword under the robe.

"Come in, then, and state your need." Her voice rasped.

We filed into a room with a ceiling so low I had to duck to fit. Our tall king could have thrust his head into the thatched roof if he stood upright. Instead, he bent awkwardly at the waist. Burning candles perched in nooks fashioned into the wall, making the room bright after the darkness outside. A platter with a half-eaten coney sat on a table against a side wall. Older scraps of food and bones were heaped on the dirt floor next to the table, scraped there from previous meals. The putrid pile added to the stench of the crowded room. In there, Zelig's robe smelled sweet as cedar shavings.

Much of the foul odor came from the woman herself. She hadn't cleaned either her body or her clothing in a very long time. I also suspected there was a full chamber pot somewhere nearby. Unkempt and unclean, she had the stooped posture of many old women, head thrust forward and back bent. Gray hair frizzed out in every direction, much of it falling over watery dark eyes.

She shuffled back away from us to stand near a rear door. "Tell me what it is you wish, and I will see if I can grant it."

Beads of sweat covered Saul's face, and he clasped his hands together in front. He darted a quick look at me before he spoke. "Consult a spirit for me," he said, "and bring up for me the one I name."

The woman wagged her head side to side. "Don't you know what Saul has done? He has driven out mediums and those who speak with the spirits from Israel. Are you setting a trap for me to bring about my death?"

Saul sank to one knee. "As surely as the Lord God of Israel lives, you shall not be punished for doing this," he said. "And I have a payment for you." He drew out a pouch from his robe and poured its contents into his hand. Silver coins gleamed in the flickering light.

The woman limped forward cautiously, eyes bright with interest. She reached out for the coins.

"Give them to me," she croaked.

The king refilled the pouch and placed it in her hand.

She opened it to look inside and jingled the coins. "This will do." Raising her gaze to Saul, she asked, "And whom shall I bring up for you?"

"Bring up Samuel."

The old hag held the pouch to her nose and sniffed at its contents while she thought. "Very well, then," she said. "Wait here while I prepare the room, then come in when I call for you." She turned her back to us and limped to the rear door, glancing back furtively at us before she opened it and passed through.

I knew then that the old woman was a fraud. My father had once warned me about magical tricksters who "prepared the room." He and I were sitting on a hillside overlooking Lo Debar when I asked him about the traveling mediums who used to stop in our village on occasion in those days.

"My son," he said, "they set up illusions in a darkened room to impress you—polished mirrors to reflect false images and things that move when an unseen black thread is pulled. The best ones will even create a sound to act as a spirit's voice. Beware of such magicians."

"Then, Father, are any of them truly in touch with the spirit world?" I asked.

He shook his head. "I don't think so. They only exist to take the money of unsuspecting fools. Even if one could reach the dead, it is a matter best left alone by us."

"How do you know all of this?" I asked.

He smiled and looked off at the hills. "I was not always as wise as I appear to be now."

That conversation had happened years before, when I was a youth. That night in the odious hovel, I ached to give my king the same advice, but I knew I wouldn't. Saul *wanted* to believe the bent little woman could help him, and nothing I could say would change that. He stared at the rear door with no thought for anything else, looking like a hound waiting to hear its master's returning step. His hands twitched except when he sleeved away the sweat on his brow. Ben-Ami and I shared a silent look.

Finally a muffled voice came through the door. "You may enter. Keep your hands together and touch nothing."

Saul led the way as we dutifully placed our palms together before passing into the next room. It felt cooler than the front of the hut. I realized it wasn't a room at all. The back of the hut had been built against a cave entrance in the hillside, a cavern opening up larger and higher than the shack itself. Two candles, set far apart on each side of the chamber, barely lit some of its interior. They flickered in the barest of breezes passing across my face, indicating another opening somewhere. The smell was better there, but I could still detect the woman's presence.

Her voice came from the darkness ahead. "There are stones before you. Sit there."

I made out the dim outlines of several large boulders arranged around an open space in front of us. We groped our way to them and sat down with the king between Ben-Ami and me. As my eyes grew accustomed to the low light, I could see the woman seated in an armchair, facing us across an expanse of what looked like white sand.

"Tell me again," she said. "Who is it you would have me bring here?"

Saul cleared his throat. "Samuel the prophet," he answered.

"Ah yes… Samuel. I have spoken with him many times already since his death," she said. "Stay quiet here until I speak to you."

The old hag rocked side to side then started a circular swaying of her torso. She moaned nonsensical words in a grating voice that reminded me of a working millstone. Ben-Ami glanced at me behind Saul's back while she babbled. My eyes searched the dark cavern, looking for hidden mirrors and threads. The king himself watched intently as the medium raised her wrinkled hands and face to the ceiling.

She spoke in Hebrew again. "Come forth, Samuel. Come across from the land of the undead. Speak to us." She lowered her arms and stretched them to her front. "Now!" she shouted and clapped once. A small flame suddenly flickered in the sand at her feet.

Had I seen her flick something toward that spot when she clapped? I couldn't be certain. The fire caused the hairs on my arm to stand up even though I knew everything the woman did consisted of trickery.

The woman bowed from the waist to the burning sand. She cupped her ears as though listening to a very faint noise. "Yes?" she asked. "It is you, Samuel?" I became aware of another low moan that gradually rose in volume. The voice seemed to come from the darkness behind her, yet the medium concentrated on the low fire in front of her. To me, the moan sounded like a man younger than Samuel had been at his death, and I wondered where Tal had gone. Saul looked transfixed.

"Ahhh!" The woman exclaimed in surprise. She leapt to her feet, her eyes bulging in shock. In the center of the sandy area between her and us, a soft bubbling stirred the sand like spring water bursting through. She screamed at the top of her voice and stepped back, knocking over the chair. She pointed a bony finger at the king. "You tricked me! You are Saul! Why did you do this?" she blubbered.

Her wailing appeared to irritate Saul. "Don't be afraid, woman. Tell me what you see," he ordered.

The medium fell to her knees. "I see a spirit coming up out of the ground," she whimpered.

Something did begin to rise up through the moving sand at that moment. A pale-gray wisp rose slowly and silently like smoke to the height of a man before it stopped and floated in the air just above the ground. It shimmered and swayed, glowing inside itself but casting no light in the cave. The bottom half swirled like a pennant in the breeze. I think I could have put my hand through it, yet it was no magician's illusion.

"And what kind of spirit is this?" Saul's voice shook even while he demanded an answer.

"It's an old man wearing a robe," she cried before lying facedown to hide herself, arms covering her head. Her whole body trembled. Clearly, she had not expected this sort of visitation.

Saul stood. "It is Samuel," he said. He bowed to the figure, now vaguely outlined with a head and torso. Then the king also stretched out prostrate on the ground.

A rumbling sound filled the chamber. Without knowing why, I sensed that that outline of a man was questioning us, but in a language that only Saul seemed to comprehend. He rose to his knees, his arms outstretched.

"I am in great distress," he said. "The Philistines are coming against me. I have prayed to Yahweh but received no answer, either through the prophets or my dreams. He has turned away from me, and so I come to you. Tell me what to do."

The figure flashed in a great white light then darkened. The rumbling intensified into a growl that vibrated through my sandals and the rock I sat on. Dust and dirt shook down off the walls of the cave. The ominous menace there was like a pride of lionesses, and my bravery turned to water. I looked over at Ben-Ami, who was as frightened as myself.

The angry grumbling noise dragged on longer than a priest's prayer while quick little red flashes shot through the outline. Finally, Saul fell forward on his face once more, and everything stopped. The figure that was Samuel went pale again and began to slip back into the sand, sinking down as deliberately as it had come up. I sat motionless in the low light cast by the medium's fire, the two candles having been put out by cascading dirt.

CHAPTER THIRTY-TWO

The woman set [the fattened calf] before Saul and his
men... That same night they got up and left.

1 Samuel 28:25 NIV

THE FALSE WITCH MOVED FIRST. She came to her knees and peered about. "I think it is gone," she muttered.

When I reached over to tap Ben-Ami, he jerked at my touch. "Damn, Beral!" he gasped. "You scared me like that."

He and I stood to relight the candles from the dying fire. The old woman got up and tottered around the spot where Samuel had disappeared to look at Saul in the dim light. He lay motionless with his face in the sand.

"Sire, you must get up. The prophet is gone. It is over," she said. When the king didn't seem to hear her, she gently shook his shoulder.

"Huh?" Saul rolled onto his side, moving away from her. I held my candle up and saw his wild expression and his hair, which he had twisted into tangled knots. "Why do you bother me, woman? Leave me alone," he snarled.

"Sire, it is safe now, but you must get up. Samuel may return," she answered.

"He may return?" Saul whimpered like a child. He sat up and climbed to his feet, aided by Ben-Ami. "Yes, I should go. I have to go." He took a step and collapsed onto Ben-Ami. I hurried to place his other arm over my shoulders. He sagged between us, unable to walk by himself.

"Here. Bring him into the house," the old crone urged as she limped to open the door. "This way."

We carried our king back into the odorous room, where we sat him down on the floor. Tal was already there and had banked a large fire in the hearth. He looked frightened and stepped aside for us.

Saul slumped forward, hair covering his face. "Water," he croaked. The woman bustled to bring him a cup she filled from a bucket on the floor.

"My king," she said, "I see you are disturbed by the prophet's visit and his words to you, but you should eat now. I fear you are greatly weakened."

Saul gulped the water and set the cup down. His head drooped to his chest. "I don't care," he said. "Leave me alone."

But the woman persisted. "Look," she said, "I have done what you asked and at great risk to myself. Now, I only ask you to let me feed you. Gather your strength and return to your army. Otherwise, Samuel may come back." She shot a glance at the closed door to the cave.

Saul leaned back to roll his eyes at the low-hanging ceiling. "No, I will not eat."

"Sire, you must eat something. We have a long ride back, and Israel needs your strength," Ben-Ami pleaded. He sank to one knee before Saul. "Please, my lord."

The king's head jerked with a grim chuckle. "Israel needs me? You did not hear Samuel just now? Israel does not need me." His words were bitter.

I went to a knee beside Ben-Ami. "My king, this nation does need you. We need our king to lead against the Philistines." I slowed my words to be deliberate. "And even if you feel that Yahweh has turned His back on you, He still expects you to stand at our front. Israel expects that too. I expect it." I looked at Ben-Ami. "And so does the captain of your guard."

Saul regarded me curiously for a moment. I feared I had said too much.

He sighed. "You're right, of course, Beral. I have a duty. If I die, I die as a king." He sat up straight. "Very well, then. Woman, where is my food?"

The medium bowed. "Of course, my king. The boy will butcher the calf right now."

She and Tal exchanged a look with meaning beyond our meal. He

215

backed out of the room, watching all of us with bright, birdlike eyes, but I was too tired and shaken to care about private thoughts between those two. I helped Saul up onto a filthy couch. He leaned back and closed his eyes while the woman kneaded bread. Ben-Ami and I stayed awake to watch her.

Tal brought in a hindquarter to present to the medium before he disappeared outside again. She worked efficiently, and in a surprisingly short time, we were eating warm bread and the charred meat of a fattened calf. All of us felt better. The events of the cave seemed far in the past. King Saul stood up and bumped against a ceiling beam.

"It's time to go," he said, but his eyes still looked dull.

We stepped out into fresh air with no farewell to the witch. She watched silently as we departed, her dark eyes darting about and regarding us in the same fearful way as Tal. I looked at the night sky and saw the time was shortly past midnight. We could still get back to camp early enough to sleep a short while before dawn.

Ben-Ami led the way down the path while I trailed at our rear, both of us wearing our swords openly. When we reached the bottom, droppings showed where the horses had been tied, but they were gone. I became instantly alert, certain this was no accident.

"This is treachery," whispered Ben-Ami. "Should we return to the hut?"

"No," I replied, "that might be what they would expect. We should leave this place quickly instead. We'll not be safe until we reach camp."

We looked at Saul, but he seemed uninterested, staring about at the stars.

Ben-Ami turned his head left and right. "Agreed. Let's be off."

We wanted to hurry, to jog back to the army, but the king was still acting detached from our situation. He walked at an unhurried pace, murmuring to himself in a voice so low I couldn't understand him. Our gentle urgings had no effect. I realized we might barely return by sunrise.

We had scarcely traveled fifty paces when a sharp rap echoed in front of us. Ben-Ami heard it too. He crouched with his sword drawn in the fighting stance of a swordsman without his shield. I put a hand to my ear. It had sounded like my oaken staff knocking skulls. I heard it again, then other noises. Sandals crunched on the hillside above. Suddenly the clash of swords rang out. Shouts of alarm and screams rose in front of us, the sounds of men fighting.

"Let's go!" I shouted. Saul shook himself out of his stupor, and we turned around to run away from the conflict, but two armed figures stepped out into the gray starlight.

"Hold," one said. "You are safe."

I knew that tall posture and that voice. "My lord?" I gasped. "Jonathan?"

With Herzi following close behind, Jonathan closed with his long strides and embraced the king. "My father, are you all right?"

Saul nodded. "Yes, I am unhurt."

Jonathan clasped my arm and then Ben-Ami's. He pointed his sword toward the sounds of the fighting on the hillside ahead of us. "Renegades—Hebrew bandits. About ten of them who thought to make their fortune by presenting Israel's king to the Philistines."

The din quieted as we listened in the darkness. It ended with a scream abruptly cut off, no doubt by a slashed throat.

Openmouthed, I turned to Jonathan. "How did you know? How did you get—"

"We followed you," Jonathan interrupted. "Zelig was concerned that my father would go off on some night errand without his guards." He gestured at figures now appearing on the road and walking toward us. "He told me, and I brought them. These are your men, Ben-Ami, returning from the surprise they sprang on those who would have set upon you."

"My men, sire?"

"Yes. Who better to protect the king?" Jonathan smiled. "We found your horses too. The bandits had moved them to another place. I suggest that you three mount and get back to the army quickly. We will be along soon."

"The danger here is past?" asked Ben-Ami as our horses were led up.

"I am certain of it," replied Jonathan, but he was watching Saul anxiously. "My father, are you truly all right?"

Saul was staring at the sky once more, nodding to himself. "These were not Philistines," he muttered. "No, I shall not die at their hands."

He inhaled deeply and returned his eldest's stare. "I am well, my son. Yes, we should be off. Thank you for your actions on my behalf."

I climbed up onto my rough ride back to our encampment, already dreading the experience to come. I leaned over to Jonathan. "Your father was betrayed tonight. An old hag lives in a stone hut near the top of that trail." I pointed out the pathway we'd taken earlier. "She is a witch."

Jonathan's eyes widened. "A witch? This is the witch of Endor? Why would you come to her?"

I shrugged and cocked my head at the king, sitting astride his horse ahead of me.

My prince saw the look, and his face dropped. "I see."

"There will be a youth with her, perhaps her grandson. Kill them both, my lord."

"I will," said Jonathan. He stepped back. "Now go, Beral. Take my father back safely. And Beral... Get rid of that stinking robe."

The horses could navigate in the darkness, so Ben-Ami dug his heels in to lead us back at a trot. I could not have suffered more if I had been bounced up and down on a wooden beam all the way. We startled the camp's watch when we arrived in the blackest time of night. Servants rushed to take our bridles, and I was happy to slide from that saddle. My back ached. I groaned to myself as I hobbled through camp to my sleeping site. When I sank down for an hour's rest, Zelig rolled to face me across the dying embers of our fire.

"I thought it was you," he said. "You're right about my robe. I should have Jemima wash it."

"I'm getting used to it,'" I replied, slipping the garment over my head to set it aside with my gear.

He rose to one elbow. "Was I a silly old woman to worry about the king?"

"No, you weren't, Zelig. In truth, you probably saved his life and ours tonight."

"What happened?"

"Do you recall those rumors about a witch—a medium—hiding at Endor? Well, those rumors were true. Saul went to see her."

Zelig bolted upright. "The king consulted a witch?"

I sat up too. "Ben-Ami and I were there. It's true."

218

"Why would he do that?" Zelig scratched his head. "It isn't right."

"No, it's not right, but King Saul feels that Yahweh has left him. He wanted the medium to conjure up Samuel to help him," I said. "The old faker surprised herself by actually bringing the prophet to us. He was real too—not a trick."

Zelig stared at me. "What did he say?"

"I don't know. The ground shook when he spoke. I think only Saul understood him. Whatever the message, it scared Saul... I know I was so scared I thought I would piss myself."

"No matter, in that robe of mine." He rubbed his face. "So how did I save your life and the king's?"

"That false medium arranged to have bandits attack us when we returned, but Prince Jonathan and the guards came across them first. They killed the bandits, and by now, they've taken care of her and her assistant too."

"False medium? You said Samuel's appearance was real."

"Oh, it was! But it wasn't because of her powers. You should have heard her scream when he came up out of the ground. I believe Yahweh Himself sent the prophet to Saul."

Zelig nodded and twisted a finger in his ear. "And you think that his message was not good."

"It didn't seem so to the king. He is truly frightened," I replied. "I think this coming battle will go badly for us."

"You may be right. All the more reason to rest now." He lay back under a blanket.

I lay down on my back and stared at the stars, unable to sleep.

After a moment, Zelig spoke quietly. "Commander."

"Yes?"

"Why don't you throw that robe on the fire?"

CHAPTER THIRTY-THREE

Now the Philistines fought against Israel...

1 Samuel 31:1a NIV

I HAD SCARCELY FALLEN ASLEEP WHEN the stirring army roused me again. Men were moving all about me on the forested slope. Shouts went back and forth.

A familiar voice spoke much nearer. "Rise up, Commander. God has given us one more day and one more chance to serve Him." Zelig stood over me, resting his spear on the ground. "And General Abner is calling for all his commanders to meet in council."

I opened my eyes enough to see that the night still held sway over us, dawn being at least an hour away. Grunting, I labored to my feet and peered around. Mazal waited with my sword belt in the dim starlight.

"Let me empty my bladder first," I said, stumbling to the tree we had designated for that task. I leaned one hand against the trunk while I tried to shake off the fatigued stupor in my head. *Did last night really happen?* When I finished, Mazal strapped my sword onto me and adjusted the leather breastplate. He followed Zelig and me to Abner's campsite. We all chewed dried goat meat on the way.

At Abner's fire, commanders stared glumly at each other without speaking. It looked as though nobody had slept any better than I. We stepped aside in silence to let Abner walk through to the center space. He paced around the fire as he spoke, and sparks crackled into the night sky behind him. "Commanders, our plans are unchanged. Deploy as I said yesterday. We stay up on this slope," he said, sweeping an arm across our front. "If the Philistines want to fight, they will have to come uphill and into the trees. Their chariots will be useless."

Men murmured approval. Those were sound enough tactics against the enemy we faced. Taking away the Philistine advantage of chariots would help, although our army would still be greatly outnumbered.

General Abner planted his feet and waited for silence. "Do any of you doubt that we can defeat these pagans once more? If you have doubts, speak them now. I would hear them."

"Is King Saul going to lead us?" Jeronn, now in command of his own brigade, asked the question.

"Of course the king of Israel will lead. He fights more bravely than any of us," Abner replied, perhaps a little too vehemently.

"Then where is he? And where is Prince Jonathan?" someone else asked.

Abner glanced at me before he answered.

I gave him a curt nod.

"The king will be here. He has never failed us," Abner said.

"I am here now. Who dares to question me?" King Saul's voice bawled from the darkness behind us. He strode into the light with Nathon at his back. "Who dares?" he repeated.

Men looked at the ground, and no one spoke.

Saul moved his gaze around the circle. "Very well. Get your units to their positions. I will fight in the center with your brigade, Jeronn. Then you will be able to see where I am."

"And me as well!" Jonathan shouted as he walked into the circle to stand next to his father.

His clothes were covered with dust, and I knew he had just arrived from the long Endor march. I caught his eye, and he nodded. *The witch is dead.*

"Does anyone doubt me too?" he asked, turning his attention to the other officers. "Do any of you doubt my father or me?"

"No!" we cheered in response.

The king had shaken off his depression from the night encounter with the medium. He and Jonathan together in the firelight looked fierce as she-bears.

"Then let's be about this business!" Saul bellowed. "Yahweh waits for us, but the sunrise doesn't. Move to your positions."

We roared in reply and went to our units.

Zelig took a hurried count from the company commanders. They stood ready, every man present. I moved us, clanking and stumbling in the night, down the slope to where the forest thinned away. There, my ten companies stood shield to shield in a line that snaked from Jeronn's center brigade back into the tree line on the left flank. We waited in silence, but I could hear militia units still organizing behind us and trying to find their positions in the darkness. The part-time soldiers had little experience at maneuvering, so Abner placed them at our rear as a reserve.

Down on the valley floor, the Philistines were already active as well. Hundreds of torches burned in the blackness below us. The rumbling of chariots took over the night sounds.

I turned to Zelig, beside me. "Give the men 'rest.' Nothing's going to happen until we can see each other."

He put a fist to his chest before he went along our front rank, telling the companies to stand at ease. I studied the movements of the Philistine torches, trying to pick out their deployments. Their main lines had moved forward to about three bowshots away in the dark. Large, rapidly moving clusters of lights gathered on each side, far beyond our own flanks. I knew those would be chariots.

We had received one piece of good news. Spies reported that David did not march with the Philistine army that day. Achish had sent him and his men back to his town of Ziklag at the insistence of the other Philistine commanders. They still did not trust him. Knowing that we would not be fighting against fellow Israelites—especially David— cheered all of us a little.

The blackness gradually turned gray. Once the eastern skyline held a pink hue, I could see our ranks. Men picked up shields and spears. They coughed and spat, but all eyes stayed fixed on the scene in front of us. Some shivered in the cool air. I recognized the voices of squad leaders straightening the lines as I began to walk across our front.

"Be sure to eat. Open your bags and eat what you have. There is a long day ahead of us," I shouted. I chewed more of the tough goat meat as an example. "I trust your water bags are full." I knew frightened and nervous men forget to eat, and when their knees go weak at the sight of an enemy, it's made worse if they're hungry.

Philistine drums started just as the sun came up. A large number of them pounded away behind the center of their army while smoke from snuffed torches hung over their lines like black fog. Weapons and armor gleamed in the growing morning light. The sea people couldn't stay still. They practically quivered with anticipation, so confident were they. Constant murmuring came from their lines, occasionally interrupted with laughter.

I looked at the two armies. We were outnumbered three or four to one, but we held the high ground on the slopes of Mt. Gilboa. With the Philistine chariots taken out of the battle and turned into spectators, our shield wall could hold, and we could win the day. I felt confident my brigade would hold, but I worried about the center—Jeronn's brigade— where King Saul would be. I could see the king off to my right, standing just outside the trees, surrounded by Ben-Ami and his guards. Abinadab and Malki-Shua, getting a first taste of battle, hovered near their father. I shook my head at the sight. Saul wore his crown and gold armbands as usual. That and the princes' bright red-and-purple clothing would certainly tempt the enemy archers. Jonathan would be with his brigade, far away on our right flank.

The drums stopped, and trumpets blew. At that signal, the enemy chariots on each flank began to move. I expected them to mass at the rear as a reaction force, but instead the two horse-drawn bodies converged toward the center on the flat ground between our lines. They met and passed by each other at a slow-footed parade clop. I watched their lead drivers skillfully swerving at the last instant to avoid a mass entanglement in front of us. This was no accidental movement—it had been planned. The chariot columns reached the opposite ends of their army's massed infantry and wheeled around. A huge cry went up from the Philistine spearmen, and they beat iron weapons against their shields.

I tensed, thinking that would be the charge, but nothing happened. The noise subsided, and the chariots repeated their maneuver. That time, they crossed much closer to us at the base of the mountain. The archers in each vehicle lobbed arrows at extreme range up toward our center. They had obviously seen our king's position, but Ben-Ami's guards deflected the few that reached there. Saul stood untouched and proud. The pagan infantry roared again when the horsemen completed that second crossing.

My spearmen stared at the chariots as they began to go by a third time. So far the Philistines had only flung a few ineffective arrows and a lot of dust into the air, yet the sight and sounds of hundreds of war machines made an impression. I could feel the ground tremble at the sheer number of hooves and wheels below us on the valley floor. The chariots bounced over rocky ground, shaking the crews side to side. Their spoked wooden wheels would smash if they turned to charge uphill through the boulders on this mountain.

"Be of good cheer, men," I shouted. "Those painted wagons are only fish. They can't come up here on the shore to fight, so enjoy the show they perform for us."

Men laughed, and I heard them passing on my words to those who hadn't heard me.

My words were braver than I felt. I looked at Zelig. He leaned on his spear, chewing thoughtfully on a twig.

"This is a feint," I said. "Do you see the quivers on their chariots? They loose only a few at us, but those quivers are packed tight with arrows."

"Aye, Commander, I saw that," he replied. "Those chariots expect more action than this." He blew out the twig. "Much more than this."

By the fourth parade-ground pass, my troops were unimpressed. They started to cheer sarcastically. "Come to us, fish," they jeered. "We'll roast you on a spit." Nobody had been hit by an arrow, and their spirits were high. I still wondered what the Philistines intended. Achish commanded their army. He would not put his forces on display here for our benefit. I thought of how he had tricked me that day at Megiddo—how his forces held our attention while he outflanked us on the rocks above.

Activity stirred at the center of our line. Abner had brought up a detachment of sixty archers and slingers and positioned them in the front rank so that, when the Philistines began to cross, we responded with volleys of our own. We held the higher position and stood on solid footing, so our accuracy proved better than the men in the jolting chariots. Arrows and stones pelted them. Horses whinnied and jumped as they were hit, twitching feathered shafts sticking out from their flesh like banners. The charioteers displayed considerable skill in keeping wounded teams under control. One man toppled out of the back of his chariot to lie still on the ground. None of the vehicles bolted, but they all finished at the trot, hurrying over the dead body of their comrade.

Our lines roared. Cries of "Fish! Fish!" filled the air. "Come let the crocodiles eat you!" the spearmen yelled.

The enemy chariots retreated behind the infantry flanks and stayed there. Spearmen cheered our archers who had driven them back. The Philistine drums, which stayed silent during the chariots' displays, began again in a fast staccato. To my amazement, the enemy ranks started backing away, stepping in unison to the drumbeat. I had never seen the sea people maneuver that way before. The massive squares of heavy infantry got a little entangled, but, overall, it was done well. They halted about half a bowshot farther away. Our soldiers went wild with glee.

"What do you think of that, Zelig?" I asked.

The old warrior let his mouth curl up at the edges. "I think, Commander, that King Achish must have watched our movements very carefully that time at Megiddo." He lifted his chin at the Philistine army. "They try to move like our crocs, and they do it too—just not as well."

"Um..."

He turned toward me. "I know that sound in your voice, Commander. What is it you see?"

I pulled at my ear. "Tell me, Zelig. Why would Achish decide to pull his lines back? They shoot a few arrows at us, then everybody retreats when we stick some horses and kill one man." I gestured at the crumpled body of the dead Philistine below us. "The infantry were already well out of bow range. Why do you think they would go still farther back?"

Zelig never took his eyes from the Philistine army as he replied. "It's not so hard a puzzle, is it, Commander? This was all staged. The chariots feint, and then they all fall back, hoping we'll come down after them." He shook his head. "Achish would be delighted at that—catching us out in the open ground there." He paused and rubbed his beard while he looked toward the center of our line. "We are blessed that General Abner leads us. This won't work with him."

"No," I agreed. "Abner is no fool."

"Sire, a messenger comes," said Mazal, his gaze on a courier running toward us from the center.

I recognized the youth as one of the king's household servants, not a military aide.

"Commander Beral, you are to make ready to move your companies forward when King Saul signals you. The signal will be his raised pennant." The young man blurted his message and stepped back. He drew in great gulps of air as he trembled with excitement.

"Hold on. Hold on, boy. The king wants me to deploy farther down this slope? Where do I stop? Is everyone moving?" I reached out and laid a hand on his shoulder. "Calm yourself. Are you *certain* the orders you were to bring me said for this brigade to move forward?"

"No—I mean *yes*, Commander. You are to go forward when King Saul signals. The signal will be a raised pennant. That's what he told me, sire." The flustered young servant clasped his hands together. "I swear an oath to Yahweh. That's what he told me to tell you."

"*Who* told you this?" Zelig came forward and thrust his face within a hand's breath of the boy. "Was it General Abner? Did Abner send this order?"

The messenger shook even more, a little basket of wheat being ground between two millstones. "No, my lord," he replied. "King Saul himself sent me."

"Why didn't he send a military courier?" I asked.

"General Abner refused to have them carry the order, either to you or Prince Jonathan," the servant answered. "The king sent me instead."

"He *refused*?" My mouth dropped open.

"Yes, sire. That is all I know, sire. Please, may I return now?"

"Go."

Relief plain on his face, the boy turned and ran back toward the center. Spearmen watched him leave, knowing orders for them would be coming from me soon. Zelig and I stared at each other.

"Abner is no fool," I said.

He nodded. "True, but he takes orders from the king. Saul is doing this."

"He can't defy the king's command. That might be a fool's act," I answered.

"And Abner is no fool," Zelig replied. He scratched his armpit and stared at the ground.

I looked toward where Saul and Abner were positioned. I couldn't distinguish anything except the two princes' colored cloaks. "I am going over there," I said to Zelig. "This needs to be clear. Take command until I return."

"Very well, Commander." He bumped a fist to his breastplate. "What do I do if a signal is hoisted to move before you come back?"

"Do as it commands."

CHAPTER THIRTY-FOUR

The Philistines pressed hard after Saul and his sons...

1 Samuel 31:2a NIV

MAZAL AND I SCRAMBLED ACROSS the face of the hillside, staying in the tree line as much as possible. Rocks tumbled and rolled down the slope under our feet. Militia standing in the shade eyed us as we passed.

When we neared the king's position, I heard raised voices before I could see the speakers. I burst out of the trees next to a group of aides and guards clustered behind our massed line of spearmen. King Saul stood in the middle with his arms crossed, looking furious. General Abner looked just as angry, his jaw clenching and unclenching while he stared boldly back at the king. The two younger princes were there, scared and looking like wilted flowers in their colorful robes.

To my surprise, Prince Jonathan had come to the command center too. He held his helmet under his arm while he addressed his father. "My lord, please. Going down to meet the Philistines would be what they want. Up here, we can repel them over and over until they tire of their losses and go home." His voice carried an air of pleading.

"And when they go home, they replenish and come back to invade us again!" Saul answered. "No! This must be the way. We finish the struggle with them today!" He saw me when I entered the circle about him and gave me a cold smile. "Ah, Commander Beral, I suppose you've come to add your weight to these dogs arguing against me?"

"My king, I—"

"Silence! Say no more. I can read your face, Beral, son of Ammiel.

You also are too frightened to advance on the enemy. You come to ask me to call off the advance," Saul thundered.

Jonathan stepped up beside me. "Father, Beral doesn't deserve these words you hurl at him. He is the bravest commander in your army—"

"You keep silent as well, you son of a perverse woman. You are all cowards today. Whatever you did before in my service has made all of you limp today, like so many empty water bags. You're of little use to me," Saul retorted.

Abner stiffened and raised his chin. Jonathan slowly shook his head. The king's words were unfair, and they bit deep.

I cleared my throat and spoke. "My king, we fear no heathen force. We will do as you command, but sire, do you think this is wise after the message you received last night?"

Saul's eyes rounded, and his face drained of color. "Enough!" he roared. "Say nothing more of that! Go to your posts, all of you, and prepare to carry out my command."

Abner said, "My king, I cannot do this. Your order will bring us to ruin. I cannot follow it." Tears glistened on his cheeks.

"Very well, Abner. Then you are no longer the general of this army. Stay up here in the trees with the tribal forces." Saul spoke coolly, but I knew that Abner would pay much more for his refusal later. Saul looked around at the group. "Katriel, you are now general of my army. You others will take your directions from him."

Katriel's face froze in shock. "Y-Yes, my king," he stammered.

I sucked in my breath. The king had just put an ass into the harness of a war chariot. Abner stepped back as if struck in the face. His mouth opened and shut once. Someone behind me groaned.

Saul ignored all of us and turned to his armor bearer. "Bring my shield," he barked.

Nathon hurried forward to fasten Saul's battle shield onto the king's arm. His hands shook as he fumbled with the fittings while Saul stood impervious to our stares. I caught Jonathan's eye and mouthed, *What do we do?* My prince gazed back for a moment before he shook his head and dropped his eyes. He put a finger alongside his nose.

"It is God's will," he muttered. "This has to come to pass."

The Philistine drums pounded again. At that sound, the king drew himself up to his full height and looked over the heads of lesser men to the valley floor. "See!" he said triumphantly. "They're still withdrawing. Look at them!" The pagan infantry did edge backward again, away from us. "General, give the order to advance. Keep the brigades in contact with each other," Saul called out. He pointed at Katriel. "You!" he shouted.

Our new general of the army appeared startled. "Y-Yes, my king." He looked about for an aide. "You there, have the king's pennant raised. We will advance."

"But, *General*, shouldn't you wait until we are back at our commands before we try to move?" asked Jeronn. Contempt showed through his question like the sheen of skin through thinning hair.

Katriel licked his lips. "Of course," he said. "That was my intention."

I walked back to my brigade in no hurry, trying not to speculate on what was about to happen. Israel had certainly defeated its enemies before when outnumbered, but then we'd always had Yahweh with us. On this day, I couldn't be sure, for King Saul's evil spirit had possession of him again. Did that mean Yahweh had turned His back on us all? *And what exactly did the spirit of Samuel say to Saul last night?*

Zelig waited for me behind the center of our brigade, his raised eyebrows almost hidden under the visor of his scarred helmet. "Well?" he said.

"Get the companies ready. We go down to the plain when the signal is hoisted," I answered. "Keep the lines as straight as you can in these rocks. We'll re-form at the bottom."

"General Abner agreed to this?" Zelig asked.

"Abner is no longer our general. We will be getting our orders from General Katriel."

"*General* Katriel?" I had never seen Zelig so shocked before, and I nearly smiled at his wide eyes.

"That is what I said."

The old veteran took a deep breath. He turned to stare down at the Philistine horde, which had stopped backing away. Now they shuffled and swayed side to side in some primitive battle dance while their drums pounded. Dust swirled and hung over them, the early morning still without a breeze.

"Well, that's it, then. I hope we kill a lot of them first," Zelig said. He drove his spear point into the ground.

"I am sure we will," I answered.

The king's banner rose above the command site. His crown glinted in the morning sun as he took his place in the front rank.

Zelig and I shouted out the familiar orders to our companies, "Advance. Shield to shield. Spears out."

Slowly, with the stiffness of a man just awakened, we started our descent down the mountain. The spearmen moved purposefully and with confidence, most of them unaware we were being led by a spirit-possessed king with an arrogant incompetent for his general.

I half slid and half walked on the loose scree of Mt. Gilboa, pained to see how difficult it would have been for the Philistines to charge us up here if we'd only held our positions. The entire army reached the bottom in a haphazard jumble.

"Forward!" Someone shouted the order up and down the line.

I looked over at Saul's position to see Katriel holding his spear aloft and waving his arm, urging us to advance. The fool wasn't giving us time to form our line properly.

"Zelig," I shouted, "get the left flank companies aligned. I'll take the right."

He nodded and left to trot along the moving ranks. I went the other direction, finding each company commander already correcting his line even as we marched. "Good work." I patted Yair's shoulder. "You have the centermost company. Put them in ranks four deep. Don't let a gap open up between you and the next brigade."

"Yes, Commander. Are we attacking the Philistines?" Yair asked. His open-eyed stare conveyed disbelief.

"Yes, and we can defeat them with the help of Yahweh..." We walked a few more steps. "If it's His will," I muttered. He looked at me sharply, and I slapped his shoulder again. "Now, get your men straightened and do your best. I'll see we survive this."

"Yes, Commander."

The army kept walking forward as I hurried back to the brigade's center, wishing I were as confident as I had tried to sound for Yair. Another house servant courier found me there and breathlessly informed me that we were to halt. By the time the order passed along our front, we were well away from the mountain and swishing through tall grasses. Men halted and caught their breath. Our army of Israel now stood closer to the Philistines than to the mountain behind us. I watched the enemy spearmen. They had stopped dancing and stared back. Their drums ceased, but I heard no shouts or orders in their ranks. The sea people waited in an ominous silence, a dark, gathering thundercloud about to break.

Suddenly, a red-and-white pennant thrust up in the center of the Philistine mass. Others popped up in succession, traveling outward along their front in each direction. I craned my neck to see all the way to the end of their infantry. Dust was beginning to rise beyond the flank that overlapped my position, and I realized what that meant.

"Take command here!" I yelled to Zelig. "I'm going to defilade our flank. Chariots are coming!"

I pointed at the dust behind the Philistine infantry as I ran toward our left side. Zelig's eyes widened when he saw it too.

"Defilade! Defilade back!" I screamed while I ran along the front of the shield wall.

Commanders and men recognized me and began shifting, curving our line back like a bow. By the time I reached the end of our left flank, the reason for my order was plain. The dust cloud rose higher into the air, and the ground shook. The first chariots burst around the Philistine flank, four abreast and coming at a fast trot, feathered headdresses riffling on the drivers' heads. More followed in a column too long to count. Some of my spearmen were still moving back.

"Hurry!" I urged. "Take your positions! Down!"

Men dropped to crouch behind their shields and plant their spears butt down in the ground with tips angled forward. I had never fought chariots before, but we had all trained for this. The interlocking spears would keep the horses from running us down, and our shields would protect us from their archers.

The short moments before the chariots actually reached us were the hardest. Zelig had told me once that the thunder and rumble of chariots did more damage than their arrows. "When you're hiding behind your shield, you can't see them, but the ground shakes when they bear down on you, and the noise reaches inside your stomach. It makes brave men retch."

I knew what he meant. My guts clenched as I held my head down, waiting for them to run left to right across our front. I heard *thunks* on the shields farther to my left. Then they came to me. In an instant, choking dust filled my nostrils. Unseen horses whinnied in front of me. I heard the shouts of drivers and the slap of reins. An arrow struck my shield with enough force to penetrate a finger's breadth through the wood and leather. I grunted.

"My lord!"

I jerked my head around. *Mazal!* I had forgotten him. He carried no shield when he followed me. He was lying prone, his only protection a hope that the archers wouldn't notice him in the grass behind me.

"Stay down, Mazal. I will come back to cover you," I said.

He raised his face to me, and blood trickled from the corner of his mouth. Too late, I saw the fletching of the arrow embedded deeply in his back, angling down into his lungs.

"No, sire—" He coughed more blood and dropped his head.

I crab-walked behind my shield back to where he lay. His body was rigid with pain, and then, when I touched him, his spirit left. He softened and settled onto the earth, a puddle of blood under his head.

"Mazal," I said quietly. "Mazal. May you go with Yahweh."

Another arrow clanged off my shield. The attack continued. I waddled up into the line and took up my spear again.

The noise was terrifying. The tumultuous sounds of rattling chariot wheels, screaming horses, and shouting charioteers could drive men mad when they cowered helplessly on the trembling earth behind their shields. However, the din quickly began to recede, and then the chariots were past. I cautiously peeked around my shield. Dust still hung in the air. The grass thirty steps in front of us had been trampled flat. I stood up to stretch my limbs, but before I could do anything more than pop my aching back, I heard the familiar rumble again. "Down!" I bellowed. "They come back."

CHAPTER THIRTY-FIVE

...the Israelites fled before them, and many fell...

1 Samuel 31:1b NIV

T HE SECOND PASS CAME FROM the other wing of the Philistine chariot corps, the one to our right. Men dropped once more to endure a barrage of arrows.

I huddled close against the shield and closed my eyes as the first ones struck. The chariots' rumble seemed louder than the first time. *Are they closing with us?* Carefully, I cracked a space between my shield and the one overlapping my right. The enemy did edge nearer. Their horses' slobber flecked on us as they ran across just outside our spear tips. Archers leaned out over the sides of their vehicles and released arrows almost without aiming, driving them deep through our battered shields. I heard my spearmen curse as iron points penetrated forearms set in the lashings.

I gripped my spear hard as I thought. The sea people had made a tactical mistake. They came too close, and no infantrymen ran alongside these chariots to protect them as they did in the Egyptian armies. Chariots were effective because they could use their speed to keep them out of danger, but they were vulnerable if foot soldiers could ever close with them.

"Spearmen! Crocodiles!" I roared. The men nearby looked at me, no doubt thinking I must have broken under the Philistine attack. I jumped to my feet and waved my spear. "Attack!" I stepped forward into the direct path of the next chariot. No one followed me. Alone, I waited while the vehicle bore down, the driver's eyes startled wide open.

The archer beside him didn't notice me as he nocked another arrow. The charioteer tried to drive his team into me, but I leaped to the side of the horses. I swung the spear shaft two-handed into his face and caught the bowman too. Both men tumbled out of the chariot to bounce awkwardly on the packed ground.

I spun around to meet the next oncoming chariot. Still alone, I concentrated on the tip of the arrow pointed at me. Before the archer released it, I fell to the ground and rolled so that it hissed past my head. The chariot missed crushing me by a hand's breadth yet trampled over the two fallen Philistines ahead of it as it rumbled on. That first team, now without a driver, chattered away to the right and entangled itself with chariots alongside, creating a sudden blockage. The wheeled column slowed to a walk in front of me. Following teams crashed into the ones in front.

Knowing I was a marked man, I raised my shield and prepared to fight the closest stopped chariot. Its driver jerked the team's heads around, trying to get out of the milling knot of horses and cursing men. The archer coolly eyed me and raised his bow. The vehicle was still. He wouldn't miss. I crouched behind the shield and ran at him, hoping he wouldn't shoot for an exposed leg. A gargled cry came from the chariot. I peeked over the edge of my cover to see the archer had gone down, writhing on the ground with an Israelite spear protruding from his side. The driver looked at him then at me before bolting from the chariot, screaming, just ahead of me. I stopped and hid next to the chariot.

"Crocodiles! Do you expect Commander Beral to defeat the heathens by himself? You want to fondle yourselves while he fights?" Zelig stood up in the front rank of our kneeling spearmen, his empty hand a testament to the spear throw that had killed the archer. "Get up off your backsides and charge!" He drew his sword and waved it.

Around him, men got to their feet. They raised spears and charged into the mix of stalled Philistine chariots. No shield wall formed. They just darted in among the unprepared charioteers and killed them. All along the line, they got up and ran into the dusty melee. The fighting only lasted until the heathens could get free of each other and drive away in panic, completely routed. I stepped away from the empty chariot as Zelig came to me.

"I need my spear back." He grunted as he bent and jerked it out of the archer's still body. He gazed about at the carnage with the air of a man enjoying a mountain view. "That was good, Commander," he said. "But next time, tell me before you make such a foolish move as that one. My bowels almost released when I saw you out here greeting chariots."

I grinned at him. "In truth, I didn't know myself that I was going to do that. I just found myself suddenly dodging them." I struck him lightly on the shoulder. "If I had thought about it beforehand, my own bowels would have released."

Zelig seemed lost in thought as he rubbed his neck. "It would have been more likely for me, Commander. I was still squatting behind my shield back there."

We killed about fifty of their elite charioteers—not a large number, but it satisfied us, for we had broken the Philistines' chariot attack. I directed that the captured horses be killed on the spot, and their chilling screams filled the air.

Remembering where I was, I hopped up into an abandoned chariot to check on the enemy. They could have come upon us in this confusion, yet they had not moved. Their front rank stood at a distance, quiet and sullen as they watched my men rifle through captured gear, taking anything of value.

"Form your ranks," I shouted. "Commanders, re-form your companies as before." The chaos ended as spearmen grabbed their sacks of plunder and hustled back into a shield wall. Soon I stood by myself amid the wrecked chariots and downed horses. I watched the silent enemy soldiers. *Why haven't they charged us?*

Their ranks stirred. A single chariot came through them slowly until it emerged from the mass of footmen and halted. Even beyond two bowshots, I recognized Achish. He leaned on the front of the vehicle and scanned left to right, seeing for himself what had happened to his vaunted chariots. His eyes came to me and rested there. He nodded. *"I recognize you, Beral the Benjamite."* He spoke to his driver, and the chariot turned around to reenter the Philistine lines. I stepped down and walked back to our standing wall, where spearmen plucked out or broke off arrows in their pockmarked shields.

Another courier waited for me there, a military aide this time. He raised his fist in salute. "Sire, the king and General Katriel congratulate you on repelling the Philistine chariots," he said.

I said nothing, knowing there would be more.

He cleared his throat. "Also, sire, General Katriel orders you to finish re-forming your ranks and be prepared to advance again on the Philistines. The signal will be a raised pennant as before."

I closed my eyes for a moment. When I opened them, the young aide still waited there, watching me. They expected a reply. I puffed my cheeks out. "Were there any casualties on the right flank?" I asked.

"Yes, sire. Heavy losses. Some of the heathen chariots broke through our lines there before they were driven off."

"Prince Jonathan?"

"He is unhurt, sire."

I took my helmet off to run a hand over my damp hair. This was madness. "Very well. Tell the general my brigade will be ready. I'll watch for his signal."

"Yes, Commander." After another bump to the chest, the courier was gone.

The companies soon stood in straight ranks again except for our curved flank. I had Mazal's body covered with my cloak. No one else had been killed, but that would change soon. Zelig positioned himself twenty paces to my left, his eyes roving up and down the back of our lines. I sensed him watching me too.

The king's pennant shot up. A murmur rippled through the ranks. They all knew what it meant. Jeronn's brigade in the middle lurched forward.

I cupped my hands and shouted, "Companies... forward! Stay in line. Stay together."

The commands were repeated in each company as we unlimbered and started forward. I caught Zelig's eye, his expression as grim as any man's expecting to die shortly.

"May Yahweh be with us, Commander," he shouted across the space between us.

"Yes."

The men weaved through the wrecked chariots and dead horses, always trying to keep their wall together. They were trained and experienced at war, and I was proud of them. My jaw tightened. A thousand good men under my command were walking to their probable deaths. Some of them had been with me since I started as a commander of a hundred.

The front rank began talking excitedly, gesturing and pointing ahead. The enemy drums had started. I climbed up into the same abandoned chariot to get a better look. The Philistine infantry actually backed up again. Staying with the cadence of the drums, they increased the distance between us, except at the far left where their line overlapped ours. That part of the foe's forces didn't retreat. Instead, the flank held its position and began to curl around toward us, threatening to engulf even our defiladed line.

As I watched in that direction, my eye caught something else. Dust! It billowed up behind their positions as it had for the earlier chariot attack. Suddenly, I saw Achish's plan. I looked behind me. The safe, rocky slopes of Mt. Gilboa were too far away. I jumped from the chariot and ran to Zelig. He and the ranks had continued moving forward while I surveyed the Philistine troops. "Stop the advance!" I shouted. "Halt!"

Zelig swung around to me, his expression puzzled. "What?"

I pointed to our far left where the Philistines moved. "The chariots are coming back! They're going to go behind us this time! Form a circle!"

He gazed at the enemy's far left as the first row of chariots rounded that flank. "We won't have time to back up, will we?"

"No, form a brigade circle."

He shook his head. "That will take too long too. Better to have them go into company circles instead," he said.

"You're right. Go to the right and give the order. I'm going to the flank."

We parted at a run.

I yelled at each company as I passed, "Chariots behind us! Form the circle! Now!" It was a familiar drill that would save us if I could warn them in time. Fortunately, the last two companies had good commanders who could see what was happening. They had already combined into one large circle when I arrived breathless as the first chariots thundered up. I dived over the kneeling spearmen to find shelter.

"Yah! Yah!" the Philistine charioteers yelled as they slapped the reins against their little horses' backs. They passed around to the rear, held away by iron and bronze spear points bristling out from our formations. They shot a few arrows but paid little attention to us otherwise, their point of attack being the center of our army. They went straight for Saul. I listened to the last of them rattle by before I stood up.

Jeronn hadn't seen them in time to face about. The chariots drove hard into his brigade, and Philistine archers had an easy time of it, shooting standing spearmen from the rear. I watched the distant carnage for a moment before I spun around to check on the enemy infantry. As I expected, they had started advancing at a walk all across our front. Soon, they would break into a run. With mobile archers at our rear and overwhelming numbers of foot soldiers attacking our front, Achish's trap would be complete. Our best hope was to get out of the jaws before they closed.

"Stand up," I roared. I pointed at Chanan, one of the two commanders there. "Take these men back onto the slope! Make a shield wall at the trees. Hurry! Their chariots will be back!"

I repeated myself until the shaken young officers understood my directions. Then, leaving them, I retraced my steps to the other companies. Glancing to my left as I ran, I saw that the Philistine line opposite us had faltered and stopped, probably unsure about our ringed formations. Once they realized we were actually retreating, they would charge again. I could hear a din of clangs and shouts at the center. The rest of the heathen army had already closed there.

I sent each company I passed back to join the others on Mt. Gilboa. The nearer I came to our center, the louder the fighting ahead of me. Guttural cries filled the air. Chariots circled behind King Saul's position in a giant wheel shooting a continuous flurry of arrows where they knew him to be. The thick cloud of them arching out of the choking dust was a horrible sight.

Yair's company, at the far right, had been embroiled in fighting the chariots. One had breached his shield wall. The dead crew and horses, along with too many Israelite bodies, lay around a smashed vehicle inside his re-formed circle. The Philistines had apparently moved on to press their attack against our middle brigades. I found Zelig standing beside Yair, both of them staring at the massacre taking place next to them. I knew Yair to be a good soldier whom I had seen in many fights, but on that day, he shook at what he watched.

It shocked me also to see how many spearmen over there were down, many still moving on the ground with arrows protruding from them. The circling chariots wheeled closer to the remnants of Jeronn's men, who clustered in a dense knot around the king. His crown still flashed in the sun when I could sometimes see it amid the upraised shields held to protect him. Arrows stuck in every one of them like bristles on a boar's back. The Philistine archers loosed so many shafts at him that, from that distance, it sounded like a winter wind rattling dead tree leaves. More men fell as I watched. The screaming was constant.

Philistine infantry pressed them on the front side. Metal clashed on metal. Swords thumped against shields already battered and broken. The Israelite wall had given way, and our troops fought separately, each man alone now. Attacked front and rear, they had no place to go.

I looked over toward the Philistines still facing us. They were starting to move again. Pennants waved along their front. I grabbed Zelig's arm, and he turned a grim face to me. "They'll be coming for us next," he said. "We've lost this battle."

"They're coming already," I said, gesturing at the advancing infantry, "but this brigade isn't lost yet. Look there."

I pointed back to the other companies, now jogging back to Mt. Gilboa, the farthest ones already at its base. The heathen spearmen pursued them in ranks but would not catch up in time to stop the withdrawal.

Zelig understood instantly. "We're falling back?"

"There's no time for anything better. This is the last company." I raised my voice above the tumult so Yair would hear me as well. "The Philistines will be here quickly. Take the company and run. They're almost on us."

The enemy lines had closed to less than a bowshot and started to trot toward us. We had seconds.

"Now go!" I shouted.

Yair shouted at his remaining men. Squad leaders echoed his orders, and the circle collapsed. He looked at me.

"Go!" I yelled. "Run!" I pointed to the slope behind us.

He broke into a run while the company fell into two files alongside him. In a short moment, Zelig and I stood alone before the oncoming Philistines.

"You too, Zelig," I said. "Go and take command of the brigade. Form a wall at the trees. The pagans won't follow you there."

"What about you, Commander?" Zelig's eyes flicked to the closing Philistines and back to me. "You're not coming?"

"You know I can't." I tilted my head toward the fighting at the center. "I have a duty there yet."

"Jonathan."

"Jonathan," I answered. I pushed his shoulder. "Go. If we stand here any longer, we'll both be dead men. I can already see which Philistines in the front rank are missing teeth."

He clasped my forearm. "Beral, must you do this—"

"Go, Zelig! That's an order. You told me once that an infantryman needs his legs." I grinned at him. "Now, prove you still have yours. Go, old friend. Find Abner. Save the men."

CHAPTER THIRTY-SIX

So Saul... and his armor-bearer... died together that same day.

1 Samuel 31:6 NIV

ZELIG AND I SEPARATED FOR the last time, both of us bounding away like hunted deer over the rocky ground. He followed Yair's company while I veered toward the desperate struggle at the center. My final glimpse of the old warrior showed him running with the speed of a man half his age. I dodged and feinted to avoid javelins hurled by the closing Philistine infantry. They were very close. I could hear their leaders shouting to pivot left toward the center. With my brigade withdrawing to the mountain, the way was clear. I found myself in front of the heathen army, leading them straight toward King Saul.

I soon came into the midst of scattered enemy looters hastily picking through Israelite bodies. Hundreds of dead and dying men—the remains of Jeronn's shield wall—lay in a rough line here. The scavengers barely took notice of me, and I stabbed at the nearest ones as I pounded by. Their outraged cries followed me across that killing ground.

Farther along the tangled rows of downed spearmen, I couldn't hear anything but the sound of battle. A solid, continuous roar rose from the heaving mob in front of me. Philistines packed together across the Israelite front, shoving and squirming up on their toes to get farther in to hack at the dwindling defenders around the king. I couldn't cut my way through that pack. I decided to try running through the arrows on the opposite side.

Chariots clattered close behind Saul's stand, their horses lathered. Everywhere, arrows stuck in the ground or in bodies. The air hissed with their sound. I took a deep breath, raised my pocked shield, and ran forward again. The archers soon noticed me circling around to enter the fight from the rear. Most of their arrows hit the shield or bounced off my helmet, but two stuck in my right thigh. I still ran unimpeded, knowing the pain would start later. Backing away from the chariots, I eased toward the Israelite stand, trying not to stumble over dead men and debris.

"Commander Beral! This way! This way!" Voices behind me guided me until I reached what was left of their shield wall and fell backward into the center.

I gasped at the pain when the arrows stuck in my leg hit the ground. I rolled away from them, got to my hands and knees, and pushed myself up.

"Sire, are you badly hurt?" Oren, one of the king's bodyguards, stood beside me, his shield up against the constant barrage.

"I'll be all right. Here, let me lean on you while I do this." I bent over and quickly snapped off one arrow before I could think about it. That sudden pain made me fall against him. "You do the other one," I said through gritted teeth.

Oren leaned down, and I passed out in a sea of red when he splintered it.

It must have been the agony in my throbbing leg that got me up again. I thought only a few moments had passed, but Oren was gone when I struggled to my feet once more. Blood oozed around the broken shafts in my wounds and dried in long streaks down my leg. I looked about, dismayed at what I saw. Fewer than a hundred spearmen still stood around me. Bodies piled up inside the shrinking circle, most with arrows in them. King Saul was easy to find. He fought in the front rank against the enemy spearmen. Two bodyguards stayed behind him, protecting his back with shields against the chariots' barrage of arrows from the rear. The shields looked like porcupines. The Philistines weren't trying to capture Saul alive.

I started to hobble toward him, thinking to help in the shield wall, when my eye caught a flash of color on the ground beside me. A bright-red toga lay rumpled within a jumble of bodies. Abinadab, the king's son, was dead. I tried to step around the pile and saw Malki-Shua's purple cloak as well. Arrows punctured him in several places.

Our entire right wing, led by Jonathan, had collapsed. I could see renegade Philistine soldiers looting hundreds of Israelite corpses over in that direction, and I thought it likely my prince had been killed there too. My heart ached at the thought. I wanted to slump in despair, but I had no time to grieve. Staring at that carnage, I could only pray that he had somehow escaped. I hoped even as experience told me not to.

Shouts from the spearmen facing the archers made me spin around. One of the Philistine charioteers, probably looking for glory, had wheeled out of their revolving circle and was charging directly at our weakened line. The chariot bounced violently as the driver urged the team faster. His crewmate carried javelins. Our spear wall looked too thin to stop them. If they broke our circle, their momentum would carry the vehicle straight through to King Saul's back.

Suddenly, a broad-shouldered Israelite burst out of our line and ran toward the oncoming chariot, his heavy spear raised—Ben-Ami. The driver bore straight at him, ducking down against a possible throw. Ben-Ami stopped instead, and laid his spear on the ground. He knelt just before being overrun, raising the spear tip quickly to catch the left horse squarely in the chest. Braced against the ground, the spear went deep before breaking. The animal's screams were louder than any other sound of the fight. The impaled animal dropped, but the chariot rolled over Ben-Ami as it flipped, spilling the crew. He disappeared under the wrecked vehicle when it crashed down. The other horse broke free to run away. The injured one lay kicking.

Behind me, a hand grabbed my shoulder and turned me around. Katriel stood before me, wild-eyed. "Beral? It's you! You got here past the Philistines? That was you?" He jabbered, trying to speak over the noise and looking ludicrous in a borrowed helmet with his puffy jowls pushing the cheek flaps out. He put both hands on my upper arms. "Beral, we are lost here! They will kill us all! We must get away!" His lips quivered as he drew breath, and his eyes pleaded. "You did it. You and I could do it again, Beral! We'll take some spearmen, and you could lead us out of here!" He nodded vigorously. "Yes, you can do it, and I will reward you too. There's no reason we should die here like the rest of them." He looked like a caged animal.

A giant roar came from the Philistine infantry. Saul had fallen out of the front rank, bleeding from an assortment of cuts. Nathon grasped him under the arms and dragged his master away. Our whole circle contracted.

I leaned in to put my lips near Katriel's ear. "You want to leave this?"

He nodded again, bright-eyed and eager as a young pup. "Yes! Yes!" he said. "Get some men. We will have to hurry."

I put my shield arm around his neck, pulling him in tight against me. With my other hand, I drew my sword. "Then I'll help you," I purred in his ear, placing the sword tip under his chin. I drove it hard into his head just as he realized what I meant.

He jerked back with eyes bulging like toads. Blood spurted from his mouth. I let him slump to the ground, another casualty of the battle, and glanced around, not caring if anyone had seen this or not. Only one person had. I started when our eyes met.

Prince Jonathan sat nearby, propped up against several bodies with a shield in his lap to cover him. A Philistine arrow was embedded above his collarbone. Blood stained the soil under him while the corner of his mouth leaked another trickle. He raised one hand to me, and it fluttered like a dry leaf before he dropped it. I limped over dead men to get to him. Unable to kneel on my wounded leg, I managed to drop down to sit beside him, keeping my shield overhead.

His head lolled onto my shoulder. "Beral... my oldest friend... and now my last." He spoke like a man without sleep, slow and labored. More blood ran out of his mouth as he coughed. "Thought you might come..."

I put my arm around him. "Don't try to speak now, sire. You must rest."

"Rest?" He tried to laugh but almost choked on blood. "Are we... hunting goats tomorrow?" Jonathan was very feeble, but I heard only his voice in that maelstrom of sounds. He rolled his gaze toward Katriel's body. "Killed him, eh? Should have done that myself... years ago." His chest heaved, his breathing obviously painful. He started to pant.

"Sire, don't—"

"'S'all right... All right." My prince raised his face to me. "Beral... I need... favor..."

"Anything, sire."

"Herzi's dead..." Jonathan looked me in the eye. "I need... armor bearer... last time."

"Of course, my lord." I tightened my grip around him. He seemed smaller than I ever remembered him. "My staff is here."

He grinned, his teeth red. "Good old Beral." He took a shuddering breath. "Need to stand... for this... Help me up."

I got up, hardly aware of my own pain. Jonathan grimaced and gritted his teeth as I pulled him to his feet. Unable to stand without my help, he dropped his shield to the ground. All around us, the circle of spearmen shrank. The arrows had stopped, for Philistine infantry completely surrounded us. Saul stood nearby, weak and unsteady. He was speaking to Nathon, who only shook his head in reply. I knew what the king wanted him to do. Our time was short. I looked up at the afternoon sun and wondered what Liora did at that moment.

Saul had his great sword out, its hilt on the rocky soil and its point resting against his lower chest. Our last spearmen fell backward, overcome by fatigue and wounds. The Philistines howled as they poured in over them. My prince and I stood alone. I remembered an old bull ox surrounded by jackals. Who would remember our stand? Who would even know of it?

"Beral... It's time." Jonathan coughed softly. "This is Yahweh's will." He leaned against me so that we stood swaying together.

"Yes, I know." I raised my sword and shield. "I am with you heart and soul, my lord."

EPILOGUE

Zelig

NOCTURNAL CREATURES CAME OUT DURING that night to worry at the thousands of dead bodies left behind on the battlefield. Little foxes barked back and forth while jackals prowled the area, avoiding the big hyenas. Dogs came from nearby villages. The sounds of crunching bones and snarling beasts filled the darkness. Wounded men moaned for help that never came. Downed horses kicked feebly. All would eventually die. The blood smell was everywhere.

An hour before dawn, the night sky was just turning gray when I came down from Mt. Gilboa. In the darkness I could barely make out a lone figure already there, far ahead of me. The animal scavengers shrank away from him. His robe marked him as an Amalekite or Edomite, but I couldn't be certain. Several had watched our battle the day before from the safety of a distant hilltop away from the fighting. This one must have seen and carefully marked the king's last position where the chariots had concentrated against him, for he confidently approached that spot under the lowering new moon. He stepped over increasingly concentrated numbers of dead men scattered about on the ground and in small piles. Studying their bodies, he never noticed me.

This lone heathen in front of me did not belong here, and I meant to kill him. I quietly crept closer, taking care not to kick anything or make any noise in the trampled grass. I came across corpses too. Israelite and Philistine alike looked the same in death. The twisted figures on the ground had dark, upturned eyes like coal smudges in the dim light. Their wounds and blood looked black. I squatted and held still, moving nothing but my eyes.

The searcher came to a large man lying facedown in the center of a cluster of bodies, his hands clasping a sword blade piercing his torso.

The man rolled the body over and exclaimed in the tongue of the Amalekites, "Ha! Found you, didn't I?"

When I realized what he intended, I stood to move forward, but the thief moved more quickly. He took Saul's crown and armband and dropped them into a sack as he straightened.

I bellowed, "Loose that! You've no right to those!" I charged at him.

The thief looked around, startled. Seeing me, he started to run away, the crown and armband clinking together in the sack he carried. He proved too young, too fast. I couldn't catch him. I stopped, enraged by the blasphemy toward my dead king.

"May you die the death of the coward you are, Amalek dung heap!" I yelled after him.

The man hurried south, away from me and away from the Philistine army, whose early cooking fires flickered across the valley. I stood near Saul's body and next to an overturned Philistine chariot with a dead horse lying in its traces. I took a deep breath.

The sky had turned lighter. Already, I could see more clearly. Others would be here soon. I began searching among the bodies, scanning quickly, knowing exactly whom I sought. At frequent intervals I raised my head to gaze about, as a deer will when watching for predators. The sky turned rose as the sun eased over the mountain behind me. I spotted two distant chariots, accompanied by about twenty foot soldiers, coming slowly from the Philistine encampment. The column carefully picked its way through rocks and the debris of battle. It became clear that its objective was this same cluster of bodies where I now stood. I needed to hide—quickly.

I dropped to my belly and crawled under the overturned chariot only to discover an Israelite crushed beneath it. Ben-Ami's contorted face told me of the agony that had gripped him in the moments before he died.

"Rest peacefully, my brother," I whispered before wiggling forward. Lying flat on my stomach, I peeked out under the front edge of the wrecked vehicle canted on Ben-Ami's torso. I drew my sword and waited.

The chariots arrived shortly. Achish stepped out of the first one, followed by his son.

An officer walked directly to King Saul's body. "Here he is, my lord," he called. "This is where I remember him falling. See, the coward took his own life."

Soldiers surrounded the body, sniggering and prodding it with their toes.

Achish looked down and grunted. "Take his head off. Use this same sword." He pointed at the great sword protruding from Saul's chest. Two men yanked the sword out.

One hefted it and swung it over his head a few times, testing its balance. "Ow, it's heavy," he called.

"Are you a boy, then? Can you handle a man's sword?" taunted one of his comrades.

The swordsman didn't reply. He pivoted around, flashing the sword's blade in a great arc and bringing it down on the neck of Israel's first king. In my hiding place, I squeezed my eyes shut.

Achish strolled about the bloody ground. "Find his sons. They're here too."

Abinadab and Malki-Shua were soon pulled out of a pile of bodies by their colorful cloaks. The same man beheaded them.

"Here's the crown prince!" yelled one of the soldiers.

Jonathan was lying on his side, an arrow in him and a deep slash in his neck. Next to him lay an Israelite commander. His arm, bearing a battered shield, was wrapped around the prince.

"This one is Jonathan. Take his head too," ordered Achish.

"What about this one?" A soldier poked at the other dead man with the butt of his spear.

The Philistine king looked thoughtfully at that body. "No... this is Beral the Benjamite—a good man for a Hebrew dog—probably the best one of them all. He can keep his head." He bent down and picked up the sword next to Beral, its handle a pair of entwined snakes. "I will take

249

this, though," he said. He glanced down as he hefted the weapon. "I told you I would return this to Anak's sons."

The bodies and heads of Saul and his sons were thrown into the second chariot. I watched them leave until they were out of sight from my hiding place before I crawled out and hurried to where Beral still lay. I gazed at the corpse.

"Yahweh, you are hard sometimes," I rasped, falling to my knees and putting my face in both hands. My shoulders shook as I sobbed quietly, unashamedly, bending almost to the ground. After several minutes, I straightened and got to my feet. I sniffed and wiped my nose on the sleeve of my battle toga then stared up at the early-morning sky. "I do not understand your ways," I whispered.

The sun was up. Looters from the rest of the Philistine army, as well as local villagers, would be here soon to pick over the dead for anything of value. I already could see specks moving about on the far edge of the battlefield. Commander Beral would not suffer that indignity. I would see to it.

Behind me, a man cleared his throat. I whirled around and crouched with sword raised but saw no one.

"Come out and show yourself, whoreson. You'll not get anything off this man!" I warned. I gripped the sword with both hands and waited. David stepped out from behind the broken chariot.

"Zelig," he called softly.

"My lord." I dropped to one knee. "You were here?"

"No. I've just arrived. I had to know." He came forward. "Tell me, Zelig, are they alive? Any of them?" His voice caught.

"No, my lord. King Saul is dead. His sons are dead. Jonathan is dead. The Philistines have just left with their bodies."

David stood motionless. He bowed his head with eyes closed, his mouth a tight line. "Then it must be so," he said to himself. "God wills it." He took a deep breath and looked up. "Zelig, what do you do here?"

Without words, I waved an arm at the body of my commander.

David stepped over to look. "Oh, Beral. They have killed you too," he moaned.

We stood beside each other, looking down at Beral in silence.

After several moments, David turned to me. "I always wanted him as a friend," he said.

"He loved Jonathan too much, my lord."

"Yes... He did." Another silence came over us. "They were both such honorable men."

"Yes." I stirred and looked sideways at David. "His wife is with child, you know."

David's eyes widened. "Truly? How do you know?"

"She told my wife that she suspects it is so. My Jemima is a wise and experienced woman. She could tell. Liora has the glow of a woman with child."

"Does Beral...? *Did* Beral know that?"

I shook my head. "No. Liora wanted to be certain before she told him. It's the way of young wives, you know."

"I suppose that's true."

"I intend to take her into my household as a daughter. Jemima will like that. Liora and the child will live as well as we do."

"Good. Beral would be pleased at that."

"My king, may I give you some advice?" I shifted my feet, scuffing at the hard ground.

"Certainly, Zelig. I know you gave Beral wise counsel."

"My king, it would be best if you are not seen here today." I pointed toward the human scavengers in the distance. "Villagers will be swarming here soon. If it were known that you were at the site of King Saul's death... people will talk. There would be rumors..."

David's smile was crooked. "I know about rumors. They spread as wide and fast as windblown chaff... So then, you think I should not be here?"

"No, my king. Go back to Ziklag, where Achish sent you. Wait there and then be surprised at the news of this battle. Hold your grief until then."

David sighed. "I think you are right, Zelig. I will leave. But you must remember, I am not your king. Not yet."

"I know, but it is plain now that this is the will of God." I gestured at Beral's body. "I think even he knew it."

"Very well. Will you come to serve me if I am king?"

"Of course, sire. I always intended that. Go now, my king."

David turned and loped away, heading southwest over the hills that lay between him and Ziklag. For a long time, I watched him flitting through the hillside boulders. Traveling easily at a shepherd's gait, he would reach his Philistine city before the morrow's sunrise. When my future king passed out of sight, I bent and picked up the body of my friend. Cradling Beral in my arms, I carried him back to Mt. Gilboa, where the brigade waited.

ABOUT THE AUTHOR

A son of the South, Channing Turner grew up in Arkansas and Louisiana before graduating from Louisiana State University in Psychology. He did graduate work in marine biology and became an estuarine biologist along the Texas coast. After retiring from the petrochemical industry where he worked in Louisiana and Montana as a laboratory analyst, he managed the 2010 US Census in Montana and northern Wyoming. He now lives in eastern Washington with his wife, Barb.

Channing served in the army and was discharged as an Armor captain. Reading and writing are his sedentary pursuits, but he also enjoys riding his Tennessee Walker in the Blue Mountains of Washington and Oregon.

CPSIA information can be obtained
at www.ICGtesting.com
Printed in the USA
DW01n2151201216
IFS